SATURNIN

ZDENĚK JIROTKA

Translation MARK CORNER

Karolinum Press

Particular thanks to Lenka Cornerová-Zdráhalová
for her painstaking work in reading through
and correcting this translation.
Translator's Acknowledgement

Text © 2022 by Zdeněk Jirotka – heirs
Translation and afterword © 2022 by Mark Corner
Illustrations © 2022 by Adolf Born – heirs

Cataloging-in-Publication Data is available
from the National Library of the Czech Republic

ISBN 978-80-246-5074-6 (hbk)
ISBN 978-80-246-3288-9 (pbk)
ISBN 978-80-246-3369-5 (ebk)

I.

could not possibly say that all the parables and comparisons interwoven into Doctor Witherspoon's intemperate speeches were entirely to my taste. But I have to admit that there is something in his graphic tale of a fellow in a cafe with a plate of doughnuts. At the very least the story may serve as a rough guide to Saturnin.

Dr. Witherspoon used to categorise people according to the way they behaved in a half-empty cafe when confronted by a plate of doughnuts. Imagine some high-class coffee-house on a Sunday morning. It is a lovely day outside and there are only a few guests in the cafe. You have already taken breakfast, you have read all the newspapers. Now you are comfortably leaning back in some cosy nook, lost in thought and gazing at the plate of doughnuts. Boredom is slowly spreading into every inch of the cafe.

This is where it can be shown to which category of people you belong according to Dr. Witherspoon's theory. If you are allegedly a person without imagination, any dynamic passions or a sense of humour, you will subject the doughnuts to a dull and thoughtless gaze until perhaps midday. Then you will rise to your feet and take yourself off to lunch.

I have a well-grounded suspicion that Dr. Witherspoon considers me to belong to this first category. I think him somewhat unjust. We will not speak about humour and dynamic passions, but about his denying me any imagination. When I recall that he is well aware of my success in satisfactorily completing an official tax return, I have to say that his accusation surprises me. But we will let the matter pass. Even if I really did belong to this category, it would be more pleasant than being in the other one. At the sight of the doughnuts a member of the second category enjoys reflecting on what it would be like if someone, quite out of the blue and without warning, employed these pastries as missiles and began bombarding the other customers in the cafe.

I do not understand how a grown-up, intelligent person can think of such things. At the same time I am in full agreement with the view that Dr. Witherspoon, as he himself admits, belongs to this latter category. For whatever inexplicable reason he is proud of the fact. He considers this second group of people to be spiritually more advanced. Of course I haven't the faintest idea what spiritual maturity has in common with doughnuts fragmenting around the heads of peaceful cafe guests. I cannot imagine it, but I have refrained from arguing the point with him. For I have a definite opinion concerning debates with Dr. Witherspoon. Whenever I let myself descend to such an argument, I feel like someone who has been foolish enough to smash a hole in the wall of a dam.

If fate had not brought me into the path of Saturnin, I would never have believed that a third category of people existed, the members of which are as rare as white crows. I mean those people for whom the idea of a doughnut whistling through the air is such an enticement that they get up and actually make it happen.

Such individuals Dr. Witherspoon holds in unholy esteem. He maintains that to carry out such a deed it is necessary not only to possess a marked sense of the comic, but also courage, a good temperament and who knows what else. In my opinion the task also calls for an unusual degree of lunacy. Indeed I cannot but feel that any reasonable person would be astonished to see people of this sort anywhere outside an institution established especially for them. Unfortunately I was fated to discover that such people actually exist and that no limits have yet been placed upon their personal freedom. For such a one is Saturnin.

If I look back today at the short period of my life which I have recently lived through, I find many things to wonder at. In fact I wonder at how much happened during this period. My life was somehow condensed, events tumbled over one another and I could hardly follow what was going on. I was like someone who upon descending from a snow-covered hill steps onto a patch of ice hidden beneath the snow.

I have a feeling that at the time when I was sliding downwards as if on glass I hardly behaved in a very dignified manner. I think that this is understandable, and I would like to know who could blame me for it. Only a person with no knowledge of what it is to engage in a desperate battle to keep one's balance and not topple over would say that I could have left the ice patch at any moment of that undignified descent. Come to that it wasn't an unpleasant experience, and I even think that it was well worth it. I grew out of boyish dreams of adventure long ago and I like a quiet and sober existence. However, I think that a passing shower of unusual events does no harm to anyone. No one is drowned by rain and one is apt to forget the unpleasant things that have happened. A miserable journey through a snowstorm seems to have been an interesting adventure when recalled some time later.

Perhaps it was not altogether wise for me, a single and relatively young chap, to engage a manservant. I daresay it even seems eccentric and too like a character in a novel. Certainly no one can deny the fact that not many young men can be found in Bohemia who have their own gentleman's gentleman. Consequently the mere recollection of having done something so strange and unusual embarrasses my normally peaceful and conservative self.

Saturnin advertised in the newspapers for the position of manservant, under conditions which I felt able to accept, and he had several very good references. His appearance and correct manner were very much to my liking. I later discovered that he was the recipient of a systematic and by no means superficial education.

His rather unusual name somehow rang a bell, but it was only recently that I first discovered the connection that had lodged it in my memory. A copy of a newspaper which must have been about two years old had come into my hands, containing an article about an attempted burglary at Professor Luda's villa. I remembered that we had talked about it at the time in the cafe. Saturnin was the hero of the hour, though the more serious-minded readers of the newspaper felt inclined to shake their heads at his behaviour. Incidentally, I still have the newspaper cutting:

EXCITING INCIDENT WITH A BURGLAR. During the night of Saturday, 5th August an unknown burglar broke into the villa of Professor Luda, historian and collector of fine objects, and tried to prise open the reinforced case used by Professor Luda to keep safe a number of valuable gold antiques. Before he could open the case, he was disturbed by a member of the domestic staff, Mr. Saturnin. What then took place between the two men is the subject of further investigation. When the police, summoned by telephone, arrived at the scene of the crime, they found the burglar unconscious from a serious head injury. Mr. Saturnin's testimony concerning the preceding events was somewhat strange. According to his statement the burglar had injured himself, making use of the mediaeval flail included in Professor Luda's collection. He persisted stubbornly with this curious explanation. The burglar recovered consciousness in hospital but claimed to have forgotten his own name. Initial investigations indicate the following course of events: the disturbed thief tried to frighten Mr. Saturnin with a loaded revolver. Mr. Saturnin knocked the weapon from his hand and threw it out of the window into the garden, where it was indeed later discovered. Then Mr. Saturnin addressed the burglar with a speech of some length, in which he elaborated upon the notion that a duel between two unequally armed combatants was hardly cricket. He forced the intruder to avail himself of a weapon hanging on the wall, which the man describes as a pole with a ball and chain, and picked one up for himself. After somewhat confusing opening formalities the duel commenced, during which the burglar was wounded. It is of interest that the injured party does not exclude the possibility that the head wound was of his own doing. He says that the weapon in question was very difficult to control and that he had been forced repeatedly to dodge the swinging ball of his own weapon. Moreover, throughout the battle he was apparently in mortal fear of breaking the chandelier. On the whole the burglar admitted to being rather pleased at the outcome of his adventure. At the conclusion of the investigation we will not fail to provide readers of our paper with a full report.

I have already pointed out that it is impossible to argue with Dr. Witherspoon. Not only does he overwhelm you with a torrent of words, but he usually carries out an intellectual somersault and delivers a diatribe against something which you never had the slightest intention of discussing. This will somewhat influence the coherence of my tale, but there is nothing I can do about it. The unexpected speeches of Dr. Witherspoon will sometimes be responsible for the existence of a chapter treating of criminality at the beginning and criminality at the end, while being almost entirely filled with a discussion of trout fishing. The doctor is like this, and a fifty-year-old person is hard to change.

When I once asked him what a person with a healthy mind is to think about the events described in this newspaper cutting, he replied that it is very difficult to decide, because these days no one has a healthy mind. He explained that we have all hitched up our brains to the service of narrow, specialised occupations and that we try with all our strength to let the other parts of our brains atrophy. As soon as this happens we are noticed by our superiors and begin to fall into a career. It is apparently amazing how even simple and straightforward considerations are already beyond the brain capacity of most people.

Dr. Witherspoon continued to speak for another five quarters of an hour, and to this day I do not recall what he was talking about. He ended with a paean of praise for Pythagoras. I did not challenge his views, but concerning his contention that no one today has a healthy mind, I rather think that Doctor Witherspoon should speak for himself.

II.

would like you to imagine how quietly I used to live before Saturnin came into my employment. I inhabited a fairly modest flat in one of those old town houses whose individual charm always had an effect on me. I felt most content there. The atmosphere of these houses – facades filled with ornamental stucco, well-trodden stone steps, intimate corridors that never saw the full light of day, high panelled doors – is so much closer to my heart than the uniform surroundings of modern buildings. I somehow feel that a pleasant and reassuring twilight is part of what makes a person's home homely.

Dr. Witherspoon says that such sentiments are inherited from our ancestors who lived in caves. Whenever he expressed himself on the subject of my flat at this time, he did so in a derogatory manner. He simply did not understand how I could choose to live in this house. He said that as soon as he stepped over the threshold his heart missed a beat and his soul filled with depressing thoughts of human tragedies. Apparently all the people who had lived there before me had taken their happiness away with them, leaving pain, sorrows and despair behind in the building. He claimed that every corner of the house was soaked with tears shed during unhappy nights, after which there was someone who never saw the dawn. In short, he claimed that terrible things must have happened here and that it was a place where he felt everything collapsing about his ears.

So far as I know, nothing terrible ever happened here. Once some scaffolding fell down, but not in any way onto Dr. Witherspoon, but rather into the courtyard. Nothing untoward took place and there was no reason for anyone to be unhappy. Dr. Witherspoon then said that he would prefer sadness to land on his head than scaffolding. Such is the manner in which he runs away from every serious discussion.

So I lived like this in a small, peaceful flat, the walls covered with faded wallpaper and pictures in broad and ancient frames. The tune on a musical grandfather clock marked the passing of time during my quiet evenings, which I whiled away in a huge winged armchair.

Yes, I would spend plenty of time at home, particularly if faced with inclement weather outside. On dark autumn nights, when the heavens open up and pour streams of rain onto the earth below, a whirlwind tears the leaves off the trees, and the shrieks of a howling gale encircle the towers of old castles and mingle with the cries of frightened crows, when lonely riders gallop along paths caked with mud in pursuit of dubious ends – these are the sort of nights on which I used to sit beside the stove and read the romantic novels of Václav Beneš Třebízský. Afterwards I went to bed and dreamt of a mistress crying, the crackling of burning roof beams and oaths of revenge. Then in the morning I was filled with wonder at the fact that trams were still running along the streets of Prague. Indeed I was surprised that the coffee which Mrs. Sweeting brought to me had not been laced with poison.

This Mrs. Sweeting was an elderly lady with black hair parted in the middle and she showed quite a maternal concern for my welfare. I lacked nothing and had nothing to complain about, which perhaps was exactly what I was annoyed about. There is a proverb about this, but on principle I don't use proverbs and maxims. My soul cries out against them. When you have learned about my Aunt Catherine, you will understand why.

And then one day Saturnin entered this peaceful environment and considered it his duty to stir my life up as much as possible. You shall see for yourselves how he succeeded in doing so.

Insofar as I can recall the circumstances, I would not want to claim that Saturnin was not a good manservant. He had all the qualities which a gentleman's gentleman should have. He was a handsome fair-haired fellow, honest, reliable and very intelligent. I always had the impression that he could just as easily have been the manager of some international concern as a butler. Of course he could not have had himself transferred from one managerial job to another in quite the same way as he moved position as a manservant.

When he produced his references, I couldn't help observing that he lacked a report from his last place of employment. Later I learned why he couldn't have one. He'd abandoned the position after an almost absurd scene. He was thrown into some kind of tantrum where he supposed that he could no longer tolerate the behaviour of his employer. In a fit of rage, which I have reason to believe was simulated, he caused inexcusable damage to the furniture of the apartment and, taking his employer by surprise in a park, threw her into a fountain. Only then did he calm down. I will not give the name of the lady concerned, even though I know her very well, but I would like to make the observation that my own experience of this lady partly explains and perhaps even excuses Saturnin's behaviour. I mean by this that I know a considerable number of people who would be quite happy to throw her into a fountain as well. Of course none of them would complete the task in quite the same manner as Saturnin. When this lady emerged waist deep in water and fixed a look of utter incomprehension upon the wrongdoer, Saturnin bowed stiffly and announced that the table was laid. Then he went off to pack his things.

I did not have to find out that the creation of such absurd situations was a passion of his until much later. By this, I don't mean that he would ever allow himself to behave in a similar manner towards me. In the first place my bodily proportions convince him that he might not be able to predict the exact outcome of such an encounter. In the second place my natural dignity inhibits him. But in spite of that, from the moment he became my employee I have not been able to predict when I will be forced to deal with a wholly unexpected situation. Something unbelievable could happen at any hour of any day, and despite its sensational character, the event would in all likelihood afford me very little pleasure.

It began with his habit, whenever my name came up in the course of his conversations with Mrs. Sweeting, of referring to me in terms of the most outlandish titles, such as His Lordship, His Grace, Sahib and His Excellency, according to whatever he had just been reading. Then he collected together various hunting trophies for the flat, such as buffalo horns, elephant tusks, an assortment of animal skins and similar objects. I later found out that he borrowed these things from the props manager of our leading theatre. In my absence he apparently regaled my friends with fictitious hunting yarns. This is the only way I can explain the fact that several ladies of my acquaintance surprised me in a cafe with the request that I explain to them how I came to kill a shark with a camera tripod. Naturally I denied that I had ever done such a thing, and from that time forth I have acquired the reputation of being too modest a hero.

I have pondered in vain the reasons why Saturnin does this. At first I presumed that he had a kind of pathological need to become the servant of some gentleman adventurer, and that out of necessity he sought to wrap my prosaic character in an aura of heroism. Later I arrived at the conviction that he simply enjoyed it.

His sense of humour was really almost beyond the pale. He once acquainted me with a very confusing theory of his concerning a special type of practical joke. As far as I could understand him, the punch-line of such jokes is that either the house burns down or someone is badly wounded. I have to say that I wasn't exactly enamoured of such humour.

After about six months Saturnin expressed his opinion that the flat in which we had lived perfectly happily until that time was not big enough. On the whole this was true. Although originally its size was perfectly satisfactory, things had changed. I don't know whether any of you has ever seen buffalo horns . . . but that would be a long story. It goes without saying that Dr. Witherspoon supported Saturnin. He said that I should have already changed my residence long before, and he said something about my health being frail and the flat damp. There wasn't an iota of truth in this. In the first place the flat wasn't even slightly damp, and so far as my health is concerned, Dr. Witherspoon knows absolutely nothing about it. He last treated me when I had measles at the age of about ten.

The outcome was as follows. One afternoon Saturnin searched me out among my circle of acquaintances and discreetly informed me that we had moved. He added that we now lived on water near to a suspension bridge.

Apparently it would have suited his book had I proceeded to faint. However, I received the news in silence and continued my game of cards. Not before evening did I avail myself of several cognacs and set off to look at my old flat. Sure enough it was empty and Mrs. Sweeting had tears in her eyes. From the manner in which the owner of the house treated me I judged that it would not be a good idea to inquire too closely into the details of the move.

Then I departed for the suspension bridge. It was a foolish thing to do, but I had to go somewhere. Saturnin stood on the embankment wearing a flat sailor's cap and hailed me as 'Captain'.

From this time forth we lived on a houseboat and I cannot say that it was an unmitigated evil. It is true that in the very first week the anchor broke loose and our boat went over a weir. It was an unpleasant experience, taking place in absolute darkness, and at first I thought that Saturnin had drowned, because a search of the whole boat failed to disclose his whereabouts. Later it was revealed that he was asleep in the crow's nest. But I have to say that despite this one disturbing event I had nothing to complain about in my new abode. One must accept life's little difficulties.

Of course I do not mean that I resigned myself to being at the mercy of Saturnin's ideas of what made for gracious living. I could not do so because I was not indifferent to my reputation, which had already been considerably affected by his hare-brained schemes. I had begun to acquire stature as a person of reckless daring and as a notable eccentric – in short, a person in the mould of Harry Piel. There was once mention of our houseboat in the newspaper and in this connection it designated me 'our famous sportsman'. Next day I unintentionally overheard an argument between Saturnin and our fuel supplier, in which Saturnin was griping that the reference was not to 'a big game hunter', despite the fact that he had explicitly stressed this appellation to the editor.

This constantly burgeoning, undeserved, and to me personally most unwelcome reputation as a man of exceptional character had some markedly unpleasant consequences. Thus, for example, I was once woken up during the night by a man in an official cap who explained to me that he was urgently in need of my assistance. Making considerable use of my powers of deduction I gathered from the man's confused chatter that the inmate of some asylum, supposing himself to be Marcus Aurelius, had escaped from confinement, and that the management of this establishment was of the view that for a man of my calibre it would be a piece of cake to recapture the fellow.

It is not easy to disappoint people who have a flattering opinion of your talents. I rose from my bed and dressed at speed. The man in the official cap claimed that he had been requested to ask whether I would kindly take a shotgun with me. I do not have one, so I steered the conversation away from this idea. I said that I would not need such a thing, and the man in the official cap looked at me with an expression of unfeigned admiration.

I gave Saturnin instructions to be carried out in the eventuality of my failing to return, and accompanied the man outside into rain and darkness. Only during the conversation which we enjoyed together on our journey did it come to light that he worked for a zoo and that Marcus Aurelius was a lion.

I am decidedly a man of at least average bravery, but you can imagine how I felt. I do not like to recall it. In the end things turned out all right. Certain employees of the zoo succeeded in capturing the lion after it had fallen asleep, having tired itself out in vain attempts to attack a number twelve tram. Hence my involvement proved unnecessary, but in spite of this the director of the zoo acknowledged in the warmest terms my willingness to contribute to the defence of the endangered citizens of Prague. He even expressed the gratifying view that on a future occasion I might be granted the opportunity of using my bare hands to apprehend some dangerous beast by the ears. Perhaps he thought that for some reason – God alone knows what – this was one thing I really wanted to do.

Next day there was mention in the papers of my extraordinary willingness to take part in the capture of poor Marcus Aurelius. You can imagine how this was grist to Saturnin's mill.

When I spoke about these events with Dr. Witherspoon, he delivered himself of a surprising opinion which almost insulted me. It was his view that the legend built up by Saturnin rather suited me. Apparently he could not otherwise manage to explain my willingness to go hunting lions in the zoo district in the middle of the night.

I have always been of the opinion that a capacity to assess human nature is something that a person must be born with. Neither the years nor experience will endow you with that capacity, as can be seen in the case of Dr. Witherspoon. How could such a thing have occurred to him in the first place? Just how foolish and vain does he think I am? If I had wanted the reputation of an adventurer, I would have obtained it for myself and would not have waited for my servant to create it on my behalf. No one can disregard the fact that circumstances drove me into situations where I had to make difficult decisions between a desire to be truthful on the one hand and my natural dignity on the other.

If you live peacefully like an ordinary and sober member of the community, you do not exactly inspire your friends and acquaintances with a wish to find out how you would behave if attacked by a raging buffalo. Try to imagine the people in your own life in a similar situation and you will see how nonsensical such a thing is. And now consider the fact that thanks to Saturnin's fantasies my friends were at once led to think about me in the manner that I have described. Where my personal courage was concerned, I was unwillingly put to the test like a guinea pig.

I have never, for example, made that foolish claim about the shark and the camera tripod, but you can imagine how you would find it if the most beautiful mouth you have ever seen should curve into a disbelieving smirk and say: "You've been with a shark?" It is certainly understandable that such situations sometimes led me to decisions reached in the hope that one day I would be able to say: "Oh yes, Miss Barbara, I've been with the shark and I've seen the lion. In fact there have been feats of derring-do the world over."

III.

got to know Miss Barbara Basnett on the tennis court. She was a leading light in the suburban club of which I was a member. I used to encounter this beautiful and inaccessible woman while she took part in practice matches with the coach or with some top player. I have Joe to thank for the fact that our acquaintance ever went beyond a polite greeting on my part and an equally polite, if cold, reply on hers.

Permit me to introduce this Joe to you. He is twelve years of age, collects tennis balls and rackets left on the courts, smokes, plays truant and is part of the furniture at the club. Despite being so young, he is renowned for his expertise on the beauty of the female leg, whose different manifestations he carefully scrutinises in the course of carrying out his duties. He is absolutely unwavering in his views on the subject, and it is common knowledge that the owner of the only two legs that have passed the test of his critical appraisal is none other than Miss Barbara.

The guffaws of male members of the club could be heard a mile away whenever Joe held forth on the subject in their company. I considered their amusement to be in extremely bad taste. Even if Joe's youth partly exonerated him, it remained indisputable that a properly brought up gentleman does not stare at women's legs. Even if the opportunity to do so presents itself.

Half an hour before I was introduced to Miss Barbara, I myself had such an opportunity. I was sitting on a deckchair in front of the clubhouse and Miss Barbara was standing on its raised verandah. She was looking out for the coach and kept consulting her watch. Attached to my deckchair was a sunshade which screened Miss Barbara from the waist upwards. This meant that I could be left undisturbed to examine her legs without running the risk of being apprehended in an act of indiscretion.

My mind was forced to reflect on the fact that several members of the club would be grateful for such an opportunity. With what pleasure would they gaze at the beautifully sculpted, tanned legs with their petite ankles, lissome shins and rounded calves, the plump, girlish knees and the full thighs moulded by sporting activity. The sun had created a pulse-quickening border of pink and brown in those places where the thighs disappeared inside her dazzlingly white shorts. They would even scrutinise a small scar on the left knee and imagine it to be a souvenir of a skiing accident earlier in the year. As I say, such people would be very grateful for such an opportunity and it would never cross their mind to act as I did and continue to read the newspaper.

The coach Miss Barbara was waiting for failed to turn up and this seemed to have put her into a bad mood. She asked something of Joe, who shrugged his shoulders and pointed in my direction. He then came over to ask whether I might like to give the young lady a game. I replied that it would give me the greatest of pleasure, but he conveyed this answer to Miss Barbara simply by looking in the direction of the verandah and calling out, "Yeah."

Miss Barbara smiled in my direction and I will tell you something. That she has attractive legs, I do not deny. So have many women. But I have never in my life seen such a mouth. The essence of her magic is that wonderful mouth. Even if I had known her a very long time I would not have been certain what her eyes were like, because whenever I was in her presence I was looking at her mouth.

I played three sets with her and lost all of them. This was not a pleasant experience, but I consoled myself with the thought that she would think I was playing the gallant. Strangely enough, however, she did not think this, and informed me after the game that she had never seen such a ridiculous forehand drive as mine. She spoke even more disapprovingly on the subject of my service. She said that I served like an old woman. I do not like it when a young lady expresses herself in such a manner. Naturally you must not be allowed to think that I am a defender of euphemistic social conventions and white lies. I would not have found it preferable if, after a match in which my level of play was almost an embarrassment, I had heard Miss Barbara coming out with sentences such as:

"Oh you play so beautifully! It is so long since I've enjoyed a game like that. You must adore playing tennis."

I would definitely not like to hear that, but at the same time it is not necessary to use suburban slang such as "You serve like an old woman". I take pleasure in people treating me honestly, but this doesn't mean that they have to speak in such a manner. It is possible for anyone to use the refined speech of good society. I read once that on no occasion would a diplomat say that someone was lying. In such circumstances he would use the sentence: "I assume that one might successfully doubt the accuracy of your information." QED.

I do not know how Saturnin learned that I was not an equal match for Miss Barbara. He looked heartbroken and I can only assume that he took it personally.

He devoted the whole of the following day to the erection of a peculiar wooden fence on the deck of our houseboat. I did not dare to inquire as to its purpose. In the evening he painted a line the height of a tennis net along the fence and announced that it was a training wall. He recommended that I exercise my tennis strokes against it on a daily basis. He particularly mentioned the forehand.

He then provided a demonstration with several drives of such savage force that I felt sure the wall could not withstand such a barrage. I asked him how he acquired his skill and he explained that for a long time he was a tennis coach in Nice.

I decided that it would be no surprise to learn that he had played in the Davis Cup. I trained in accordance with his instructions for perhaps half an hour and discovered that he had built the wall in an ingenious manner with barriers on each side. Consequently only a handful of balls fell into the River Vltava.

So a training wall was added to the manifold alterations, repairs and extensions which our boat was subjected to under Saturnin. I preferred not to think about what the owner of the boat might say about it.

The thing was that Saturnin behaved from the outset as if the boat was ours. I watched with growing apprehension, because I presumed that the owner would not approve of the changes which we carried out. At the very least I could not imagine him enthusing about them. For the moment, however, I had no opportunity to discover what view he took of Saturnin's modifications. I had never met him personally and I didn't long to do so. Saturnin, who was the one to rent the houseboat, described him to me as small and extremely tubby.

When I say that Saturnin rented the boat, you must not suppose that he followed the usual practice of agreeing the level of rent and term of notice, signing a contract and suchlike. Saturnin cannot act in such an unromantic and pedestrian manner. At the time he informed me that the boat was a free loan for fifty years. Then he explained something to the effect that he told the owner we were preparing to set off on a polar expedition and that nowhere on the seven seas was there a more suitable boat than his. That it would be for him – for the owner, that is to say – a great honour that one day his vessel would be as well-known as the famous polar explorer Nansen's boat *Fram*, and so on with more nonsense.

The owner agreed to all this on condition that we gave the boat a name like *Lily*, *Fifi* or something – I have already forgotten what the name was, save that it was something awful – and that when we come upon some hitherto undiscovered land we name it after him. Saturnin promised to do so, but forgot to ask the man his name. He did not even remember to do so at their next meeting, when the man called on him in order to explain that he'd fallen out with his girl and now wanted the boat to be called *Cleo*.

I cannot imagine where people get hold of such tasteless names. As if there weren't already enough beautiful names for women. Over and over again I found myself driven to the conclusion that if I managed to acquire a respectable forehand and service, there would be no reason why we couldn't give the boat the name *BARBARA*.

In the evening we received a visit from Dr. Witherspoon. He examined Saturnin's handiwork and hankered after the opportunity of delivering a major speech on the decline of craftsmanship.

I remember as if it was this very day how we sat on deck in small wooden chairs while Dr. Witherspoon declaimed. It was a warm evening and the first stars were coming out in the sky. As we sat on the deck the hodgepodge of sounds that make up the buzz of a city – car horns, tram bells sounding in the distance and the peaceful murmur of the river – provided a muffled background to Dr. Witherspoon's speech.

If Dr. Witherspoon's speeches are not confined to personal matters, they are well worth hearing. He is a lively narrator, knows how to imitate various people in their verbal mannerisms, and at the same time he gets so worked up about the issue at hand that the result is entertaining. The darkness of night gradually descended upon us, leaving only the glow of the occasional cigarette when the doctor stole a puff during the intervals between speeches.

There was a time, Dr. Witherspoon declaimed, when a person who made shoes called himself a shoemaker. Not only did he give himself the name, but he also had it written on a signboard, where an inscription such as *Albert Little: Shoemaker* would hang next to a picture of a lady's laced boot. And this Mr. Little, the Master Shoemaker, would be sitting of an evening over his beer and make the following speech: "My dear boy, when I have made you new shoes, you will be able to go on foot making a pilgrimage to the Holy Mountain and back in one day. When you return you won't be too lazy to come and thank me, even if it's ten in the evening. That's the sort of cobbler I am."

As you know, Dr. Witherspoon continued, shoemakers have died out. It did not happen because some illness overtook them, nor because Baťa's factory destroyed them. An even worse calamity befell them. In the following generation, for some absolutely inexplicable reason, the shoemaker began to feel ashamed of being a shoemaker, the joiner of being a joiner and the locksmith of being a locksmith.

The son of Mr. Little works at his father's last in the same cubby hole, but the inscription above the entrance to his business reads: *Manufacturer of Footwear*. I am well aware, continued the exasperated doctor, that his father, were he to rise from the dead, would take the sign down with his bare hands and would say to his son: "So you are ashamed of your father's profession, are you? What's all this about a manufacturer of footwear? You're a shoemaker! It really is disgraceful. And what about that man Bullock opposite? Another one to go the same way. His inscription says *Furniture Warehouse*. Does he own a factory?" The son would explain in a condescending manner that Bullock did not have a factory and that his father should understand that it was simply a question of promotion. "Promotion?" the old man would fulminate, "it's not promotion so far as I'm concerned. It's deception. It's misleading people and it's false pride. Promotion to me is a shoe or a wardrobe honestly made."

Dr. Witherspoon explained that this elderly gentleman would be appalled by such things, but that we ourselves were already accustomed to them. We read the sign and at once translate it mentally into simple common parlance. *Gentlemen's Fashion Emporium*, that is surely a tailor's. *Designs, Decorations, Interiors*, that must be a house painter. *Manufacturer of Iron Structures*, that will be a small-time fitter with a single apprentice, because if he had two that would make them an *Amalgamated Engineering Works* or some such title. *Tar Production Plant* – you would hesitate at that one. But don't be confused, this is our well-known old friend the Master Slater, and the tar products which he needs he buys from a real factory. I happen to know him.

The fact that most craftsmen are nowadays ashamed of their craftsmanship is overshadowed by the the way in which today's products are ashamed of their producers. The articles are only there in order to fetch a suitable price, but they obstinately refuse to serve their purpose. And don't tell me, Dr. Witherspoon went on, that I am looking on the dark side. Do not tell me that there aren't still craftsmen today who make good and reliable things, or that it isn't still, for instance, possible to get furniture at which the heart rejoices, such as wardrobes that surprisingly enough open, without having to be shaken first, and bookcases whose glass fronts slide across without difficulty. Don't tell me that there's no more of the type of furniture that will keep its quality for decades.

I take pleasure in this fact, but for most people it's of little use. I am thinking of the vast majority for whom fifty thousand crowns probably represents a lifetime's savings rather than the cost of furnishing a single room. These people have for the most part reconciled themselves to their standard of living, but it is understandable that they should insist on having wardrobes that open, a bookcase with a glass front that's willing to slide and that they do not wish to find themselves in the paradoxical situation of having to buy new furniture every three years just because they are not well off.

My own family, continued Dr. Witherspoon, was not wealthy either, but you can come to us and see for yourselves what an old oak wardrobe looks like!

It would be somewhat more bearable if today's craftsmen at least offered to compensate for their low levels of skill and honesty by adopting a helpful manner. But the very opposite is the case. Master Little used to deliver new shoes to your own flat. That was in the past. Evidently it makes no sense to ask for a personal visit from a footwear production plant.

When, for example, the children used to damage some piece of furniture at home, their father would call out to the joiner in the street: "Master Craftsman! I need such-and-such repaired." The Master Joiner would thank him for the order and promise him that little Joe would be there in a jiffy with his cart. And upon my soul, he was there with his cart. You can go and ask anyone who still remembers those times.

My daughter, the doctor went on, has some kind of play-pen with perpendicular staves for her child at home. One of those staves recently snapped, leaving the split wood pointing menacingly upwards, and what might happen if the little chap fell onto it as he toddled around there doesn't bear thinking about.

So I said to myself that I would handle the matter, that everything would be put right, and at the same time the toddler would discover what grandfathers were for. Because I had had some contacts with craftsmen before, my expectations were rather modest and it never even crossed my mind that I might behave like my late father. I picked up the playpen myself, with as much skill as I could muster, and took it to the nearest large-scale manufacturer of furniture.

I did not expect him to behave with me as if I had brought an order for a million living-rooms, but at the same time my journey was not tormented by concerns about whether Mr. Manufacturer slept well or whether perhaps I might be arriving at an inconvenient moment. I needed him to effect a repair for which I was willing to pay and would even forego the customary haggling.

I walked through a gateway followed by a filthy courtyard and entered the factory which consisted of a small salesroom and a mucky little storeroom. I explained to the factory baron what I needed, after first greeting him in a very respectful manner.

My greeting was not reciprocated and the plant overlord scowled at me in a morose and malicious manner that made my explanation somewhat diffident.

Before I could finish speaking Mr. Manufacturer had scarpered, the door slamming behind him.

Two apprentices exchanged awkward glances before turning in my direction and shrugging their shoulders. All of a sudden Mr. Manufacturer showed his head through the door and he addressed me furiously: "We don't have the time to deal with things like that!" Then he slammed the door shut even more loudly than before. I reckon that if anyone turned up at *Amalgamated Timber*'s largest factory hoping to have a broken ladder mended, they would be treated more decently than I was.

I wish ill of no one, concluded Dr. Witherspoon, and my nerves do not clamour for stimulants in the form of thrilling spectacles. However, if it were to come to my attention that in accordance with some unjustly neglected procedure, used in the time of King Charles IV of blessed memory, they will be committing this particular Master Joiner to the Vltava in a basket, then I would be there first thing in the morning, in order to be assured of a place on the edge of the parapet from which to view the spectacle.

IV.

believe that I have already mentioned the fact that I have an Aunt Catherine. Accidents will happen. Aunt Catherine has a son. He is eighteen years old and bears the name Bertie. It never rains but it pours. My aunt is widowed and Bertie is an orphan, because Uncle Francis died ten years ago. He certainly did not regret doing so. To spend one's whole life listening to proverbs, sayings and nuggets of wisdom is no easy matter.

Aunt Catherine is a lady of some years, but refuses to take any notice of them. She dresses as if she was goodness knows how young, wears outlandish hats and showers on the face paint, although with no idea of how to do so properly. When out walking she prances about in her own inimitable manner and pouts her lips. It often happens that one of the men my aunt comes across is astonished by her appearance and stares at her in a somewhat bewildered manner. At which point my aunt arranges her face in a peculiar grimace which is intended to suggest that she is fighting back a smile, and a few steps further on comments in a low voice: "Such an impertinent man!" She then glances back over her shoulder, discreetly but definitely, making passers-by concerned that she might collide with a lamp-post.

She proceeds to hold forth to all her ladylike acquaintances in the cafe about some young man who eyed her up in the street and about how she found it a distinctly unpleasant experience. She explains that she is well aware of the fact she's no spring chicken, and a boy like that should find himself some young girl and not stare at her. Yes, that's the way Aunt Catherine always goes on, but I ask you, what does it all add up to? Men will go on giving her the eye.

Bertie is an exceptionally empty-headed and conceited adolescent. My aunt spoils him and invariably comes out with the remark: "He really is something, our Bertie!" She claims that he has an unusual talent which has surprised everyone. As to who has actually been surprised, that is something I have never been able to ascertain. Once my aunt told me that Bertie's talents so impressed his teachers that it was decided to send the young genius to a special school. Later someone explained to me that this unusual and particular establishment was designed for the education of children with 'special needs', i.e. those who would hold up the progress of others in a normal school. I do not know whether this is true and I will not say that it is for fear of sounding malicious.

Although I don't have any special liking for Aunt Catherine, I do sympathise with her in this respect.

The point is that her son's prospects are presumably rather bleak. The property she inherited from my uncle has depreciated greatly in value and I think that the necessity of Bertie finding some form of employment will soon become clear.

I once asked my aunt whether she had already thought about a future career for Bertie. She started by indicating that this was none of my business. Then she added in a conciliatory manner that Bertie's ice-skating was exquisite. If only I could have seen the turns he did! Nothing could match him! I found this answer somewhat strange. Even if my aunt was right, what, for goodness sake, would he do during the summer?

My aunt proceeded to change the subject and started reminiscing about her late husband. She held forth as if I'd never seen him before in my life. In fact I remember him very well.

He was an admirable fellow. He underwent several career changes for the simple reason that he considered it beneath his dignity to be anyone's subordinate. My aunt put this down to a natural sense of pride. Opinions differ concerning the position which he eventually secured.

Aunt Catherine claims that he became a research worker. I myself am of the opinion that he had a small concern producing cleaning products of some kind. Saturnin once told me that from what he'd heard the whole outfit was a disaster area. I could almost say that none of us was wide of the mark.

Saturnin's assertion was, as usual, exaggerated, but it cannot be denied that a whole series of misfortunes had really befallen my uncle's business, and that it was almost unbelievable that they hadn't led to any deaths. Saturnin was alluding to this when he referred to my uncle's concern as a disaster area. At least I presume that this was his meaning, because the cleaning products which my uncle manufactured were certainly quite disastrous, but nonetheless they were hardly enough in themselves to warrant Saturnin's description.

Nor is it possible completely to refute my aunt's opinion that uncle was a research worker. In a certain sense of the word he definitely was a man who discovered a whole series of chemical theorems and laws of the most various kinds. These precepts had all been discovered by others before him, but my uncle knew nothing of this and therefore cannot lose any credit on that account.

His own path to discovery, as someone who had no understanding of chemistry, was thick with brambles and bathed in sweat. However, all this was outweighed by the pleasure of gaining experience. No one could deny his sporting character. He resembled a person who, after mastering a few easy multiplication tables, announces to his teachers: "Don't tell me anything more. I don't want to hear about how Pythagoras, Eudoxus, Euclid, Archimedes and others invented this and that. I do not need to sponge off other people's discoveries. Just give me pencil and paper and a pair of compasses and leave me in peace. I will arrive at the answer of my own accord."

Uncle really did make all sorts of discoveries. Thus, for example, he found out during one experiment, which took a very exciting course, that it is a foolish idea to add water to acid. He was not at all concerned by the fact that he could have acquired such information in a more formal manner and without at the same time burning his fingers, not to mention a waistcoat that had once looked as good as new, from a chemistry textbook aimed at the junior forms of a secondary school.

To him chemistry was virgin territory. It meant constructing castles in the air with solid doors that opened to the sound of secret formulae. He knew no technical terms, ignored chemical formulae and marvelled at the spluttering test tubes and retorts hosting violent chemical reactions.

Like a mediaeval alchemist he was chasing phantoms, tripping up and hauling himself to his feet again, with the difference that his own quest ended not in the glittering prize of the philosopher's stone but in an all-purpose soap. The soap was manufactured from worthless waste material with minimum production costs, but the outcome was a real gem.

Before the altar of his dreams Uncle Francis offered a sacrifice in the form of injuries and burns, windows blown out in the laboratory and grave accidents in the workplace. Once he even received a beating at the hands of enraged employees who had mixed two raw materials at his command and had then hardly been quick enough to jump through the window.

The endless run of accidents finally compelled his staff to live their lives on constant alert. This was the reason for a false alarm on one occasion. The workers had created some strange concoction in a vat, and the foreman asked Uncle Francis what they were doing. Uncle knit his brows and in a sudden attack of honesty replied: "Exploring." He was most surprised when his fellow workers responded to this laconic answer by giving way to panic and diving for the exits. They thought Uncle had said "Exploding".

According to Saturnin's version of events, the older employees abandoned Uncle's factory, pointing out that they had their wives and children to think about. They opted for safer employment in a nearby factory producing explosives.

After each mishap Uncle lay down on an ancient divan upholstered in green plush and emitted low groans. Friends and acquaintances arrived and with a reproachful cry of "Sir!" or "My dear fellow!" sat themselves down on a wicker chair and asked about what had actually happened.

Uncle suggested in a tired voice that he had been conducting an experiment with far-reaching implications. He weaved a few technical terms into his explanation, and with the insouciance of an expert spokesman confronting the laity he spouted a chemical version of hogwash. The acquaintances then shook his hand, expressed their conviction that everything would very soon be working perfectly well again, and made their way out down the creaking wooden stairs, thinking to themselves: "This is a Prince among men!"

In the afternoon the housemaid, Libby, took charge of looking after my uncle and my aunt set off eagerly for the coffeehouse with a spring in her step. She puckered her lips as the men eyed her up. In the cafe she regaled some acquaintance with information about how my uncle met with his accident. Science, she explained, was a sublime and beautiful thing, but sometimes cruel towards those it loved.

Meanwhile the lover of science fell into a fitful sleep on a plush divan and dreamed of inventing soap – the best soap in the world, whether for cosmetic or cleaning purposes. From ingredients consisting of nothing but worthless waste material he would produce a real gem.

After my uncle's death I used to see my aunt very occasionally. Our mutual feelings were made clear by that reluctant affability which people show towards one another when they are less than overcome with joy at being related.

My aunt took the opportunity provided by several family meetings to make an obvious show of indifference towards my private life, something that filled me with a sense of pleasure which I made no effort to conceal.

Unfortunately this lack of interest was only a pretence. Later I gradually came to understand that where I was concerned there wasn't a single deed, trait or uttered sentence that escaped the strongest criticism. The whole lot came under censure, beginning with my tie and ending with my character.

I think that even my other relatives failed to judge me any more favourably. A silent but bitter conflict raged between the members of our family. It broke out something like a decade ago, and was occasioned by a worthy attempt to ensure that our Grandpa bestowed neither favour nor affection upon anyone who didn't deserve them. People are bad and Grandpa is so innocent! He could easily be deceived and leave his property to someone who would let it go to rack and ruin, as Aunt Catherine used to say.

The other relatives used to remark caustically that Aunt Catherine was speaking from experience, in view of the fact that she had herself already let a property to go rack and ruin.

I suspect that Grandpa finds this tasteless family quarrel, pitching each against the others, entertaining. I believe he does not even find it appropriate that I will not lower myself to taking part in trying to win his favour, but this is something I cannot help. Not that I wouldn't care for an inheritance. People for whom it is a matter of indifference whether they become millionaires are to be found only in novels, just like those human spectres who live happy and contented lives even if they have to go without lunch. Then when they come into unexpected riches they sink into a state of pure misery for some absurd reason and heave a sigh of relief only when they lose the fortune all over again. These are heroes made from paper. You can see the sawdust oozing out of them.

I cannot therefore truly deny any interest in an inheritance, but I cannot bring myself to show my concern in the way our family does. I have never in my life tried to deceive people in a doctor's waiting-room by claiming that I only needed something signed and could be admitted ahead of the others. I have never tried to buy a ticket by mistaking the front of the queue at the ticket-office for the back. I have never tried to push in front of people who were at the post office counter before me. I am not boasting in saying this. I merely want to show a certain character trait which makes it impossible for me to use sharp elbows in the attempt to secure Grandpa's estate. It is interesting to note that my relatives nevertheless consider me to be a dangerous front-runner. God knows how they have arrived at this view.

It is understandable that, relations between us being what they were, I was considerably surprised to encounter Aunt Catherine springing to intercept me one evening as I made my customary appearance on the deck of our houseboat. She looked as if she expected her presence to trigger a rapturous response on my part. Her playful banter was accompanied by the usual salvo of sayings discharged in quickfire succession. Among other things she pointed out that a guest in the home represented a visit from God.

When I had finally brought my dismay under control, and felt a desire to exploit the minor pauses in my aunt's rendition in order to get a word in edgeways, I spotted Bertie emerging from my cabin in the bow, dressed in pyjamas with a cigarette between his lips. I do not know what expression my face wore at that moment. What cannot be denied is the fact that words failed me, while Aunt Catherine hastened to tell me something along the lines of Bertie being ill. Allegedly the doctor had instructed him to stay in the fresh air. Because sending him to a sanatorium was beyond her means, she was beside herself with worry. Apparently I would have no difficulty imagining what it was like for her: she'd spent the whole night in tears. Yes, she was not ashamed to admit it, she'd cried her eyes out all night long.

There was no way out, however hard she thought about it, though the solution was simple and staring her in the face. It was Bertie who lighted upon it with the idea that he could spend his time convalescing on my boat. The more there were holes, the more there were moles. Besides, many heads found many meanings. Furthermore a lot of eyes did a lot of seeing. I believe that my aunt had a further saying in mind, but I anticipated her by pointing out that many dogs mean the death of a hare, whereupon she threw me an uncomprehending glance.

Meanwhile Bertie sauntered up to us and greeted me with the words: "Good day, old chap!" I do not care to be called 'old chap', and was on the point of making this clear when Saturnin was suddenly heard saying to Bertie: "There's no smoking allowed here, laddie."

This wasn't true. We smoked on the deck every evening, but I had the feeling that Saturnin's outburst was a response to the 'old chap', and took pleasure in observing Bertie go red. He then said something which brought out the full flavour of his foolishness.

"I didn't ask you anything, servant," he told Saturnin.

"Oh do excuse me, young sir, I really didn't mean to offend you." Saturnin's humble apology came as he snatched the burning cigarette from Bertie's lips and threw it into the River Vltava.

The contrast between Saturnin's submissive words and his disrespectful deed proved so confusing both to Aunt Catherine and to Bertie that Saturnin had time to make a triumphal exit before a word could escape anyone's lips.

Only then did Bertie manage to shout out "What an impertinence!" in a high-pitched voice before running off, evidently in order to procure another cigarette. My aunt declared that my servant had very peculiar manners. It was to be wondered at that I should allow such a person anywhere near me.

You will doubtless have noticed that my view of Saturnin is a decidedly critical one. However, at that precise moment I saw him simply as a person who had hastened to my side at a difficult moment.

I allowed my aunt to sit on a deckchair. She wanted to continue with her explanation of Bertie's poor health, but at that moment Saturnin, on the pretext of having some work to do, came into the vicinity once more. My aunt asked me to send him away. I replied coolly that as she could see it was a small boat and I could hardly order him to jump into the water.

She replied that she had the impression of not being entirely welcome. To some extent this was only to be expected. Had the health of her child not been at stake, she would never have set foot on this boat of mine. Furthermore, she had not come to beg, because in her view the family was under an obligation to do something for the young gentleman. When her husband, Uncle Francis, had been alive, the whole family had benefited from the floor polish she supplied it with. If the family maligned her nowadays, she could only make clear to them that she'd always had the best of intentions and that it was neither her fault nor that of the polish if Uncle Michael saw fit to break his leg on the shiny parquet and if this had become a source of so much unpleasantness.

I would like to know whether Aunt Catherine deliberately lies or simply doesn't recognise the truth of what took place. Uncle Michael did not break his leg on the parquet floor but on a bicycle when he collided with some cyclist. Moreover the unpleasantness over the floor polish resulted from the fact that it turned the parquet black and created masses of tiny holes when applied to it. When the owners of the houses affected saw what had happened, it nearly brought on a fit of apoplexy in several of them. I can perfectly well remember how around 140 people brought charges against Uncle Francis as manufacturer of the polish.

The more my aunt spoke, the clearer it became to me that she had decided to stay on the boat with Bertie for as long as she deemed it worthwhile to do so, and that when all was said and done I myself had no say in the matter. Finally she announced that there could be no proper home without a conscientious housekeeper. Even a corsair like myself was in need of the considerate female touch. Apparently I would only now appreciate the profound truth of the saying 'east or west, home is best'. In the past she'd had no time for the scatterbrained notion of living on a boat, but now she could see how very romantic it was. Indeed she realised now that this was what she had been longing for. Leaving other things aside for a moment she had a yearning to repair the mainsail.

I have remarked elsewhere that Saturnin usually behaves in an absolutely proper way. By this I mean that he would never intervene in any discussion unless specifically asked a question or in some similar manner invited to participate. However, he appeared to make up his mind that in the case of Aunt Catherine and her son these rules did not apply. With regret I have to confess that that I refused to admonish him.

When the announcement about patching up the mainsail came to his ears, he remarked that we didn't have any sail. My aunt snapped back that we should buy a sail. Saturnin asked her what we would do with it. He made the point that our boat had no mast. It had a propeller to satisfy any possible requirement to go anywhere. To buy a sail would be stuff and nonsense. Finally he commented that even if I, as his Lord and Master, had for reasons of my own decided to buy a sail, it would be a new one and would not need to be patched up. I must admit that there are moments when Saturnin's logic overwhelms me.

V.

r. Witherspoon always says that the most reprehensible form of absent-mindedness comes about when people forget to enjoy life. They take the bountiful gifts bestowed upon them by fate as a matter of course. If a person wakes up of a morning healthy and refreshed, in a clean bed and with the assurance that a hot breakfast is not too distant, then he has every reason to get to his feet for a song of thanksgiving or pen an ode to the glories of life.

Dr. Witherspoon maintains that too long a period of bliss blinds us to our good fortune. Fate would then do us an inestimable service if it took us by the scruff of the neck and chucked us out into the cold for a while. Then we would forget about the smoke from the stove and we would only remember that it kept us warm. Besides, we could have made sure that the stove provided heat without any smoke.

Fate took me by the scruff of the neck and threw me out of my cabin onto the foredeck. I regret that I cannot say it chucked me out into the cold. It would be very impressive if I could. However, I can recall quite well that it was during the first days of July and insanely hot.

On this particular occasion Fate appeared in the guise of Aunt Catherine, who took over the cabin as if it was her own territory, Bertie in tow. The moment my aunt and Saturnin had finished discussing whether or not we should buy a mainsail, so that my aunt should have something to mend, I was left to brood on my own. My aunt explained that she was dead tired, and gave concrete expression to her state of utter exhaustion by going gracefully weak at the knees. Then she departed for my cabin in her prancing manner.

Saturnin threw me a glance of deepest sympathy as he went out too. A moment later I spotted him on the embankment boarding a tram. I sat down on a deckchair and without thinking pulled out my cigarette case. I was on the point of lighting up when I remembered Saturnin's prohibition, and in a spirit of solidarity ushered the cigarette back into its case. Yes, while the affected Bertie was sauntering and lounging around in the vicinity, a smoking ban must prevail.

I caught myself thinking with malicious pleasure of the moment when Bertie's cigarette flew across the deck. I blame my own hardness of heart for being unable really to accept the fact that the lad was ill. The one circumstance which somewhat excused my attitude was his healthy demeanour – he had never looked so well. However, in the last resort, I said to myself, it can only be to his benefit if he stops smoking.

If Uncle Francis, his father, had been alive, he would surely have forbidden him to smoke. The man was a non-smoker himself, and never let a drop of the hard stuff pass his lips. He believed that this regime would prolong his life. He used to say that if there had never been such a thing as alcohol his own uncle, who drank himself to death before he could reach sixty years of age, would still be fit and well in the land of the living.

Uncle Francis used to recall this all the time and became a sworn enemy of the demon drink. I recall how he once flew into a rage when through some oversight he bit into a chocolate liqueur. He assumed it was a trap deliberately laid for him.

Thanks to this strict ordering of his life and methodical breathing exercises he remained admirably hale and hearty right up to the day of his death, as is well attested by the fact that he died between two press-ups, the demanding ones where the hands must lie flat on the ground, at the ripe old age of 48.

Someone once pointed out to Aunt Catherine how extraordinary it was that Uncle Francis died at a relatively young age, seeing that he didn't drink and his own uncle, who used to enjoy thirty encounters with the beer bottle each day, had almost lived to see sixty.

Aunt Catherine replied that this proved absolutely nothing, because it was possible and even probable that had Uncle Francis taken after his own uncle he would have died even sooner.

The devotee of alcohol then asked my aunt whether this meant that if Uncle Francis had drunk thirty beers a day, he would have died as a two-year-old infant. My aunt took offence at this question.

Until Saturnin returned I whiled away the time reflecting on the depressing prospects for the immediate future. The sun was slowly setting and my hopes of something unexpected happening, which would compel Aunt Catherine to change her mind and depart, were disappearing with it.

I would be most unhappy if you were to think of hospitality as foreign to my nature. It really isn't, but if you knew Aunt Catherine as I do you would understand my feelings. It was not the first time she'd descended upon a member of the family out of the blue, and everyone afflicted in this way maintained that the best thing a person could do in such circumstances was to say: "This is an Act of God. I have lost my flat and all its furnishings. It is true that I have lost everything that I ever had. A terrible thing has taken place, but worse things could happen to me. I have come out of this alive and well. I have hands that can work, a clear head and the world is big. How long does it take to get a passport?"

That is certainly easily said, but not so easily done. It is no small thing to set forth empty-handed into the world. Courage is a wonderful quality, but everything must be done within reason. Not even the fact that my grandfather's brother made his fortune living abroad for ten years is grounds for everyone else immediately to follow in his footsteps.

In any case, I don't think that I could get leave of absence for such a long period. The office has its rules. But let's keep to the case in question, as they say in court.

An unpleasant sense of disappointment in Saturnin added to my gloomy thoughts. Perhaps it seems to you that I was doing him an injustice and that he made an effort, doing what he could to acquaint our guests with the fact that they weren't welcome. However, as you are aware, he didn't pull any rabbits out of the hat on this occasion. I had always been convinced that even the impossible was not beyond him, and I felt really disappointed at our having to look on powerlessly while Aunt Catherine made herself at home in my cabin, as if she intended to accompany us on our purported polar expedition.

You will already be aware of the fact that I was not enthusiastic about Saturnin's strange ways, but that isn't to say that I couldn't conceive of a situation where his peculiar qualities were just what was needed. Saturnin usually engaged in actions which left normal people completely baffled. He lured people into impossible situations. He compelled them to do things which they had absolutely no intention of doing, and confronted them with a fait accompli. Now here we were, faced with such a simple matter as persuading Aunt Catherine to go back to her flat in Nusle near the centre of Prague, and Mr. Saturnin was completely at a loss.

I reminded myself that if a gentleman's gentleman is out of ideas, this does not mean that his master must sit around twiddling his thumbs. While the soft violet shadows slowly lengthened on the opposite bank of the Vltava, plans for disposing of Aunt Catherine whirled about in my poor head. I decided that with the assistance of Dr. Witherspoon and Saturnin I would make out that some ghastly contagious disease had broken out on board ship.

Alternatively, I would so arrange it that my aunt had to visit the town some day with Bertie. In her absence we would start the engine and take the boat several kilometres upstream. We would then return and wait for her on the embankment with a few suitably drenched personal effects. We would explain to her that the boat went down after a collision with a steamer. Then again, perhaps we could . . . in short, pending Saturnin's return I thought up a dozen schemes, several of which bordered on criminal offences.

Saturnin turned up at about half past eight carrying a small parcel. He asked whether he could impart some information which he thought might be of interest to me. However, before speaking of it he would like to ask a question of a somewhat personal nature, and he was unsure whether he might be permitted to do so, given his lowly status.

When I had finished telling him to stop beating about the bush, Saturnin asked me whether he was correct in supposing that I would receive the news that the dear lady and her wee laddie had decided to abandon ship with a certain degree of relief. I replied that his supposition, that I would receive the news that the dear lady and her wee laddie had decided to abandon ship with a certain degree of relief, was correct.

Then he told me that according to the information which he had been given, young Bertie was as sound as a bell. He did not mean to imply by this, that in explaining the circumstances which compelled her to decide on an extended stay on my boat, the dear lady had lied. He was simply suggesting that she had not deemed it necessary to divulge the true reasons for her decision. This was all the more understandable in that the aforesaid reasons were somewhat humiliating for the dear lady. Reputedly there were squabbles between Aunt Catherine and the other tenants in the apartment building, the reasons for which were not entirely clear. Consequently the other female residents had closed ranks against the dear lady and had refused her entry to the establishment on pain of a severe physical beating.

The dear lady had indeed attempted to gain entry to her flat that very afternoon, but was forced to retreat by the combined forces of the other harridans in the building. Saturnin expressed the opinion that it was the height of injustice that I should have to bear the consequences of disagreements between the dear lady on the one hand and the other residents of the apartment building on the other.

He went on to mention that it was not practically possible for these women to spend all night preventing the dear lady from entering her flat, and even if that were the case the dear lady could call for assistance from the police. Saturnin explained that these facts called for the following conclusions:

1. Young Bertie was perfectly well and could be treated like any other healthy fellow.

2. The dear lady employed a warlike cunning in order to advance her designs, and it is permissible to waive the rules and use the same weapons against her.

3. Because the dear lady moved into her cabin in the bows in a somewhat inconsiderate manner, without ever expressing any interest in where or how its previous occupant would be able to sleep, she must be prepared for the same lack of consideration to be shown towards her.

4. There is no danger of the dear lady becoming homeless. Things could be arranged so that she gains access to her flat without sustaining injury.

And finally:

5. Even if she did not succeed in avoiding the punishment promised for her, she couldn't reproach us with anything. Besides, these vengeful women had expressed themselves very precisely concerning what they intended to inflict on the dear lady's bodily person. They had chosen a part of the body where it is difficult to do serious damage in normal circumstances, and certainly not when the part in question is of the dimensions applying in the case of the dear lady.

Saturnin asked whether I would agree to his making an attempt to change the dear lady's mind. Naturally I did agree, but I did not conceal my doubts as to whether he would succeed. Instead of responding to these doubts Saturnin pointed out that it was nine o'clock and that by a quarter past nine the cabin on the foredeck would once again be vacant.

Then he untied the packet and to my complete surprise masks of St. Nicholas and the Devil emerged from the wrapping. At the same time he explained that buying a mask of St. Nicholas in July was one of the hardest tasks he had ever had to undertake. He stroked the whiskers glued on to the ruddy face of the saint with relish, and smoothed the red plush tongue poking out of the Devil's mask. He asked that, in the event of his failing to return, I would remember that he died in my service. Should the worst happen, he required me to seek out any attractive girl whom he might have married. I was to take care of her as if she were his widow.

I was a trifle confused by all this and glanced after the departing Saturnin with a whole series of unexpressed questions on my lips.

Why, of all things, did he buy those masks?

What did he mean by his allusion to some young lady?

I could not imagine what was going to happen and I confess that I was in a state of agitation. I expected to hear the cabin resonate with the sound of terrified shrieks from my aunt or else a blazing row. Nothing like that happened, and the hand of my wristwatch showed that six minutes had already gone by since Saturnin entered the cabin, wielding a mask in each hand.

Dusk was falling, although high in the sky the ethereal realm was still full of sunlight. I leaned back in my deck-chair and a strange contentment came over me. It was as if the whole episode was not my concern. The embankment lights came on and I felt like the audience in a theatre at the moment when the front of the stage lights up and the curtain rises slowly upwards. The strange blend of fading day and blazing arc lamps made everything around us seem like a piece of stage scenery, flat and unreal but unusually beautiful.

The white doors of the cabin, illuminated by the slanting beams of the electric lights, attracted my attention and led me to suspect that they would take centre stage in the forthcoming play. At that moment the first actor appeared through them. He was a handsome fair-haired man holding masks of the Devil and St. Nicholas in his hands, as if he was in the process of deciding which of these roles he ought to play. Then he fastened unhappy eyes upon the doors of the cabin, as if he was afraid of some inevitable and

unfortunate event. He gave a start at the appearance of a Queen in travel clothes with a Prince in tow. He made a gesture as if desirous of preventing her departure, but then lowered his hands to his sides looking broken-hearted. The masks fell to the ground looking once again like the empty shells they were. The Queen pranced over to the gangplank and the Prince hurried after her. As the footsteps of the departed faded out of earshot, the man raised his head and announced: "There we are. It is a quarter past nine."

It was a very long time before I managed to find out what took place inside the cabin on that occasion. Saturnin said that it was not worth mentioning and that for aesthetic reasons he didn't like to talk about it. It was indeed a drastic measure that he took and I will mention it only briefly. Saturnin announced to Aunt Catherine and Bertie that he had bought them masks and recommended that they cover their faces with them during the night.

Naturally they thought that Saturnin had gone mad. They asked why they should do anything so ridiculous. Saturnin replied that they must surely know that on boats it is impossible to exterminate certain troublesome rodents, those of which it is said that they are the first to abandon a sinking ship. He added that the two of us already knew from experience how disagreeable it was when such animals scurried across an unprotected face during the night. My aunt said – as a matter of fact she didn't say anything and began to pack her things in a hurry.

The river grew dark and on the boat a peaceful silence reigned. Some voices wafted over from the opposite bank and a stray canoe made its way to the boat-house. Saturnin disappeared for a while and returned with freshly-made black coffee. I offered him a cigarette and indicated an empty deck-chair. The sky was now pitch black and the atmosphere had cooled to a pleasant temperature.

VI.

Naturally Grandpa's pocket watch doesn't run on electricity. Only Saturnin could make up such nonsense. Evidently he wishes to allude to the way in which everything you look at in Grandpa's house is electrically operated – from the opening of doors, heating, cooking, ventilating, lighting, and shaving through to igniting your cigarette.

Grandpa is a solidly built elderly gentleman with a ruddy complexion, grey hair and jovial eyes. For many years he was Director of the City Power Station, President of the Society of Electrical Engineers, Chairman of the Provincial Association of Power Stations, Member of the Board of Directors of Electrical Enterprises and in fact a member of all those corporations within whose titles 'electrical', 'electro-technical', 'electricity' and suchlike terms are to be found.

Throughout his life he has campaigned on behalf of electricity. They say that he worked out a plan years ago for the electrification of the Elbe valley. Along the entire length of the river's upper reaches he designed one power station after another, so much so that in the end the water in the Elbe stopped flowing and had to be put into barrels and transported to Hamburg by train. That's only a joke, of course, but when people recounted this apocryphal tale you could tell from their tone of voice that they rather liked Grandpa. This was even the case where Saturnin was concerned. Indeed I think that he and Grandpa understood each other very well from the moment when Saturnin introduced himself to the old man with formal courtesy.

This all happened when I went to the countryside around mid-August in order to idle away three weeks of holiday in Grandpa's house, bringing Saturnin with me. At first I hesitated as to whether I should take Saturnin or send him off on leave and go alone. After all, I knew that Aunt Catherine had seen to it that Grandpa got to know how eccentric his grandson was. 'A young chap like that, and he has to have a servant!' I could well imagine Aunt Catherine saying such things. In the end I made up my mind to take Saturnin along.

Grandpa accepted this as a matter of course. Saturnin stood before him, clicked his heels as if on parade and apparently satisfied Grandpa with his turnout. Then Grandpa turned to me and remarked, as he did on the occasion of my every visit, that he hoped I would like it in his secluded and remote neck of the woods and that I should spend plenty of time in the forest. He added that this particular year he would have several more guests. Dr. Witherspoon would be arriving in a week's time. He had already spent a fortnight in his log cabin in the mountains, and had promised to rejoin the human race here below. The granddaughter of an engineer called Basnett, an old friend of Grandpa's, would be coming from Prague at about the same time.

I believe that I blushed at this point, but Grandpa took no notice. Saturnin also looked as if he hadn't quite caught the name. I lost track of what Grandpa went on to say and only pulled myself together when he jokingly asked me why I hadn't taken the river route in the houseboat. I wanted to reply that I was prevented from doing so by the weirs imposed by a surfeit of electrical engineers, but I thought better of it. In the event he gave a contented chuckle and didn't even wait for an answer. His eyes twinkled roguishly and then suddenly he was slapping me on the back with an even more contented chuckle.

In the evening I sat in my room and reflected on the precarious nature of our opinions concerning fellow human beings, even our relatives. Until that moment I had considered Grandpa to be a grumpy old man, of a somewhat malevolent and selfish disposition. It now seemed to me that I had done him a great injustice. How he had learned of my interest in Miss Barbara was of course a mystery to me, but that was beside the point. The main thing was that he had invited her and that the most delightful holiday that I had ever enjoyed now lay before me.

I regretted only one thing, the fact that Miss Barbara wasn't coming for a week. I examined my pocket diary and considered what I would give in order to be able to delete, vault across or pluck out that week which separated me from our reunion, so that I would be able to wake up next day knowing that a walk in the woods with Barbara at my side awaited me. A moment later, however, the sober reflection which was so much a part of my being gained the upper hand. A week of my life! The price made me wince. A week of a young life, a week of which I could have no idea what delights it might bring. A week of being alive, of wandering through woods, savouring the perfume of thyme, hearing the babbling brook, going to fish, basking in the sand beneath a crag after bathing. How magnificent it all was!

Then I decided that I would not delete this week and that I would carry out an interesting experiment. I would write down everything that happened during these seven days in my pocket diary, so that the following Saturday I could carefully consider both the good and the bad things that would have happened, before once more shaking my head in disapproval and repeating the observation that a week of one's life was too high a price to pay.

When I now look back, I can see that it wasn't necessary to set anything down in diary form. The events which occurred had such an impact that I would have remembered them in any case. Judge for yourselves.

The following day was a beautiful Sunday morning. I lay on cushions breathing the fresh air which came streaming in from the garden through the open window. After living on a houseboat I savoured staying in Grandpa's solid residence to the full. I felt a pleasant sense of security, an assurance that the deck would not reverberate to the sound of Saturnin's warning cry calling on me to hold on in the face of wake from the steamship 'Prague'. At the same time I realised that I had to have a serious word with Saturnin. The thing was that Dr. Witherspoon sometimes applied a heavy dose of his usual sarcasm when speaking of Grandpa and Saturnin responded to his words with unconcealed delight. I was concerned that he might have acquired a somewhat disrespectful opinion of Grandpa and was sorry that I had ever put up with such talk.

I do not want to imply by this that Dr. Witherspoon would have maligned Grandpa. He even says such things to his face. When Grandpa disclosed on one occasion that he probably wouldn't be with us much longer, Witherspoon carefully observed: "I imagine that you will pass away quietly surrounded by your relatives, each of whom will be beating you with something solid, since otherwise you'd never die." Grandpa must have chuckled at this for half a year.

I prepared a speech in which I sketched a brief life of Grandpa for Saturnin, outlining his contribution to the education of our country in matters electrical, and concluding with a rousing passage on the great man's many virtues.

I had just decided to get up when a discreet knocking sound could be heard and in came Saturnin. He wished me good morning and explained that it was the early bird which caught the worm. He added that youth spent in idleness would mean old age holding the begging bowl. He informed me that it was fine weather outside, but that one shouldn't count one's chickens before they're hatched, besides which we knew neither the day nor the hour and the old hag rushes in where the Devil fears to tread.

You will not be accustomed to the strange manner in which Saturnin expresses himself, but I understood from this hotch-potch of sayings that Aunt Catherine had arrived. I cannot say that I welcomed the news with open arms. Aunt Catherine definitely did not conform to my idea of a holiday. To me hers was a name that spelled all manner of trouble.

From as early as that very morning my apprehensions began to prove justified. Aunt Catherine caused an embarrassing scene when she complained to Grandpa that Saturnin had not greeted her and had even insulted Bertie.

Saturnin begged to differ in a polite manner and maintained that he'd had no intention of insulting the young gentleman. Moreover he had not failed to acknowledge the dear lady and could even recollect the form of his address. He had apparently greeted her with a respectful "Oh, hello!".

My aunt shouted that he was a shameless liar, that Saturnin had distorted the truth in his smart alec way and that she was nobody's fool. Apparently he had made a face upon seeing her and his comment had been "Oh Hell!". She did not consider this a greeting. She was most annoyed, but this was as nothing compared to Bertie. The young man had never forgotten the affair of Saturnin and the cigarette. Now he had once again been offended to the very core of his being. He had spent the whole of the last month growing a moustache, the evidence of which was something like eleven undisciplined hairs, and the insult which he'd had to endure concerned this manly decoration.

The thing is that when Bertie, true to his resolution that he wouldn't pay any attention to Saturnin, sauntered off with a conceited look on his face, Saturnin placed himself in the young man's path and, staring fixedly at his upper lip, asked in mock horror: "What happened to you?" Bertie was so taken aback that he stupidly asked: "When?" before fleeing to his room and shutting himself away. Grandpa admonished Saturnin, but told Aunt Catherine when Saturnin had gone that if he himself had grown something similar to Bertie's eruption, he would hold a clean handkerchief to it while in contact with other people.

It rained in the afternoon. I played chess with Grandpa and was thoroughly beaten. Grandpa made mincemeat of me. It is remarkable how well he plays despite his advanced age. After the fifth game he smiled indulgently and said that we would do something else. He proceeded to tell me a gripping story from his youth concerning his military service in Italy and how a countess had fallen madly in love with him. What a dear old chap.

The moment it became dark I went off to my room so as to avoid having to play rummy with Aunt Catherine.

It rained yet again on Monday. Grandpa was very grumpy and tormented by gout. He swore like a trooper, but this was understandable. When nothing is bothering him, he is sweet, jovial and more than willing to challenge all-comers to Graeco-Roman wrestling.

But more of that later. The day dragged on endlessly and it was evening before Grandpa's pains began to ease. Then it was time for me to hear the story of his military service in Italy and how a certain countess fell in love with him.

I listened with only half an ear because Grandpa had told me the story already the day before. I was reminding myself of the admirable fact that two days had elapsed without Saturnin putting into practice one of his madcap ideas. I touched wood rather noisily and Grandpa remarked absentmindedly: "Come in!" Then he went on with his story.

The very next day Saturnin made up for his omission. He maintained to Grandpa that he knew how to drive a car. Grandpa welcomed the news and expressed a wish to go for a drive in an old Ford which had spent several decades rusting over in the garage. Saturnin got hold of a can of petrol from somewhere and they set off secretly at about ten o'clock. None of us knew anything about it and the alarm wasn't raised until Grandpa failed to materialise for lunch.

At about three Saturnin arrived on a bicycle and a hansom cab delivered Grandpa. I hadn't the least idea of what had happened, but Grandpa didn't stop shaking all afternoon and kept repeating "Jesus Christ! Jesus Christ!" to himself. Saturnin had once again made himself scarce.

Aunt Catherine asked me for an explanation, even though I knew as little as she did. Then she offered some confused observations about impatient heirs apparent and assassination. Finally she commented that whoever digs a pit for another falls into it himself and that hell is the reward for those who treat the devil kindly.

It rained all day Wednesday. Aunt Catherine wouldn't allow me near Grandpa, so I gave myself over to reading. I worked my way through a book called Germinator or something like that by some professor or other. It didn't exactly make my day. In the evening Grandpa summoned me and told me about his military service in Italy. I felt sorry for him, but surely he had ended up there through no fault of mine. Before going to sleep I reflected on the fact that even rainy days like this would be lovely if I could only spend them in the company of Miss Barbara.

On Thursday Grandpa felt much better and wanted to play chess with me. I was not at all keen, because it had only just stopped raining for a while and I wanted to go and have a look at the river. Nevertheless I reminded myself of my duty to Grandpa. When all was said and done, Saturnin was my employee and I was responsible for him. My aunt was astonished that Grandpa hadn't turned against me, something she put down to the fickleness of old age, observing that a horse is only a foal once while a human is twice a child. In any case I went to play chess with Grandpa.

Although I had the best of intentions, things did not turn out well. I am no genius at the game, but in spite of that it struck me as surprising that Grandpa castled three times during one of our encounters, changing sides each time he did so. When I drew his attention to this, he became very upset and said that he had nothing to learn from me, having been playing chess for nigh on a century. He dismissed me in a most ill-tempered mood.

As I left the room Aunt Catherine drew a deep breath, which could only mean that she was preparing to come out with another saying. I managed to shut the door before she could launch into it.

On Friday Grandpa was in a very good mood and even asked after Saturnin. Saturnin reported for duty and presented Grandpa with a proper military report. He explained that everything was in order, that the tobacconist's had been restored to its original location and that the car had been sent for repair. However, the mechanic had urgently requested a photograph so that he could find out what the vehicle used to look like. Moreover he wished to know whether by chance one of the car doors had remained in the garage. Saturnin searched the garage but couldn't find the door. He still had to enquire as to whether it might be in the tobacconist's.

Apart from this the accident apparently had no more serious consequences. The owner of the tobacconist's suffered shock, though not from the accident itself but from returning from lunch to find that his shop had disappeared. Grandpa chuckled, offered Saturnin a cigar and then the two men amused themselves in each other's company all afternoon. Aunt Catherine even maintained that they took exercise together. I couldn't confirm this, since I spent the whole time in my room.

In the afternoon Grandpa wanted to hold forth to me about Italy and the countess, but I asked him whether we might do something else. It was a most foolish suggestion on my part, but who could have guessed what would result from it. Grandpa explained that Saturnin had been teaching him ju-jitsu wrestling and that he (I mean Grandpa) would in turn teach me the sport.

What followed will seem unbelievable to you. Please bear in mind that the last thing I intended was wrestling with the dear old man. It was an error on my part to respond passively to his comical attack. His initial hold, with which he tried to upset my balance, coaxed a condescending smile from my lips and led me to drop my guard. Suddenly Grandpa leaped aside and in a flanking attack knocked into me with a surprising degree of strength.

The consequences were terrible. I flew across the room over the parquet floor and landed with a bump some four metres away from where I'd originally been standing. When I tried to get up, an agonising pain shot through my right leg and everything went black. Still chuckling as Saturnin and the housemaid Maria led me to my room, Grandpa shouted after me that the pain would pass.

They conveyed me to my bed and sent for a doctor from town. I do not really know what doctors are for, certainly not in view of what this man did to me. My ankle was hurting enough as it was without someone trying to twist my leg so that the heel stopped pointing forwards. This done, the doctor announced in a sombre manner that I had to undergo an X-ray and that the following morning he would send an ambulance for me. The following morning, if you please, when Miss Barbara should at last be arriving. You will understand how I felt, and this perhaps somewhat excused the fact that I turned down in exasperation Grandpa's offer of the story of his military service in Italy.

As the door of the ambulance slammed shut behind me on the Saturday morning, I saw Miss Barbara in the garden drive as her white *Rapide* pulled in. She wore a fetching little sports cap and looked so very charming.

VII.

THEY TRANSPORT ME TO HOSPITAL
RAIN, DOWNPOUR, CLOUDBURST, DELUGE
DOCTOR LEVERET
THE HOSPITAL IS A TRAP
THE ADMINISTRATOR HAS HIS REGULATIONS
BARBARA SORTS US OUT
BY PURE ACCIDENT WE FAIL TO DROWN
DOCTOR WITHERSPOON

I lay on a stretcher and the ambulance slowly made its way towards the river. It began to spit with rain again. Saturnin sat beside the driver and drew my attention to the dangerously swollen river just as we were about to make our way across it on a narrow wooden bridge. Torrents of muddy water raced underneath a bare yard below the wheels. Swift as an arrow a length of pine driftwood disappeared under the bridge and re-surfaced on the other side carried along by a yellow wave.

Full of apprehension, I fixed my attention on the mountains which were shrouded in low clouds. Water was tumbling from the trees, sliding over the saturated moss, slipping from the stony slopes and gurgling in the gorges. It was plunging towards the river, and as it strengthened and intensified it bore in its wake pine needles, loose soil, clumps of grass, pebbles and larger stones which it tossed about vigorously. It eroded the steep hillside, broke up stacks of logs, tore into the riverbanks and carried off massive tree trunks.

I was glad when through good fortune we had the bridge behind us. I spent the whole trip to the hospital imagining the grotesque situation which would unfold if the swollen river washed away the single link between Grandpa's remote refuge and the rest of the world.

I do not think that I have yet said enough about the peculiar location of Grandpa's house. It was built at the foot of Castle Hill, and the plot of land on which it stands is an elongated triangle squeezed between two rivers. Dr. Witherspoon claims that it is the proper location for a power station rather than a private residence, but Dr. Witherspoon complains about everything. To my knowledge there is no more beautiful place in the world. It shares with certain other people, objects and landscapes the capacity to radiate a protective aura all its own. There are people at whose side you would willingly cast your lot in with some chancy entrepreneurial venture. There are objects which give you a sense of security and there are places on earth which you feel protect you from anything dangerous. Embraced by streams and backed by the hush of Castle Hill, Grandpa's triangle is such a place.

The only way from Grandpa's place to the neighbouring small town with a railway station is over Grandpa's private bridge.

If I was imagining how the flood might have destroyed the link between the inhabitants of Grandpa's house and the outer world, my fears were not focused upon a disastrous traffic accident so much as upon the possibility that Miss Barbara and myself might be be marooned on different sides of the river. That was not how I had envisaged my holiday turning out.

The ambulance drove through the town and turned into a road lined with cherry trees which led to the hospital. The spots of rain stopped falling and an unbearable closeness set in. I had a vivid impression of the august sun burning behind those clouds, beating down into the valley. From somewhere in the distance there was a roll of thunder.

The vehicle came to a halt in front of a small white building. Saturnin and the driver wanted to take me inside on a stretcher. I refused and hobbled into the Outpatients Department with their assistance, putting as little weight as possible onto the injured leg. They sat me down on a bench which had been painted white. Then

61

the driver went off to announce our arrival. It was just the two of us now, Saturnin and I, keeping our thoughts to ourselves. Saturnin had a slightly bad conscience and blamed himself, not without good reason, for my injury. He inspected the medical equipment in the glass cabinet with such interest that I felt rather disconcerted.

The air was full of some pungent disinfectant and a large circular clock made a strange ticking sound like water dripping into a basin. From the corridor came the sound of approaching footsteps. The door opened and the driver glanced around the room as if he was looking for someone before exclaiming "Where the hell . . ." and disappearing once more. The uneventful stillness returned and overpowered me with a pleasant languor.

I nodded off and a host of muddy waves, hurling tree trunks like terrible battering rams against the bridge supports, appeared in my mind's eye. Then a thought occurred which left me wide awake. "Saturnin," I asked, "do you think that these floods have reached Prague as well?" "Undoubtedly," he assured me. I closed my eyes once again and saw our boat pitching and tossing on the waters, rearing up in protest at the tight leash of its mooring, while its tubby little owner howled on the embankment.

My sombre imaginings were interrupted by the arrival of the nurse, who informed us that the consultant had not yet turned up. She removed several thermometers from the cabinet and went out again. Saturnin must have been able to read my thoughts, because he proceeded to inform me that I needn't worry about our houseboat. Before leaving he had requested the owner to insure the boat for a considerable sum of money. He added that he had allowed those of my possessions which were kept on the boat to be insured at his own expense.

I was flabbergasted. I asked where the money to pay for insurance came from. He explained that in insuring the boat he had acted as a representative of the insurance company, and had made use of the commission he'd received in order to pay the annual premium for insuring my belongings. He confirmed that it was absolutely unnecessary for me to be embarrassed. Attending to the interests of his master's property was one of the duties of a good gentleman's gentleman. He observed that our departure had been a hurried one in view of the fact that until the last moment I had not known the precise dates of my holiday. Consequently he had lacked the opportunity to explain the advantages of insurance and secure my consent for it. The sum which he had paid for insurance in my name was not a large one. If his course of action happened to meet with my approval, I could add the amount to his next salary payment. I nodded and we fell silent once more.

About half an hour later the nurse appeared with the news that the consultant had arrived and was doing his rounds. He would take about twenty minutes.

It was forty minutes later before the nurse put in another appearance, returned the thermometers to the cabinet and informed us that regrettably the consultant had already left. This was more than I could take. I leaped to my feet, but a searing pain in the ankle forced me to sit down again.

I demanded to know from the nurse why the consultant had already left, when he knew that we'd already been waiting for ninety minutes. She hazarded the opinion that he'd forgotten about us. I asked whether there was another doctor around who could do the X-ray. She was surprised that it was merely a matter of an X-ray. Judging from her expression, she must have thought I'd come to have the leg removed. She explained that Dr. Leveret could do the X-ray. This was my view too, and I asked when Dr. Leveret would be available to do so. She replied that Dr. Leveret had been there since early morning. Saturnin wished to be told where Dr. Leveret was skulking. She laughed and denied that he was skulking. He was in the examination room. This was welcome news to us. Saturnin wanted to know whether the doctor would come to see what was happening if someone opened fire in the Outpatients Department. The question slightly puzzled her, but she supposed that in such an eventuality the doctor would certainly arrive. Saturnin asked whether his appearance could be secured by any other means besides shooting. She responded that she could put the question to him directly. Saturnin said that putting the question directly to him was the wisest course for her to take.

Dr. Leveret arrived in a somewhat dishevelled state, with traces of lipstick on his face. He looked preoccupied, and after asking me four times which leg was affected he X-rayed the healthy one. When I explained that I had injured my right ankle, he looked at me suspiciously, as if I had made him the victim of a conjuring trick. He pondered my words with such an intense look of concentration on his face that I had the impression he was counting my legs. At last he reached a decision, took an X-ray of the right ankle and disappeared into the darkroom.

He returned after about half an hour and informed me that it was nothing to worry about. I should apply an aluminium acetate compress and avoid taxing my leg. He said goodbye as if he was quite a normal person and went on his way.

Glad that it was over, I hobbled towards the exit with Saturnin's assistance. The ambulance was waiting outside, with the driver laid out asleep on a stretcher inside the porter's booth. The porter himself was sitting by a small table, his head nestled in his curved arms beside the telephone. He was also asleep. It looked like a scene from Sleeping Beauty.

Saturnin sat me down on a bench and gently roused the driver. He informed him that we were ready to go. The good man explained that there was no need to wake him up in order to tell him this. He wished us a safe journey and wanted to continue his nap. Meanwhile the porter woke up and managed a dull glare in our direction. Saturnin told the driver in his good-natured way that we wished to leave in his ambulance. He added that we regretted waking him but such a step had been absolutely necessary.

The driver rose to his feet and asked us whether we had official authorisation for him to make this journey. He explained that he was referring to written authorisation from the hospital. We said that we had nothing of the kind. What's more, we had no such permit in the morning when he brought us here. He agreed with this, but explained that in the morning he himself had such authorisation, and proceeded at once to pull it out of some dog-eared wallet. This document applied only to the journey to the hospital and not to the journey back. For that it was necessary to procure some green slip of paper from the office. Otherwise he couldn't drive us.

Saturnin asked whether someone would be in the office, it being the lunch hour. The porter thought that the administrator would still be there and that he could reach him by phone. We asked him to do just that. The administrator was in and Saturnin took over the receiver from the porter. He was informed that it was strictly forbidden to make use of an ambulance for journeys from the hospital. It was meant exclusively for the speedy delivery of the sick to the hospital, and even then only in really urgent cases where any delay would be dangerous. A journey away from the hospital could never be classified as 'urgent'. The administrator found it astonishing to think of permission being given for the use of an ambulance to treat such a minor ailment as an injured ankle.

Saturnin ventured to remark that it was nevertheless beyond my powers to walk on foot for two hours with such an ailment. The administrator accepted this, but claimed that he must abide by hospital regulations. He recommended that we rent a car through Mr. Perrin. Saturnin thanked him and telephoned Mr. Perrin. He was told that Mr. Perrin had taken his car to Pilsen and would be back by the evening of the following day.

Saturnin rang the administrator back and made the difficult nature of our situation clear to him. He explained that I was absolutely incapable of walking, quite apart from the fact that the doctor had expressly forbidden me to exert my bad leg. Mr. Perrin, the owner of the car hire service, was away and not returning for another day. The ambulance had brought us to the hospital, it was now idling here without any purpose and the journey to Castle Hill and back wouldn't take more than half an hour. His employer was willing to be charged at a high rate.

The stickler for regulations answered that such a thing was completely out of the question. He would have to enter such a ride into the books as a fresh journey to the hospital, and this would mean pretending that the ambulance set off empty and returned with a sick patient. Saturnin asked whether he could do precisely that. However, the administrator replied that for Saturnin to ask such a question was insulting. Not only would it mean circumventing the regulations, but it couldn't be done for the simple reason that there would then be one patient missing in the hospital. Suppose there was an inspection: inquiries would be made and he would end up having to pay for the journey himself. Saturnin pointed out that he wouldn't have to. We would pay and were willing to divest ourselves of the money in the office right away. The administrator insisted that this wasn't possible because according to the regulations there could and should be no advance payment for a journey. Saturnin then proposed that we pay afterwards. The administrator responded that according to the regulations . . .

Quick as a flash, like a conjuror's spell, Saturnin's behaviour changed. His respectful and patient efforts to explain and negotiate gave place to an outburst of coarseness that took my breath away.

Among other things he recommended that the administrator go and lie down in the ward for sufferers from dementia, where in the case of an inspection he could personally fill the gap caused by the missing patient. He could enter the journey in his accounts as if the ambulance both left and returned empty, which would without doubt be perfectly in accordance with the regulations. Furthermore, if paying for transport either before or after the journey was forbidden, then let it be done during the journey.

He proceeded to express himself in a frightful manner concerning the gentlemen who devised these regulations. He explained that we would be leaving by car, without the administrator's permission, and advised him against trying to stop us. He said that the moment he laid eyes on anyone looking even faintly like the administrator of this madhouse he would beat his brains out with a rubber hose. As a matter of fact we didn't have a rubber hose and I don't know where Saturnin could have got one. This wasn't something on my mind at the time, however, because I caught sight of what had caused the abrupt change in Saturnin's behaviour. Miss Barbara's white *Rapide* had stopped just in front of the hospital and its owner was at that very moment heading into the entrance hall. She smiled at us, took over the entrance hall with the sound of her soft alto voice and paid no attention whatsoever to the horizontal driver or the porter. She asked what had happened to us and why we hadn't been back home ages ago. She removed a deerskin driving glove and offered her hand to Saturnin and myself.

In a moment we were sitting in the car and Miss Barbara was driving down the avenue at full throttle past the cherry trees. Without turning her head she informed us that the water was still rising and that she didn't know whether we'd make it home. Although about half past twelve, it was almost too overcast to see the time on my watch. Miss Barbara stopped for petrol and as she switched off the engine an oppressive silence set in. After the experiences of the morning I was surprised when the petrol attendant arrived at once.

Heavy black clouds grew ever darker and hung ever lower in the sky. I remarked that instinctively we'd all ducked down. Miss Barbara paid for the petrol, turned the ignition on and within ten metres we were in third gear. We shot through the town and Miss Barbara switched on the headlights. Headlights at noon! I kept my eyes fixed on the road ahead with grim foreboding, expecting all hell to be unleashed at any moment. There was a strange gleam in Saturnin's eyes. I had the feeling that he liked both the fact that something unusual was happening and the course of action adopted by Miss Barbara. Her daredevil driving was admirable. She stepped on the gas in the frivolous manner of one who has not yet managed to write off a car.

As we approached the river Miss Barbara pointed out that as far as she could see water was already streaming over the bridge, although the bridge itself was standing firm. She eased off the accelerator a little and asked: "What do you think? Shall we go for it?" Such a suggestion was utter madness. The moment brought to mind the way her beautiful mouth once shaped itself into a smirk when she asked me: "You've been with a shark?" My response was firm. "Let's go for it!"

Saturnin threw me an approving glance and nodded in appreciation. Barbara nodded too as she grabbed the steering wheel and stamped the accelerator into the ground. At that moment my blood ran cold at what met my eyes between the edge of her sports cap and Saturnin's head. The bridge was completely underwater – whether to a depth of two inches or two yards, it was hard to say. All that could be seen breaking the surface above those wild and muddy waves were the twin parapets on either side of the bridge, vibrating from the force of the current as if they were ready and willing to fly away at any moment.

The white *Rapide* flew between the parapets at breakneck speed. I was horrified to see that Miss Barbara jerked the steering wheel firmly to the right at the last moment. That was when I felt as if we'd driven straight into the river. The whole vehicle shuddered under the sudden blow of torrents of water throwing themselves against all the windows. The engine roared and the wheels seemed to be revolving on the spot. I don't remember how long this lasted, but all at once we had broken free and were out of it. Miss Barbara switched on the windscreen wipers and we continued on our way to Grandpa's house. She merely remarked that it was a good thing the water hadn't stalled the engine. I turned round towards the river, observing the place where I had just enjoyed the most dangerous moment in my life, and I was somehow offended that the bridge had not collapsed immediately in the wake of our crossing. That's what would have happened in all the movies. However, the parapets were still poking up out of the waves and quivering from the pressure of the current. On this occasion I had to be content with the fact that the bridge collapsed some two hours later. When we were about fifty yards from the covered approach to Grandpa's house, the heavens opened.

I have lived through many a mountain storm, but never have I seen anything like that. Brilliant flashes of lightning forming an almost continuous blaze of light and thunderclaps every few seconds meant that we were surrounded by a deafening racket. Barbara shouted something, but no one could catch what she was saying. Saturnin turned and tried to say something to me, but no one could hear him. I asked both of them something, but was just as inaudible. Then we all burst out laughing. We made our way into the covered drive-in and our laughter prevented us from getting out for a long time. It was a kind of release, and though it made me think I was going mad it also seemed to be a source of amusement at the time.

As Saturnin escorted me into the hall there was a tremendous report and I thought that lightning had struck the house itself. Something flashed on Grandpa's formidable instrument panel and Saturnin gave a nervous start. This was enough to send everyone into fresh fits of laughter.

A figure was leaning across the polished banisters of the staircase facing the hall and a well-known voice was saying something to the effect that hysterical laughter can frequently be observed among people of below-average intelligence as a reaction to living through a real or perceived danger. But that's Dr. Witherspoon for you.

VIII.

Grandpa's house shook to its foundations. I was sitting in a deep armchair, marvelling at the way the living room was alternately filled with violet light and plunged into pallid gloom. Torrents of water streamed down the windowpanes. Aunt Catherine crossed herself after every flash of lightning, threw a worried glance at the window and then returned to her speech.

She was explaining that no one would believe that someone of his age didn't know better. He could pay for this with his life. It surely wouldn't end well. The body is a beast of burden that can bear so much ill treatment, but one day comes the straw that breaks the camel's back. A cold was quite enough to carry away an old fellow like that. Surely everyone must be aware of this. But no, all men are alike and think they know best. It would only hurt them to listen for once to what a woman could tell them.

I registered what my aunt was saying as if it was part of a dream and thought of other, pleasanter things. Of Miss Barbara waiting for me to return from the hospital. Of how she jumped into her *Rapide* and went after me when I took too long to come back. I liked such thoughts so much that I didn't hesitate to bring them to mind over and over again. I had only to half close my eyes and I saw her walking into the entrance lobby of the hospital with that radiant smile on her face, making friendly inquiries concerning our whereabouts and asking what had happened to us and why we had been there so long.

I am surprised at people who are not satisfied with the women of today and raise all manner of objections against them. They make disdainful comments about the way young women nowadays only care about playing sport or smoking, driving cars or visiting cafes and cinemas. When it comes to work in the kitchen, however, it's the other way round. Through sport they have coarsened and even abandoned the gentle character of the fair sex. The charm of their pitter-pattering walk has given way to long strides.

I dispute the notion that sport would divest womanhood of its magic and Miss Barbara is a shining example of this. I can perfectly well imagine a woman as a partner for life even without any flirtatious displays of helplessness, neither given to shrieking at the sight of a little mouse nor routinely feeling faint. If someone imagines that a young woman will make a bad mother because she knows how to drive and triumphed on skis in the Alpine Combination in her twenties, then perhaps he has never seen a young mother at the cradle. What are all world records in comparison to that tiny tot!

Perhaps someone will object that there do exist cases where maternal love does not manage to drown out a host of other interests which a young woman takes with her into marriage and for the sake of which she neglects her children. Quite so, and there are also instances of a mother killing her child. But they are exceptional cases which have always occurred and which cannot be associated with a particular generation.

There was a peal of thunder outside and a shriek from Aunt Catherine inside. She proceeded to point out that those who didn't take advice received no help. She had warned him but what was the use – it was like dealing with a small child. She asked whether anyone else could make sense of it to her. He spent days sitting around indoors and then all of a sudden, when this tempest arrived, he had to go out.

It was Grandpa she was endlessly wittering on about. He's a passionate devotee of storms and at the first peal of thunder there's no holding him indoors. He puts on his plastic mac and wide-brimmed hat to fend off the rain and then splashes around outside in his Russian leather boots until the firework display is over. Dr. Witherspoon says that it is a work-related aberration. Grandpa goes there to see how the competition in the electricity business measures up.

My aunt said that it was enough to give anyone a stroke and time for us to have lunch. We wouldn't wait for Grandpa. Time and tide wait for no man. She left to issue appropriate instructions in the kitchen. The room fell pleasantly silent. I longed for the door to open and for Miss Barbara to make her entrance.

The door did indeed open but in order to admit Bertie. He sported a dressing gown in livid yellow and the inevitable cigarette hung out of the corner of his mouth. He acknowledged my presence with a slight elevation of the right eyebrow followed by a nonchalant 'Hiya'. God knows whether anyone will teach this lout some manners.

He sat in the armchair facing me and declared that it was all a terrible bore. Nobody should imagine that he was going to spend three weeks staring out of the window at the rain. He was definitely returning to Prague. After lunch he would ask Barbara to run him to the station. Perhaps the bridge would still be standing.

"You will be asking whom?" I inquired. He repeated the name Barbara. "Has Miss Basnett given you permission to call her by her Christian name?" His patronising look was accompanied by the playboy smirk of a film star. He told me not to be silly. He indicated that he had designs on Miss Barbara and began to elaborate on her physical attractions in an indelicate manner.

Then he noticed how furious I was. He reacted by half closing an eye in amusement and using a stiffened thumb and forefinger to stroke his upper lip. By doing so he affected a moustache. He told me that wouldn't have imagined a man of my age taking an interest in Miss Barbara too.

To clear this point up I would like to point out that I am thirty years of age. Bertie has some strange notion that my life is all behind me. He said that it now seemed as though life in this backwater wouldn't be as dull as he'd feared. He offered me a wager as to which of us would be the first to win Miss Barbara's favour. I looked at this conceited eighteen-year-old boy with a knowing expression on his sybaritic face and a wave of nausea surged over me.

Bertie paid no attention to this and perhaps even understood the fact that I was lost for words to mean consent. He explained that he didn't like to boast, but it was clear to him from Miss Barbara's behaviour that his chances in the contest were better than anyone else's. To balance the odds he would wager at two to one, his two thousand against my thousand. At the same time he began to outline what must be accomplished in order to win the bet, but I did not give him time to finish his sentence.

I have never liked Bertie but at this precise moment I felt that my one aim in life was to kill this swollen-headed slug, to destroy it, to crush, tear and break it into pieces. I leaped out of the armchair like a madman and jumped on him.

Unfortunately, I got nowhere near hurting him. The attack ended halfway between my armchair and Bertie, because for the second time that day I had forgotten about my injured ankle.

White from the agony and purple with rage, I sat on the carpet and felt my forehead bathed in sweat. My leg hurt so much that I could barely stifle a groan. During this short period the expression on Bertie's face underwent a double transformation. From the complacent smirk of a ladykiller it mutated into the look of a frightened rabbit accompanied by a peculiar squeak of panic. My helpless collapse onto the carpet brought the original mask rapidly back into position while he told me how surprised he was at such a fit of temper and explained that this would make things all the more interesting. He added that he would send Saturnin to help me back onto my feet and went off in a manner which he probably took for effortless grace.

Saturnin came running up and conveyed me back to my arm-chair. It was evident that he didn't understand how I had come to find myself on the carpet and why Bertie himself hadn't helped me, but he was too practised a butler to ask any questions. He used to say that there were two alternatives in cases like these. Either one's master wishes one to know what has happened, in which case one will be informed about it, or he prefers not to mention anything, since any kind of explanation would be embarrassing.

I invited Saturnin to take a seat opposite me and asked him whether he was content in my employ. He assured me that he was most content. I asked him how things would be if I gave him an instruction of a rather unusual kind. His face lit up and he replied that he had always longed for someone to give him such an instruction, but that such an opportunity had never come his way. I wanted to know whether he would have any twinges of conscience if he had to take my cousin, the one who rejoiced in the name of Bertie, to some quiet spot where he could knock the stuffing out of him.

He replied that he would indeed have such twinges, because if such an opportunity presented itself then mere compliance with my wishes would mean that certain ways of responding to the situation remained rather foolishly under-explored. He then took me completely by surprise with a list of things that could happen to Bertie if a suitable opportunity ever arose. Evidently he had his own score to settle, but I didn't wish to pry.

Then I put Saturnin on oath to pursue Bertie relentlessly by air, land and sea for as long as I was unable to stand on my own two feet and punish him myself. In the furtherance of the cause he was to exploit every favourable circumstance and use all his ingenuity and cunning. He was to make sure that during our stay in Grandpa's house an uninterrupted series of embarrassments and horrors would be provided for this haughty Don Juan. He was to be on his guard every step of the way and punish the slightest impertinence towards Miss Barbara by administering a good thrashing. He was to . . . I can't remember now exactly what he said but it added up to vowing that a terrible revenge would be visited upon Bertie for the way he'd expressed himself concerning Miss Barbara.

Touched by the glorious and unforgettable moment, Saturnin rose from the armchair and in a slow and distinct rendition repeated all the details of his sworn duty. His words mingled with the rumbling of the receding storm and I couldn't resist getting to my feet with him. I stood on only one leg, but I stood to attention.

The solemn occasion was disturbed by Aunt Catherine arriving. 'Bursting in' would be a better description, because she doesn't make an entry in the way normal people do. The doors flew open as if a hand grenade had exploded behind them and my aunt rushed into the room. She called out something it was impossible to make sense of and threw herself into an armchair.

Saturnin had the temerity to observe that this couldn't be happening. My aunt pointed out that unfortunately it was. Saturnin expressed the opinion that no doubt there would be an explanation for everything. My aunt explained that if everyone minded their own business the world would go round a deal faster than it does, adding that flamingoes and mustard both bite. Saturnin asked whether the moral of that was that birds of a feather flocked together. My aunt looked nonplussed and asked what birds. In default of a reply Saturnin inquired whether Bertie had been beaten when he sneezed from too much pepper. My aunt wanted to know whether Bertie had said something to that effect and where the pepper was.

I found myself wondering whether they'd both taken leave of their senses. I asked Saturnin what had so upset my aunt and what she had been shouting when she came running into the room. Saturnin claimed not to have the slightest idea, because he never understood a word she said. My head went into my hands as I tried asking him what he had just been speaking about with her. He replied that he'd been practising a tried and tested method of pacifying over-excited persons.

My aunt jumped up from her seat and protested against being called a 'person'. I calmed her down and asked for a precise account of what had happened. Her features slowly rearranged themselves into the earlier look of fear and she cast her eyes around the room as if expecting to see a ghost. Then in a strangled voice she explained that the cook and Maria the maid had vanished.

I confess that I was confused at first, simply because of Aunt Catherine's look of alarm and the vagueness of her explanation. If someone told me that the cook had vanished into thin air, I would take this to be either a cheap party trick or something related to occult practices. It would be, so to speak, a case of dematerialisation. That would mean that the cook grew pale, formless and blurred before evaporating into the astral realm via the ventilation system. I would then understand how someone who'd witnessed such a terrifying event might burst into a room scared out of their wits and cry out about the cook's disappearance.

Nothing like this had been spelt out, however, and there was absolutely no need for panic. My aunt had simply failed to find either the cook or Maria the servant-girl in the kitchen and I couldn't understand why she was so upset by this fact.

At this point Dr. Witherspoon came into the living-room closely followed by Miss Barbara. My aunt swooped on them to discover whether they'd seen the missing women. Then Bertie sauntered in and thus it happened that when Grandpa returned he found us all together, busy inventing solutions to the case of the missing cook and maid.

Dr. Witherspoon was just observing that he was keener to know what would be done about lunch than to discover the fate of the cook when Grandpa walked in. Aunt Catherine made straight for him with a shriek and had soon submerged him in the shower of her tender reproaches, in order that he might be in no doubt as to her fears for his well-being. She tried to enshroud him in a camel hair blanket even though he was still in his wet plastic mac. This was a strategic error on her part. Not only was it ridiculous to try to wrap someone up in a blanket without first removing his hat, but apart from anything else such behaviour rather revolted Grandpa himself. He is proud of his health and hardiness and takes great exception when anyone fusses over him too much.

Whatever Aunt Catherine said later, it is clear that the responsibility for what followed lay with her for going too far and for making such an exhibition of herself over Grandpa's welfare. Perhaps Grandpa would not have been so annoyed if his feathers had not been ruffled in front of so many witnesses. He felt the eyes of everyone present upon him. Only Bertie, standing behind his shoulder, was more interested in Miss Barbara's knees than in any soul-stirring display of concern for Grandpa on the part of my aunt. The usual cigarette was lodged in the corner of his mouth and he looked as if he could hardly keep his eyes open in the dense smoke, but I was not deceived by this stratagem.

I don't know whether you have ever had the experience of seeing your wishes hardly formulated in your mind before they have been translated into deeds. Such things happen in fairy tales. For example, you get angry about something and wish for lightning to strike the source of your annoyance. There is a flash and it's done. Something like that happened to me on this occasion. I remember how I was desperately longing to give Bertie a hiding when all of a sudden he received one: with a bad-tempered snarl Grandpa threw both hands in the air in order to liberate himself from the blanket Aunt Catherine had smothered him in. At the same time he struck Bertie in the face with the back of his hand, forcing the burning cigarette into what he liked to call his moustache. Bertie yelled out and Grandpa followed with a startled shout because he'd also taken fright and burned himself into the bargain. Quick as a flash he turned and clouted Bertie. Before anyone could respond, Saturnin weighed in. With a cry of alarm he snatched the blanket out of Aunt Catherine's hands, threw it over Bertie's head, forced him to the ground and with all his strength pressed the blanket into his face as he called out: "His moustache is on fire!"

Grandpa gave another start and the whole group looked on dumbfounded as Saturnin sprang into action. My aunt called hysterically for someone to bring water. Saturnin shouted "Not water! Sand!" and Dr. Witherspoon muttered under his breath, "It's gone up in flames, thank God."

When Saturnin finally let Bertie go we thought that a madman had arrived in our midst. Bertie's eyes wandered over us with a dazed expression that either took us for an apparition or as people who should long ago have been hidden away in their graves. Evidently he didn't understand a thing that had happened. Then he began frantically looking for something in his pockets until after a while he suddenly stopped without finding anything. He rotated his head from one side to another, leaned back and I couldn't avoid the impression that he was about to crow like a cock. My aunt pounced on him and asked what was the matter. She sat him in an armchair and wanted to wrap him in the blanket as she had earlier tried to do with Grandpa. I think that if someone had a piece of grit in his eye, my aunt would have his head wrapped in a blanket. This was her remedy for all complaints. She did not succeed in applying it to Bertie and I don't think anyone else could have managed it either. As soon as he spotted the blanket coming his way he broke out in a squeal and fled the room.

My aunt ran after him.

There was a moment's silence before Dr. Witherspoon observed that he hoped it would not be necessary to amputate the lad's moustache. I suspected Miss Barbara of suppressing a smile by holding a handkerchief to her mouth. Grandpa took off his plastic mac and his hat and announced that he had two important items of news to impart.

He explained that ten minutes beforehand the floodwater had swept away the bridge that was our link to the rest of the world, and that the cook and Maria the servant-girl were stranded on the other side. They set off on bicycles in the morning in order to buy provisions in town. At the moment when the bridge gave way they were standing helplessly on the opposite bank, shouting to Grandpa and asking what they should do. Grandpa added that they both came from a nearby village and that by now they would both be safely home. We couldn't count on their returning to us for the next few days, because the path to White Saddle Ridge, where the river has its source, and the descent via Castle Hill would take them two days, even assuming that they dared to make such a trek in weather like this. Then he explained how glad he was that Aunt Catherine had made herself scarce, because it enabled us to discuss how we might prevent her from taking over the cooking. He pointed out that he was admittedly a man of advanced years, but if Aunt Catherine was going to cook then he was going to make an effort to swim across the river. He asked Miss Barbara whether she was prepared to come to our rescue.

Barbara's head nodded in just the way it had done when she signalled her decision to let fly with the *Rapide* at the flooded bridge. Grandpa responded with the ardent assurance that he would never forget her assistance. She had probably imagined that her holiday would not turn out like this, but he would try to make it up to her. Perhaps Mr Saturnin would be so kind as to assist her, at least in serving and setting the table. Saturnin stood to attention and sonorously clicked his heels.

Miss Barbara set off for the kitchen in order to see what we had in stock and find us something to eat as quickly as possible. We were all famished. Then Grandpa surprised me by expressing regret over my injured ankle and asking what the hospital had made of it. He was delighted to learn that it was nothing serious and told me that I ought to make a speedy recovery because he was concerned that our supplies were low. It was quite possible that after a while our isolated position would compel us to replenish them through hunting. At that point it would be necessary to conscript every healthy man.

This was a scenario which Dr. Witherspoon found hugely amusing, but I remembered how during my last holiday I had missed a roebuck at three paces and my spirits fell at the prospect.

Miss Barbara returned from the kitchen with an announcement popular among all of Prague's tram drivers: the power was off. Grandpa scowled and tried a switch. Miss Barbara's information was shown to be correct. It was little short of disastrous.

I have already mentioned that everything in Grandpa's house runs on electricity. Anyone else would have remembered that an ordinary stove can outperform an electric one during a power cut. However, this was not something one could point out in Grandpa's presence. It all meant that we suddenly found ourselves in a situation where not even a cup of tea could be brewed. But for the roof over our heads we resembled a strange bunch of castaways. There was Grandpa, given to irascibility and childishness,

Dr. Wither- spoon with his malicious remarks, serene Miss Barbara with a smile on her face, whose beauty took my breath away, affected Aunt Catherine spouting proverbs with her eighteen-year-old fop in tow, I myself with my damaged ankle and last of all the hazardous presence of Saturnin.

I ran over in my mind the events of the week just passed and it dawned on me that Saturnin had not been idle during this time. He had destroyed Grandpa's old car, damaging a tobacconist's in the process. He had taught Grandpa ju-jitsu. He was responsible for my injury, without which Miss Barbara's daredevil drive across the waterlogged bridge would never have taken place. I even suspected his fingerprints on events surrounding the cook and Maria the servant-girl. I think that the one thing he couldn't have been held accountable for was the flood, but I'm not even certain of that.

IX.

An extract from the Koran concerning the cow

Bertie is sent to fetch worms

Miss Barbara cooks our first lunch

The duty to deliver a story at bedtime

My aunt offers Grandpa various delicacies

The return of Bertie

And when Moses said to his people 'God commands that ye sacrifice a COW,' they replied: 'Art thou trying to make fun of us?' He said: 'God forbid that I should be associated with anything foolish.' They replied: 'Go unto the Lord and ask on our behalf whether He would show us what sort of cow He wants.' He said: 'Ye shall know that the Lord's word is: This cow should not be old, neither should it be a heifer, but of an age which is between the two. Therefore do what is commanded of ye.' They replied: 'Go unto the Lord and ask on our behalf what colour the cow should be.' He said: 'Ye shall know that the Lord's word is: The cow should be bright yellow, in order that it may give pleasure to those who gaze upon it.' They replied: 'Go unto the Lord and ask on our behalf whether He would make it absolutely clear which cow He's got in mind, because to us all cows look much the same and surely, if it pleases God to do so, He could point out the right one to us.' He said, 'Ye shall know that the Lord's word is: Let it be a cow that has not been tired by working in the fields and irrigating your land, a cow that is healthy and unblemished.' They replied: 'At last Thou hast made clear what Thou wantest.' Then they just about managed to get round to sacrificing a cow. Your grandfather would like you to take a tin and fetch worms, because he intends to go fishing in the morning. You ask me what sort of tin, where it is to be found, what sort of worms you should catch, how many of them you should collect and whether the whole thing couldn't be put on hold. The director has not given me such detailed instructions, and I can therefore only reply to one of your questions, that concerning the tin. If you're asking what sort of tin, then I can only offer my recollection that the precise words of the director were 'a tin'. He did not say anything about a willingness to add a host of further explanations and my personal opinion is that you would do better not to burden him with so many unnecessary questions. I suppose that he wouldn't have the sort of patience with you that God had over the cow. Aren't you familiar with the Koran?"

Bertie pulled a face to show that Saturnin's speech was of no interest, and then asked him whether he always talked so much. Saturnin explained that it depended on the circumstances. With an intelligent and quick-thinking person it was possible to be brief, but in other circumstances many words and illustrations had to be used before a bulb could be lit in the listener's little head. There were other cases where he didn't speak a word but instead took prompt action. In this manner he had already brought benefit to many people and he was sorry that he had to remind someone of this fact so forcefully, when only the day before he had saved that person's life by his prompt intervention.

Bertie grabbed his ruined moustache, recoiled in irritation and went out. I asked Saturnin whether Grandpa really wanted Bertie to collect worms. Saturnin said that the old man hadn't expressly issued an order to that effect, but that for people like Bertie idleness could be very damaging.

I had guessed something of the kind. I could not imagine Grandpa wanting to hook fish in a torrent like this. I told Saturnin that I was concerned about Grandpa taking offence when it came to light that Bertie had been commissioned for such work in his name. Saturnin thought that the old gentleman would certainly not take offence, besides which he was convinced that Bertie would

83

not find any worms and would be only too pleased not to mention the matter.

He explained that his main reason for sending Bertie away was Miss Barbara. Miss Basnett was minded to exploit the fact that it had finally stopped raining outside and wanted to take a look at the river. Master Bertie was doggedly determined to accompany her, and had fitted himself out in exotically stylish gear to this end. Saturnin explained that in all likelihood being ordered to fill a rusty tin with worms would rather thwart Bertie's original plans and Miss Barbara would certainly breathe a sigh of relief.

Privately I reflected that I'd breathe a sigh of relief myself, but I did not mention anything to Saturnin. I changed the compress on my swollen ankle and stretched out comfortably in a deep armchair. A tempestuous morning was behind us.

Aunt Catherine was irked by Grandpa's request that Miss Barbara deal with our empty stomachs. When she first heard of it she pretended that it was a laughing matter. She made us repeat for her benefit that the girl with painted nails was really going to be let loose in the kitchen, and shook with laughter once again.

This really infuriated me, not only because my aunt was trying to make fun of Miss Barbara, but also because she made a mockery of one of the most beautiful sounds I know, that of human laughter in all its brightness and warmth, a gift given by God uniquely to human beings among all His creatures.

Aunt Catherine laughed, but with vicious little flames blazing in her eyes, and her malicious laughter erupted in such a manner that someone might have been treading on her stomach. Then she screwed up her face for a moment as if she had at last managed to get the better of her fit of laughter, told us that Grandpa couldn't really mean it seriously and set off for the kitchen.

I was glad that Miss Barbara did not witness this. Her presence would not have had the slightest deterrent effect upon my aunt's theatrical performance and would merely have provided her with the occasion for a more effective ending. I can vividly imagine Aunt Catherine dubbing Miss Barbara her dear young lass and commending her with a play of kind-heartedness to tickle the ivories, play bridge or tennis, have a cigarette, paint her nails or venture an opinion about art – only in God's name would she please leave culinary affairs to women of the old school. As I say, it was all to the good that Miss Barbara was not present.

After the departure of Aunt Catherine the three of us, that is to say Grandpa, Dr. Witherspoon and myself, remained in our seats without saying a word. I think that we all had different things on our minds. Dr. Witherspoon was surely wondering to himself why Grandpa, who was so terrified of my aunt's cooking, did not employ every means at his disposal in order to ensure that the decision to put Miss Barbara in charge of the kitchen was complied with. Of course I know Aunt Catherine better and Grandpa's behaviour is scarcely to be wondered at. My aunt is one of those people who can be held in contempt or even hated, but who for all that affects your decisions, wearing you down with pressure that is gentle but constantly applied. There comes a day when you realise with horror that you're under the thumb.

My aunt has some kind of sixth sense enabling her to divine when it is not advisable to oppose Grandpa, but with which she can also unfailingly ascertain when he is not spoiling for a fight but just wants peace and quiet, and when whatever happens it's all the same to him. This is the moment for one of her limited displays of force. She is clever enough not to go too far, but the inches of ground which her methods deliver into her hands are lost to Grandpa forever.

When the old boy becomes aware of his losses it annoys him and he becomes hard as nails for days on end. Oddly enough, this is a period during which my aunt does not try to put any pressure on Grandpa. Then the old boy tires of his bad mood and at this point Aunt Catherine is at his side again, working her mouth in words of angelic sweetness and devilish cunning, until Grandpa finally raises a weary arm and concedes another inch of territory. Aunt Catherine says that the constant drip wears away the stone, but she would be highly offended were it to be suggested that the maxim might provide a suitable description of her own behaviour towards Grandpa.

Shortly afterwards Aunt Catherine returned from the kitchen and informed Grandpa that we had a power cut. Testily he observed that we'd found that out the day before. My aunt asked how she was supposed to cook anything. Grandpa replied that no one had asked her to cook anything. My aunt said that this was perfectly true and a disgrace to boot. Any decent family of normal people would have invited her to take over the kitchen and no one would have insulted her by entrusting the cooking to a slip of a girl who couldn't so much as peel a potato.

Then she sighed and explained that the whole thing came as no surprise to her. She had long grown used to the family treating her like this. Grandpa asked whether when saying 'family' she meant him. My aunt somehow avoided the question and then with a sudden outburst of laughter informed us that at last she understood why we had asked Miss Barbara to do the cooking. It was the best joke she'd ever heard. The electricity was down and there wasn't a hint of a stove run on anything else in the whole house. In such circumstances the cook with painted nails was a harmless figure of fun.

Then my aunt became serious and asked what we were actually going to eat. The old boy told her: "Softly, softly catchee monkey." My aunt frowned. She does not like it when she is the one to be brushed aside with a saying. She makes so much use of maxims and proverbs herself that she assumes anyone else quoting one must be making fun of her. With a sarcastic comment about being curious as to why anyone would catch any monkeys, let alone breakfast on them, she retreated to an armchair with a romantic novel. At about half past eleven she was unable to resist paying a visit to the kitchen. She found no sign of Miss Barbara and returned pacified but with added venom.

It was a few minutes after twelve when Saturnin entered and announced that luncheon was served. My aunt went pale and was first in the rush to the dining room. Grandpa and Dr. Witherspoon followed with myself bringing up the rear, supported by Saturnin. Let me say at once that Miss Barbara had excelled herself. She did not fall at the first hurdle of being without power, but used her energy and imagination in order to improvise. With the skill of an old frontiersman she had set up a field kitchen in a meadow just a few steps from Grandpa's house. We could spot her through the window, charm and planning equally in evidence as she moved between two fires adding the finishing touches to our lunch, the first course of which Saturnin was just serving. It was a vegetable soup. Tinned sausages and mashed potatoes came next, followed by pancakes with jam and finally black coffee. I am aware of the fact that my feelings for Miss Barbara are such that she could produce a piece of toast and I would pronounce it the best meal in the world. But you must believe me when I say that it was an excellent lunch, and Grandpa said that he'd not eaten anything so tasty in a long time.

Dr. Witherspoon asked Aunt Catherine several times over whether she was enjoying her meal, and on each occasion received the cool response, "Thank you, I am." Bertie replied to a similar inquiry that the food was not too bad. Aunt Catherine couldn't hide the fact that she was trembling like a pressure cooker under too much strain. She was simply waiting for an opportunity to blow her top. At last it came to her. On one of the pancakes there was a minute speck of wood ash.

Considering the fact that Miss Barbara had to prepare the food over an open fire, this was hardly a matter for surprise. For that matter, I know of few people for whom a morsel of ash ground between the teeth would spoil their enjoyment of potatoes baked in the embers of an open fire.

When the incident occurred Aunt Catherine stiffened and then curled her lips in an unpleasant sneer. She held a handkerchief in front of a mouth full of food and proceeded to leave the room. A while later she returned and ostentatiously wiped her mouth at some length with a cloth. She then remarked that she didn't know whether or why the others would put up with this, but at any rate she couldn't. Grandpa asked her whether she might prefer to try another restaurant.

I do not know what she would have said to him in reply, because at that moment Miss Barbara appeared and both Grandpa and Dr. Witherspoon greeted her with fulsome words of praise and enthusiasm. I did not allow myself to be left behind and Miss Barbara turned pink with pleasure from head to toe. Then she pointed out that she didn't know how she was going to satisfy us in the future. There were still some tins in the larder, but not many. She had used up the last of the milk making pancakes and the bread had run out.

Grandpa said that she would certainly not allow us to die of hunger. After her performance that day his faith in her was boundless. He sat her in an armchair and showed his consideration by asking whether in devoting herself to our needs she hadn't forgotten about her own. Pleased by her success I looked at Miss Barbara and privately thought that she was more beautiful than ever. Her hair was slightly ruffled, her eyes shone and she had a smoky fragrance. She chatted happily with Grandpa and then turned to me, inquiring after my ankle and asking whether I had yet prepared a story to tell in the evening.

The previous evening Dr. Witherspoon had proposed that since we had to spend our evenings in the dark we should take it in turns to tell interesting stories. I was to be the first narrator, apparently because spending the whole day in a sitting position meant that I was likely to be well placed for thinking up things to say.

I told Miss Barbara that something might come to me by evening, and at once felt ashamed. The truth was that since the morning I'd had a story prepared which I had every intention of telling. I'd been going over it in my mind all the time, looking for the best way of expressing myself, weighing every word and polishing my style. On the whole it was an unassuming tale which I had to tell, but I hoped that I could add to its interest by narrating it well.

Grandpa said that I should put on my thinking cap. He drew attention to the fact that it would have to be a wonderful story, one that would repay Miss Basnett for today's lunch. We spent the afternoon amusing ourselves in a pleasant and convivial manner, and Miss Barbara completely forgot about wanting to go to the river. As for Bertie, who was probably collecting worms somewhere or other, we didn't miss him at all. Even Aunt Catherine failed to spoil

our good mood. It was getting on for five o'clock when she arrived in the dining-room and asked Grandpa what she should make him for dinner.

Grandpa explained that he'd eaten a full lunch which would be enough for him to last until dinner. Aunt Catherine responded that say what he will he must eat something. Let no one try to tell her that such gypsy fare cooked over a camp fire would satisfy the needs of an elderly gentleman. She had kept her silence for a long time, but Grandpa could not be allowed to endanger his health like this.

She proceeded to bring Grandpa various titbits at roughly ten-minute intervals, but he stubbornly turned them down. Pig-headedly my aunt kept coming, with an announcement each time she appeared at the door: "I have brought you a little egg yolk with sugar. I've got you honey. Here's some fruit preserve. Try this cheese." After the fourth appearance an infuriated Grandpa leaped to his feet and my aunt beat a hasty retreat. He had scarcely been able to resume his seat when the doors opened once again and Bertie came in with a rusty tin in his hands. "I have brought you some worms," he informed Grandpa. Grandpa's eyes opened wide and then with a fearful bellow he drummed the panic-stricken Bertie out of the room.

The rest of the day passed peacefully. As we were sitting together in the living-room after dinner, we all had the feeling that this holiday was not so bad after all. Then Miss Barbara came over to my armchair and with a hint of conspiracy asked me for a cigarette. My God! How the simplest of things can set a man's pulse racing! Dusk fell gradually and I told my tale.

X.

was a boy. I wished that I could find myself all alone on a great ship, able to explore wherever I wanted, walk on the deck, visit the engine room and examine its intricate workings before lighting the boiler and seeing whether it would go. I couldn't imagine anything more thrilling. To be alone in an unfamiliar setting like that, not knowing what I might encounter behind the next door, was a far more enticing prospect for me than the thought of eventually ending up on a desert island. But like so many childish fancies this dream has never come true, and it comes to mind only because of another situation, unfortunately a much less romantic one, to which it bears some comparison.

On that other occasion I spent the night quite alone in a strange house. I had gone to a town in Central Moravia with a key in the pocket of my winter coat which my friend Otto Johnson had pressed upon me with some friendly advice: "My dear chap, are you out of your mind? You don't want to sleep in a hotel when I've got an empty house there." I argued that I was arriving late and that it would be difficult to find his place during the blackout among the hundreds of other houses, each the spitting image of all the rest. To no avail. He explained that I couldn't go wrong. His was the third street from the bottom, then the seventh house on the left. Finding it would be a doddle.

In fact it was not so easy. I arrived there well into the night in impenetrable darkness and with snow falling heavily, but at last I managed to find it. I could make out even less inside the house. Johnson had entreated me to close the curtains before I switched on the lights. I do not know whether you have ever been in a strange flat after dark, but I can assure you that it's no laughing matter. I had neither torch nor matches, so it took a very long time to make sure that no light could escape through the windows without my damaging or breaking something in the process.

Then things took a turn for the better. Johnson had said that the switch was to the left of the door. So it was. The stoves had been prepared with wood and coal and it remained only to light them. All well and good, I told myself, but where were the matches? It did not take me long to find them, and once I had a cheerfully crackling fire in the stove I set to work following my friend's instructions as to where to find tea (really a minor consideration) and plum brandy (the all-important one). I found everything and spent a pleasant hour in an armchair beside the stove with book, tea, plum bran-dy and cigarettes. Johnson's cigarettes had that especially pleas-ant taste which is shared by all cigarettes which someone else has paid for.

At about midnight I retired to bed, once again following in-structions on how to go about it. Everything was where I'd been told it would be, the bedclothes inside the sofa, the alarm clock on the side table and in one of its drawers some literature specially designed to induce sleep. It was so effective that I do not even recall when I dropped off.

It seemed to me that I had only been asleep a short time when persistent ringing of the doorbell summoned me back to life. Even if you are sleeping at home, in the flat you have slept in for years on end, and a shrill ringing drags you out of the deepest slumber, then you may find your peace of mind, sense of balance and power of judgment somewhat disturbed. Perhaps you will come out with inarticulate sentences born of drowsiness and then blush that you ever said them. You will begin dressing in some muddle-headed manner that you'd consider ridiculous if you were fully conscious. Your head will spin in a whirligig of ideas about who could be calling you at this hour and why. You rule out the possibility of its being a salesman who has dropped by at this late hour in order to commend the virtues of life insurance, and so you are left hesitating between fire, a burst water main and murder.

If you are in unfamiliar surroundings and happen to be dragged out of sleep by a bell screeching in the darkness, then the chaos in your head can reach dangerous levels. You will leap out of bed and grope for a switch in the dark or, to put it better, you will grope towards where the switch would be if you were at home. It begins to dawn on you that you are not at home when you have collided several times with objects in unusual places. Then you come to a confused halt and try to organise your thoughts. This is a time when you need some peace and it is highly disagreeable when at that very moment the bell is ringing more furiously than ever.

Under these conditions the constant din drove me into several panic-stricken attempts at finding a switch. This is where I would like to point out that I have never considered a cactus to be a suitable indoor plant. Then I recovered enough composure to begin a systematic search. I edged forward with care until I found a wall. I followed the line of the wall around the room until, after some minor setbacks, I eventually located a switch. I put on the light, wrapped a coat around my pyjamas and went to investigate the troublemaker who had disturbed my sleep.

At the door of the house stood a man with his head underneath a snow-covered hat. That hat was sitting on his head in a rather uncertain way that one tends to associate with a generous consumption of beer. A chubby little hand was keeping time as he murmured some complaint about a deaf publican and an unrefreshed glass. I asked him what he wanted and why the devil he was ringing my doorbell at two in the morning.

"Forgive me," he replied, "but I cannot find where I live. I don't understand what's happened. Whenever I get to a house I find someone else living there."

I am not able to recall how I looked at that moment, but I don't think that my face lit up with any gleam of comprehension. I simply couldn't understand how anyone could be so brazen as this little man. The thing was that I could observe a trail of footprints in the freshly fallen snow winding from one front door to the next like a chain binding the whole street. A whole legion of unfortunate people had had to forsake their warm beds just as I had, in order to listen to complaints about a house that was too irresponsible to remain in its proper place. It was a miracle that there was no obvious sign of anyone having laid a finger on him. Perhaps they were all struck by a wave of pity for this little fellow lost in a sea of box-like dwellings, each of which was just like all the others.

"Do you live here?" he asked me. It was an endearingly silly question. He didn't realise that this question caused me mild embarrassment. When I'm speaking to a fellow whose mind is befuddled by alcohol, I choose short clear sentences, carefully avoiding anything that I have to explain at length. But this time it could not be avoided. His inflamed eyes were filled with the light of victory when I failed to respond immediately. Apparently I was the first person who hadn't responded to this innocent question with a diatribe and he cried out in triumph:

"So you don't live here! This must be my place."

"No sir, it's not!" I replied. "This flat belongs to my friend Mr. Johnson."

"Then I've no idea where I live," was his helpless reply.

He was so downcast that I had to battle against an impulse to invite him indoors and offer him hospitality overnight, but I quickly dismissed the idea. The flat did not belong to me and besides it is difficult to deal with people in his condition.

"The name is Alan Lock," he added quite unnecessarily. It seemed to me that considering how many people this good man had got out of their beds he could just as well be called Alarm Clock and make a ringing sound. We stood in silence for a short time while he dug an earthenware ashtray belonging to the pub out of the pocket of his winter coat. A look of surprise came over him before he sank back into deep thought. I was beginning to shiver from the cold and I was relieved when he shoved the ashtray back into his pocket and said:

"If you say that your friend lives here then I must be moving on once more. Good night."

I watched him make for the door of the next house and then closed the door. Back in the room I took a wee warming dram of plum brandy and was just getting ready for bed when the ringing started all over again. Once more it was Mr. Alan Lock. My patience wearing thin, I asked him what he wanted this time, but before he could answer me there was a sound from the neighbour's house, where Mr. Lock had apparently just rung the bell, and a hoarse male voice broke the silence of the night. "Hoi! Are you the one who's just been ringing my bell?" he asked in a menacing tone. Mr. Lock glanced over his shoulder, gestured with his hand and with an unflappable calm said:

"That's right. Wait there, I'll be right with you."

The neighbour slammed his door with an expletive. Mr Lock turned his attention back to me and said:

"What was it I wanted? Oh yes: this friend of yours, Mr. Johnson, what does he look like?"

There are times when a person seems to have infinite reserves of patience, and this was one of them. Rather than start to yell my head off I described Otto Johnson to him as best I could. I explained that he was of medium build with brown hair and eyes.

"Don't you think we look alike?" Mr. Lock asked.

"No, I don't."

"You could have got us mixed up."

Such was my consternation at his train of thought that I was lost for a reply and simply stared after him as he departed.

Back in bed I thought over what had happened and on falling asleep I dreamed that I was living in a town full of identikit little homes, the inhabitants all wearing the same clothes and living in rooms equipped with the same mass-produced furniture. It was one of the most terrible dreams I have ever had, because all the people in this town looked exactly alike, the same build, the same faces, the same eyes and hair, a vision so appalling that I broke out in a cold sweat. I tried to recognise my friend Johnson among these countenances, but time and again the same mask stared back at me from all the faces.

There was frost in the air when I left in the morning, and the tracks of the errant pilgrim were half obscured by fresh snow, making me reflect on how his journey might have ended. I was just locking the door when I suddenly felt faint. There was a brass name-plate above it. It said:

ALAN LOCK

This was the end of my story and before long we retired to bed. On the whole my audience was satisfied. Miss Barbara in particular showed her appreciation, which was what mattered most. Grandpa promised that the following evening he would tell the story of how he served under General Radetzky in Italy where a beautiful countess fell in love with him.

Privately I thought to myself that worse things could have happened to us and that we would somehow survive Grandpa's story. I knew the tale by heart. I'd heard it for the first time when I was a small boy and could never rid myself of the feeling that I'd read something similar in an almanac of some kind. Naturally I could be mistaken and I wouldn't like to do Grandpa an injustice.

Miss Barbara offered me her hand to say good night and then we all stumbled to our rooms in the darkness. I opened the window and lit a cigarette. I could hear forest murmurs on Castle Hill and in quiet moments the babbling of the river. The stars were shining and the night was warm. A bat winged its way past my window.

XI.

IT IS BEAUTIFUL OUTSIDE AND THERE IS
NO PAIN IN MY ANKLE
MISS BARBARA CANNOT FIND A ROE DEER
AUNT CATHERINE ACCUSES ME OF SCHOOLBOY
PRANKS
MISS BARBARA COMES TO MY DEFENCE
THIS TIME IT'S SATURNIN'S TURN TO DISAPPEAR
BERTIE IS BEHIND BARS
NO SHORT STRAWS FOR ME
WE GO MUSHROOMING
IT WAS WONDERFUL

I woke up early in the morning and was pleased to discover that I had hardly any pain in my ankle. I walked carefully around the room a few times and it was not at all bad. It was a glorious day outside and the sun, shining onto me through one of the room's windows, already had a pleasantly warming touch. I shaved with care and while the house was still quiet stole outside. I wanted to examine the place where Miss Barbara had prepared a fire the day before.

I found a flat rock to sit on outside, breathed in the fragrant and refreshing air of morning and wondered whether I dared to throw pebbles at Miss Barbara's window. In the clear light it seemed as if the mountains were much nearer than they actually were. The slanting rays of morning sunlight highlighted every detail on the mountain slopes. I could discern bare ledges of rock, mountain trails shining on the bare slopes and then fading away into the fir trees, and tree trunks felled and stripped of their bark, looking like a haphazard collection of matches. In a large clearing somewhere around the middle of Holy Mount I even saw a roe deer. Regrettably I didn't have my binoculars with me.

Then I stopped paying attention to the roe, because Miss Barbara was approaching from the house. I greeted her cheerfully and she expressed pleasure at the fact I could already walk. She tested the grass with her palm and since the sun had already dried away the dew she sat down on the ground. I offered her a cigarette and then we spoke about the beauties of nature. I showed her the roe but she couldn't make it out, although I explained that it was directly in the line of the top of a certain fir tree on the edge of the forest. She said that the view must be different from her vantage point and tried to look from where my head was. I discovered that to point something out in this way to a young lady whose presence sets your pulse racing was a distinctly pleasant experience, and I was actually sorry when she spotted the roe. Somewhat awkwardly I suggested that I would find her another one, but she smiled and said one was enough.

She asked me whether I could help her clean up around the fire and prepare a new woodpile. Although she could have left me to look after one fire and herself taken care of the other, she went to the same one as I did and got in the way in a charming manner. I regretted the fact that there weren't ten of these fires, fifty, a thousand.

Before we had finished the work Aunt Catherine emerged from the house, looked about her in all directions and then began prancing towards us. She was tight-lipped and looked greatly huffed. She did not react to our greeting and in a sharp tone asked me to give her the key at once.

When I inquired as to which key, she angrily stamped her foot. She told me to stop pretending and informed me that while she'd never had a good word to say about me this latest affair really took the biscuit. It was all too much. What I'd done was nothing but a schoolboy prank.

I took offence and told her that I would not allow her to speak to me in such a tone. I was not accustomed to anyone behaving like that towards me. I didn't have the foggiest notion what she was going on about, and I did not intend to carry on with such a pointless debate. I turned away and continued to prepare the fire.

My aunt went on speaking to Miss Barbara, telling her that someone had locked Bertie in his room and gone off with the key, and that only a stupid little boy would do such a thing. Miss Barbara said that in that case it would seem that Bertie had locked himself in, since he was the only boy among us. At this point Aunt Catherine took umbrage and told her that in the first place Bertie was definitely not a stupid boy and in the second place he was the one locked in the room and could not have gone off with the key. She remarked that someone had chosen to make Bertie the butt of bad jokes and she wasn't going to stand for it. Some very unsavoury things were happening this year. Grandpa should be more careful in his choice of guests.

That showed disrespect of the first order towards Miss Barbara and I was so incensed by it that I forgot about my decision not to have any more words with my aunt. I told her that Grandpa's guests were selected very carefully, at least so far as the ones actually invited were concerned. Unfortunately there were also some guests present who had arrived uninvited and had nothing to say except that the family owed them favours. They drifted from one place to another like floodwater, oblivious of whether or not they were welcome, and they demanded that every consideration be given them whilst lacking every courtesy themselves. Such a thing seemed beyond belief, but I knew it from my own experience. Recently I endured an occupation of this kind on my boat. Incidentally, I would take great pains to provide my aunt with an opportunity to explain to Grandpa personally just what she thought about this need to select his guests more carefully.

While I was speaking to my aunt Miss Barbara moved on to the more distant of the fires. My aunt shot me a momentary glance, her lips pursed in anger, and then commented that he who laughs last laughs longest. I replied to her that I wasn't laughing at all, besides which I was fed up to the back teeth with her maxims.

My aunt gave a sudden start and pranced off back to the house. The thing was that she had spotted Grandpa, who had just emerged with Dr. Witherspoon, and apparently wanted to get her word in with him before I did. Then she returned in their company, subjecting Grandpa to a quickfire delivery of words on some issue. The old boy heard her out absent-mindedly and at the same time smiled at Miss Barbara, waving affably. When they caught up with us Grandpa was saying that he couldn't understand how it had happened and was asking where the key was.

My aunt said that that was just the point – the key had vanished. Grandpa recollected some nursery-rhyme from his childhood which ran that the fish was in the stream, the key was in its mouth, when a woman came on the scene, the fish had headed south. Then he said that as soon as the water had receded and a new bridge had been built we would be able to send for a locksmith. Bertie would have to hold out until then.

My aunt pulled a wry face and served up the maxim that the injured are immune to mockery. She looked defiantly in my direction, as if she wanted to point out that she would use as many sayings as she pleased, and commented that a friend in need is a friend indeed. She asked us immediately to dedicate all the resources at our disposal to the liberation of Bertie. Grandpa said that he too would be guided by a proverb, that which spoke of letting sleeping dogs lie. Surely my aunt did not want him to break down the door or call upon Bertie to jump from a window and be caught in a sheet. Finally he advised her to ask for assistance from Saturnin, who was a very capable fellow.

My aunt went off and I was on the point of going into the whole unsavoury business with Grandpa when I noticed Miss Barbara looking at me beseechingly, making pleading gestures and shaking her head behind the backs of Grandpa and Dr. Witherspoon. She looked so sweet and appealing that I could not refuse, despite my great indignation at Aunt Catherine.

Grandpa and Dr. Witherspoon parked themselves on the ground and asked our charming cook what was on the menu for breakfast. Miss Barbara said that she could provide them with baked potatoes and black coffee. She made both men laugh by apologising in the manner of a head waiter for the lack of choice. She explained that there was also a little streaky bacon in the pantry but that since we didn't know how much longer we'd have to play at being castaways the bacon would be more suitable for lunch. Then she lit the fires and the two men each took one to keep an eye on.

A while later my aunt reappeared to announce that Saturnin had vanished into thin air. Grandpa told her not to lift her expressions from popular romances. Dr. Witherspoon intervened with the comment that such disappearances were a favourite device for the authors of detective stories because they heightened the tension. After a few days the missing person would be found in some remote spot showing signs of having been murdered several times over. If someone disappeared in real life they usually came back very soon, saying that they'd been for a walk in the fresh air or had gone off to post a letter. Seeing that, in the situation we were in, it was out of the question that Saturnin had gone to the post office, it was clear that he'd gone for a walk. In all likelihood he'd be back in three minutes. Dr. Witherspoon explained that he was basing this judgment on the altitude of the sun, the direction of the wind and the fact that Saturnin was already to be seen heading their way.

Saturnin arrived from the forest carrying a basket. He wished us all Good Morning and surprised us with what must have been a dozen prime mushrooms. Miss Barbara showered him with praise and proposed that in the afternoon we would make for the forest in larger numbers and try to emulate Saturnin's example. We could have fried mushrooms for dinner. Everyone was willing to join the hunt except Aunt Catherine.

Then we stretched out on the grass and waited for our baked potatoes. The sun was scorching and I noticed that Miss Barbara's petite nose was a little sunburnt. After breakfast I had a chance to have a private word with Sa-tur-nin. I told him that someone had incarcerated Bertie in his room and Saturnin replied that he was aware of this fact. I asked him how he knew and Saturnin retorted that as a matter of fact he could perfectly well remember locking Bertie's door himself. He pointed out that he was only fulfilling the terms of his pledge to punish Bertie at every opportunity.

I had assumed that the great event happened at night, but in reality it had already taken place by evening. Sa-turnin told me that he wasn't sure whether Miss Basnett would wish him to say what he was about to say, but she had not expressly forbidden it, so he would conceal nothing from me. When Miss Basnett departed during the evening for her room, she found Master Bertie there. At first she supposed that Master Bertie had mistaken the rooms in the darkness, and she asked him to leave. Master Bertie had refused to do so and began to declare his love for her in a rather crude manner. Miss Basnett fled from the room that very moment and asked Saturnin, who happened to be in the vicinity, for his assistance. Saturnin had then escorted Bertie to the room assigned to him and sternly warned him not to be confused in future about where he was staying.

I asked Saturnin how he escorted Bertie to his room and he told me that it was by the ears. In view of the fact that Master Bertie received his well-meant advice rather resentfully, there was a danger of his disturbing Miss Basnett again, perhaps by hammering on the door where she'd locked herself inside her room. Therefore Saturnin had taken a necessary precautionary measure. He had locked Bertie in his room and hidden the key. Unfortunately he couldn't recollect exactly where he'd put it that evening and would have to go looking for it. He supposed that Master Bertie would have to remain in confinement until about seven in the evening, because until that time Saturnin was fully engaged with matters of more importance than playing Hunt the Key.

I was therefore forced to accept that Bertie would be locked away for the whole day, and I cannot say that the realisation upset my good mood. In the meantime my aunt moved from room to room like a female apparition, trying every possible key in the door of Bertie's cell. She made a racket with everything that came into her hands and kept repeating that no one would ever catch her coming to this place again.

While we left after lunch for the woods – Grandpa, Dr. Witherspoon, Miss Basnett and I – my aunt stayed behind on the terrace and tried to target Bertie's open window with baked potatoes. In this mission she was actually successful, but Bertie spoiled her pleasure by putting in an appearance at the window where with a nonchalant movement he flung the baked potato back out.

At the edge of the woods Grandpa proposed that we divided up into at least two groups, which would enable us to find more mushrooms than if we hunted as a single pack. Dr. Witherspoon pointed out with a smile that this was not a good idea, because we would fall out over who was going to enjoy the company of Miss Barbara. Grandpa weighed in with the suggestion that an even worse outcome could be envisaged. Wars had already been fought the world over for women whose beauty paled into insignificance beside that of Miss Barbara. In the end he decided that we would draw lots.

We racked our brains for a while over a method of drawing lots, before Miss Barbara pointed out that she had matches. She turned her back to us and we could hear a sound like breaking twigs. Then she explained that those who chose the matches with their heads intact would hunt together, as would those who selected the broken matches. In the drawing of lots age should have precedence.

Grandpa pretended to consider for a while and chose a broken match. When it was Dr. Witherspoon's turn, I tried to will him into making the same selection as Grandpa. So intense was my concentration that it must have been written on my face. Grandpa glanced in my direction and chortled. Dr. Witherspoon closed his eyes, blindly grabbed at a match and then, as if he was in two minds about it, replaced it and chose another. It was also one without a head. My wishes had come true and any further drawing of lots was unnecessary. Then we parted from one another, Grandpa and Dr. Witherspoon heading towards Holy Mount while Miss Barbara and I made for a rocky overhang known as The Balcony. After a while the pair of elderly gentlemen were out of sight.

It was the first time that we had been alone together. There was a certain awkwardness between us as we walked silently through the forest. I couldn't avoid the feeling that Miss Barbara was not too enthusiastic about the result of drawing lots. Perhaps she would have been happier accompanying Grandpa or Dr. Witherspoon. Naturally I found this thought upsetting. I told myself that although she had been through an unpleasant experience with that pest Bertie, she wouldn't have to be afraid of receiving the same treatment at my hands. I hoped she understood that behaving like a seducer in the manner of Bertie was absolutely foreign to my nature.

We made our way slowly in view of the fact that my ankle had not yet healed completely. The forest was moist, lush and aromatic after the recent rains. As we climbed we passed through small clearings warmed by the sun and from time to time turned round to see whether Grandpa's home was still in sight. Then Miss Barbara found the first mushroom and reacted to her discovery with child-like enthusiasm. She couldn't get over it and it brought back the amiability she had shown in the morning.

We moved twenty yards or so apart from each other and heralded the discovery of every mushroom with a cheerful cry. Then I spotted a group of about fifteen mushrooms on the edge of a small clearing. I was about to record my breakthrough with a triumphant yell when, with the generosity characteristic of all those smitten by love, I considered how to arrange that Miss Barbara was the one to discover this treasure trove of mushrooms. I imagined her cry of delight. I sat down on a tree stump and shouted to her that my leg was troubling me and that I was unable to go any further.

She came running up with a concerned look on her face insisting that we should have a rest, that she should have remembered not to walk too quickly and would I please not be angry at her. I felt an immediate pang of conscience at having wanted to deceive her. She sat on the moss and looked in the direction of the hoard of mushrooms. I waited to see what would happen but the shriek of pleasure did not materialise. Instead she gave me a searching look and asked whether I was now better. I couldn't understand how she failed to notice the mushrooms. We stayed sitting for several more minutes and then she got up, saying that we should be moving on. She made no mention of the mushrooms and I didn't know what to do. Miss Barbara threw me a glance with little green sparkles playing in her eyes and said that I should pick the mushrooms myself. We both laughed and then got on with the job together. We rounded up so many for the basket that Miss Barbara announced we could now take a proper break in the clearing, without my having to pretend that my leg was in pain.

It was a lovely spot. The short grass typical of mountain clearings was growing around us under a warm sun. We lay down for a long time listening to the manifold sounds of the forest. In the unassured manner of townsfolk we guessed the names of the birds chirping and twittering on the slopes. I think that the cuckoo was the only one we guessed correctly. It cuckooed continually and Miss Barbara imitated its voice charmingly. She proceeded to lie on her back in the grass and close her eyes, leaving me to admire her to my heart's content. Then I noticed something that made me insanely happy. A small pocket in her skirt had formed a little cave which one could see inside because the sun had penetrated the material. In that small interior where the light was gracefully subdued lay the two matches left over after we'd drawn lots and which Miss Barbara had kept in her possession. Both were headless. Dear, sweet Barbara! She had broken off the heads of all the matches, giving Grandpa and Dr. Witherspoon no chance. We were bound to be drawn together whichever matches the other two had picked. So Miss Barbara had wanted to be my mushrooming partner. Ye Gods! Ye Humans! Is life not beautiful!

After a while Miss Barbara opened her eyes in order to find out why I'd kept quiet for so long. She saw me looking at the matches and a glimmer in her eyes gave away the knowledge that I'd discovered her little deceit. I stroked her hair while she blushed to its roots. She looked up at me and smiled sweetly. Then she jumped to her feet declaring: "We should be getting back."

We returned through the mild August evening carrying the basket of mushrooms between us. We were silent for almost the entire journey, but in spite of or perhaps because of this it was a beautiful experience. We stopped at the edge of the forest. We gazed at each other for a moment and then I held out my palm with an imploring look. She looked me in the eyes for a second and then in mild embarrassment handed over the two broken matches. I have kept them as a memento.

XII.

Grandpa did not re-acquaint us with the memories of his youth that evening. He went to his room after dinner because of an insult from Aunt Catherine. As might have been expected, she accomplished this by means of a proverb. Subsequently Dr. Witherspoon, quite impervious to the presence of Aunt Catherine, delivered a diatribe against proverbs.

He explained to us that, when all was said and done, everything in the world was quite well arranged on our behalf. Many people in the past and even in our own day had made sure that we would live in comfort and wouldn't have to exert ourselves too much. You can see this from the fact that you are no longer required to travel everywhere on foot. The railway will transport you wherever you wish to go. There is no need for you to climb any giant mountains. The funicular is ready to haul you up. You don't have to read the books that are published, because the cultural section of the newspapers will not only summarise the content of the latest editions but will even dissect them for you, pointing out each and every mistake or omission. All you have to do is commit to memory, say, the third sentence from the end of a review, where the whole piece has been distilled into a few words of wisdom. If you can repeat the words of this sentence on a bar stool without faltering, you will be taken for a great critic.

But even this is not a necessity if you want to be considered witty, clever and good company. There are other ways of acquiring such a reputation. An inexhaustible supply of proverbs, maxims, sayings and turns of phrase has been built up by others through the ages. All you need to do is select the right one in order to equip yourself with a bon mot for every occasion.

It is, of course, essential that you avoid using proverbs which can't be applied to the given situation or perhaps are as helpful as a hole in the head. Otherwise you could become a laughing stock or get hurt. So, for example, it is not suitable to tell someone whose wife and children have already died and whose uninsured barn has been struck by lightning, that everyone is the architect of their own misfortune. Only an idiot would say things like that, and indeed it is possible that in such a case a person really would be the architect of their own misfortune, since they are likely to have their head split open at the hands of whoever they have persecuted with their little piece of wisdom. Thus it would perhaps be more suitable to quote the proverb that God visits suffering upon those whom He loves. Such a saying is a great comfort to the afflicted. Nor is it a good idea to tell someone who has been waiting fifteen years for promotion that patience is a virtue. In this instance it would perhaps be better to offer the adage that all things come to those who wait.

The funeral of someone you know presents an ideal opportunity for making use of brand new sayings. You can comfort the bereaved family with the dictum that what may cut short a young life always ends an old one. Where appropriate you can observe wittily that the dead have everything behind them while we still have to encounter the Grim Reaper. Even more sharp-witted would be the remark that wherever they've gone we'll all be following sooner or later. Such a surprising observation will earn you the heartfelt thanks of the bereaved and will substantially lighten the burden of their grief. All the more so in view of the fact that you will not be alone, but rather many other people will say these things to them. All the beautiful sayings will be repeated so many times that a detached observer would have the impression that all those present were foreigners, people who had learnt Czech from one and the same phrasebook which had presented all these pearls of wisdom under the heading 'At a Funeral'.

There are of course instances and situations in life where it can never be legitimate to use a proverb. Heaven help the prison officer who helps the inmates to escape and then justifies his actions with the maxim that 'just as well to be an addled egg as an idle bird'. Or suppose you find out that some acquaintance called Matthews used to be the treasurer of some society and at some point has spent time behind bars for defrauding it. The news comes as a great surprise to you, because you presumed that Matthews was an upright fellow who managed his life according to the maxim that honesty is the best policy. You meet someone else well-known to you called Marks, and he swears to you that he's known Matthews all his life. He maintains that the whole story is a tissue of lies and that the man was never locked up. So was he or wasn't he? You are in a quandary, but there's a proverb already coming to your rescue, the one which claims that there's no smoke without fire. This goes to show that Matthews was at least partially locked up.

You later find out that everything can be explained in terms of misreading a saying. Several years ago Matthews told a young boy by the name of Jamie Lucas that newborn babies are brought to their parents by storks. When he grew older the young boy remembered Mr. Matthews as a liar and a few years later falsely accused him of fraud, backing his claim up with the compelling logic of the saying that whoever tells lies must also be a thief.

Nor is it advisable to apply in real life the saying that if someone casts a stone at you you should respond by offering him bread. We can illustrate the point from the Bible itself, where the giant Goliath can hardly offer any bread to a certain David in view of the fact that he's just dropped down dead. It is a principle of such doubtful value that it is firmly rejected even by small boys, whose battles with stones are conducted on quite different lines.

From what has been said we can see that all that glitters is not gold. Take for example the saying that whoever's late harms no one but himself. How does that apply to the case where some people arrived at the railway station too late to catch a train which later collided with an express somewhere near Prague? Once I practised listening to my echo and shouted into the forest. As luck would have it there was a gamekeeper around who was enraged by my frightening away the animals. I would prefer not to repeat what he yelled at me. The adage that what you say to the forest the forest echoes back to you is plainly stupid. What I had said to the forest on this occasion was perfectly decent.

Then there's that completely bewildering saying that whoever sits on the stove at home must be looking for someone else there. Imagine if you will a typical peasant dwelling with a timber ceiling and a stove. A person is sitting on the stove looking for someone else. Because the space behind the stove is limited and the presence of someone else can be ascertained by a single glance, any sort of search will be unnecessary and a sign of mental derangement. A plain contradiction of the saying that you don't try to extinguish a fire that isn't burning you is provided by the setting up of volunteer fire brigades. Since we're hardly likely to reject the activities of the fire brigade, we are compelled to reject the proverb I have quoted.

Clearly anyone who denies the validity of a sentence so widely accepted that it has become a saying must have a certain mental fortitude. It isn't an easy thing to do, but sometimes there's no avoiding it. Even the man who clung to the saying that a dog who barks won't bite was eventually persuaded of this, after he ended up without a single item of clothing in one piece and had made five visits to the clinic for vaccination against rabies. He had been bitten by every single dog he met.

You have to admire the lively imagination of the people who mint these maxims. Take for example the saying that a cow cannot catch up with a hare. It is self-evidently the case, but I cannot imagine any cow chasing a hare or why it would do so. Don't try to tell me that such a cow exists.

Naturally there are also sayings which have not so far received the recognition they deserve. We need only refer to the dictum that personal hygiene is halfway to health or that a similar effect comes from a cheerful disposition. It is remarkable that these two maxims, which when added together account for the entirety of our health, have so far escaped the attention of the doctors in our spa towns. Put into practice they could effect cures on a grand scale.

Although there are as many proverbs as there are grains of sand in the sea, there are still people who cannot get enough of them. They usually complement the common repertoire of sayings with their own self-made pearls of wisdom and often interrupt their own speeches with the remark "I always say that . . ." Their friends and acquaintances are totally flummoxed by what they come out with on each occasion.

A strong caution must be issued against taking sayings literally. Taken literally, a bird in the hand is hardly worth more than two in the bush. A sparrow in the hand, for instance, is not going to sell for anything substantial. Nor can you imagine a fox boasting about its own tail. I spoke to a local forester and he strongly rejected the idea. He insisted that the furrier was the one who boasts about the tail when he sells you the fox. To say that the well-fed don't understand the hungry means that they don't understand what it's like to feel famished. It doesn't mean that they don't understand them when they say that you must change trains in Prague or that touching live wires even when they've fallen to the ground is dangerous to life and limb. They will understand them very well and avoid touching the wires. Otherwise they will learn the truth of the saying that there's no help for those who refuse any advice.

There is little sense to be made of the saying that it's too late to go chasing 'ifs'. It originated as a gibe against people who turned up late for everything, even other people's funerals, saying things like "If only I hadn't missed the . . ." You must be clear about the meaning of the saying so that you can point out that if you didn't chase the 'ifs' in question it wasn't because you didn't know what they were but because you realised that it was too late.

I don't know whether Dr. Witherspoon intended to conclude his reflections with this last sentence or would have wanted to continue had not Bertie walked into the living room. What is clear is that he fell silent and then growled to himself about some escaped prisoner. Aunt Catherine shot a look at Bertie before showering him with questions about how he was feeling and whether he was all right. Then she dashed off to raid the larder.

Dr. Witherspoon, Miss Barbara, Saturnin and myself then discussed why there was still no supply of electricity. We swapped conjectures as to what could have happened. Because Grandpa wasn't with us we assumed a very technical manner of speaking, running through everything that might have gone wrong, starting with blown fuses and ending with the power station being washed away by the flood. We even discussed another thing. In order to see whether the power had been restored, we'd tried the switches so many times that we didn't have a clue whether the lights or any of the other electrical appliances were in the 'on' or 'off' position.

While we were on the point of leaving the living-room, Aunt Catherine was trying to wrap Bertie in a blanket, despite its being a warm August evening. Bertie accepted it compliantly and gobbled down some food which she'd brought him. In the hall Saturnin inquired as to whether we were in need of anything, bade us Goodnight and retired to his modest quarters. We climbed the staircase in the darkness to the first floor while Dr. Witherspoon held forth on an affliction of the eyes known as night blindness and then went straight into reciting some poem about King Solomon and how darkness slept on the marble columns. Then he told us that if he was younger he would accompany us onto the terrace, but such an activity apparently didn't agree with elderly men. He bowed to us like a courtier and tried to convey his Goodnight in verse form. Then he disappeared to his room.

We would certainly never have had any intention of visiting the terrace, had Dr. Witherspoon not spoken about it. Until that point I don't think that I would have dared to suggest such a thing to Miss Barbara, but now the proposal was a simple and obvious one to make. So it came to pass that I spent about an hour with Miss Barbara looking for shooting stars, most of the time without speaking.

Then Miss Barbara went off to bed. The house was in silence and I could hear the forest murmurs outside. I lay in my bed, disinclined to sleep, smoked a cigarette and looked out into the darkness. I was thinking about Miss Barbara, about myself and about whether I had behaved properly on the terrace. More often I think that when it comes to relations with women I behave like a hopeless idiot. I could imagine what Bertie would say if he got to know that I spent the best part of an hour looking at the stars with a woman I was in love with, and that I didn't even venture a kiss.

This didn't mean that I cared about Bertie's opinion. I was much more concerned about what Miss Barbara thought. Once, during my student years, I fell out with a girl to whom I was attracted. She was pretty and good-natured, but grew tired of the way I managed myself so correctly. I was upset and made up my mind to behave in future in a direct and manly way. I was going to turn over a new leaf, but I never did. I have my own ideas and my own dreams where such matters are concerned, and have waited too long for them to come true to be able to abandon them easily.

Maybe it was naive, but among other things I decided that if I came across a woman whom I loved and who loved me, then we would never mention our feelings for one another. Words can be superfluous and there is so much beauty in keeping silent. In this realm everything has been spoken far too much and the words of the poets have grown cheap in the mouths of marriage cheats.

A hairdresser from our street was performing in the theatre. He knelt down in front of the headmistress of the local school saying: "Madame, I am in love with you," stressing the 'e' of Madame. The headmistress, who had an ill-fitting wig, perspired, sighed and announced to the audience "And I am in love with you, sir" in exactly the tone that she might have used to say, "It is hot in here, folks."

In the shrine which I have dedicated to love hangs the inscription: 'Silence, please.'

Commit all manner of folly, weep or be mad with joy, suffer and die of love but do not speak about it.

I do not know whether I really behaved properly on the terrace, but I felt that I would never manage to steal a kiss from Miss Barbara. If the moment for which I was longing ever arrived, it would not be through my kissing her but through our kissing each other.

A violet flash of lightning broke into the darkness of my room. The storm had arrived with a suddenness common only in the mountains. I closed the window and then heard the rain beating against the panes. I went through everything that had happened from the moment when I met Miss Barbara on the tennis court and – God knows how this happened – at the same time I recalled something which was to have such a profound effect on the further progress of the night as it took its stormy course above the mountains.

When the drift of my recollections brought me to that daredevil ride in the car across the flooded bridge and to the storm which broke out shortly afterwards, I came across as if by magic a small remembered detail in my mind. At the time it had apparently escaped my attention and had lain dormant in my memory ever since. Recalling it excited me so much that I sat up in bed.

There was no doubt about it. I remembered it quite clearly. Outside the storm had raged just as it was doing now. We got out of the car under the covered entrance. I took my time about it and had some difficulties owing to my injured ankle. Saturnin assisted me, holding me under the right arm. Miss Barbara locked the car and then supported me in a friendly manner on my left side. We were laughing at the rolls of thunder and slowly made our way into the hall. We were just passing the control panel awash with fuses when an ear-splitting thunderclap could be heard and something flashed on the control panel. Saturnin started in fear and we all broke out in laughter once again. From the first floor we could hear the voice of Dr. Witherspoon. I was listening to him talking but at the same time out of the corner of my eye I could see Saturnin disconnecting the main switch on the control panel with his free right hand.

Then this superficially insignificant detail receded to the back of my mind and I did not even recall it when Miss Barbara later observed that we were without electricity. I did not even recollect it this very evening when we were telling each other how we couldn't understand why the supply had not yet been restored.

I reflected that if I had surmised correctly then everything about the power cut was clear and the one cause for surprise was the fact that Grandpa had not solved the problem. It was Saturnin's prudence which had led him, perhaps unwittingly, to cut off the electricity supply to the whole house. Either he had then forgotten the fact or he had deliberately left us in a tight spot, and responsibility for all the bother with camp fires and stumbling on unlighted staircases could be lain at his door.

I hardly ever show an inventive turn of mind, but on the rare occasions when I do I have a spontaneous longing to check whether my theory is correct. That's how I came to do something that I shouldn't have done. I slipped on a dressing gown and went to switch the electricity supply back on.

XIII.

SOMEONE RINGS THE BELL
ALARM ON THE FIRST FLOOR
I AM CAUGHT WITHOUT MY UMBRELLA
THE SOUND OF GUNFIRE LIKE A PARADE ON
CORPUS CHRISTI DAY
I AM ATTACKED
SATURNIN LIES
LOOK WHO'S SPEAKING SPANISH

I went silently out of my room. The corridor was alternately lit up by flashes of lightning and plunged into pure darkness. There were two routes to the control panel in the hall. I could head right and descend the main staircase or I could turn left and reach the ground floor via the spiral servants' staircase.

The latter alternative seemed to me more suitable for two reasons. In the first place, the main staircase was made of wood and sometimes creaked very noisily. Secondly, in order to reach it I would have to take the corridor which passed the rooms of the other guests, whereas I could locate the spiral staircase with no trouble and then cover the distance to the hall on the ground floor by passing merely the kitchen, pantry and other places that would be empty at night.

I decided on the second route and made it to the control panel without mishap. I waited awhile until the fuses, the meter and the main control switch were lit up by a flash of lightning from outdoors, and at that moment applied my hand to the lever.

When I look back on it now, I would like to know why I didn't stay happily tucked up in bed, and I reflect upon all that we might have been spared had I restored the power supply in the morning after breakfast. My reflection only goes to show what folly it is when so many people try to peep behind the dark curtain of the future, given that we don't even know what awaits us in a few seconds' time.

"You will enjoy a happy marriage and be burdened by liver disease in your old age," says the fortune teller, and doesn't foresee that within the hour she will herself be knocked down by a bus.

When I shifted the lever of the main switch, the lamps in the hall came on and the ear-splitting noise of a doorbell filled every corner of the house. I held my breath in fear. Quick as a flash I switched the power off again. The hall returned to darkness and the shrieking bell went quiet. A deep silence reigned in which I thought I could hear my pulse racing as my heart tried to make up for the beat it missed during my moment of panic.

Nothing happened for a while and a seed of hope began to germinate in my brain, the hope that I would be able to return to my room without having to explain to a fearful audience what had been going on. However at that very moment the sound of doors opening upstairs could be heard, and the clamour of confused voices penetrated to the ground floor. The first plan of escape which flashed through my mind was not a bad one and it wasn't my fault that I couldn't put it into practice. I wanted to run to the corridor which led past the kitchen and Saturnin's cubby hole to the spiral staircase, and wait there until the panic-stricken occupants of the house had either gathered in the hall or returned to their rooms, whereupon I could beat an inconspicuous retreat back to bed.

What took place next was so much a case of one thing following immediately upon another that describing what happened would take longer than the events themselves. My scheme of retreating via the back staircase lay in ruins when I heard the door of Saturnin's room opening. If Saturnin had known what was afoot he would certainly have covered my escape, but I didn't have the slightest idea of how I could explain anything in these circumstances. Moreover I had the vague feeling that the one thing I could earn for myself by trying to skirt round Saturnin in the darkness would be received squarely on the chin.

I could hear the voices of Dr. Witherspoon, Bertie and Aunt Catherine. It seemed as if a whole crowd of people was massing on the upper part of the main staircase. Several precious seconds went by before I ran to a hall window looking out onto the lawn at the front of the house and opened it quickly. Before I could jump out, a draught of cold air hit me in the face and a shower of rain made me gasp. The storm outside was little short of a downpour and understandably enough I didn't have any umbrella with me.

At that moment another flash of lightning lit up the heavens outside and the group gathered at the top of the staircase glimpsed the outline of a dark figure against the backdrop of the illuminated window. Aunt Catherine screamed in terror and Dr. Witherspoon tried to strike a match. Because of the open window it went out almost at once in the draught, but its momentary gleam was enough to let me observe something that made my blood run cold. Bertie had Grandpa's double-barrelled shotgun in his hand and was loading it with cartridges.

I admit that my behaviour was foolish throughout. Right from the start I could have called out that it was only me, that there was nothing to worry about, that some faulty electrical connection seemed to have corrected itself, that the bell had some kind of short circuit and why didn't we have a proper look at it in the morning. How ridiculous it is that what we should do always becomes crystal clear when it is too late to do it. Come to think of it, I could at least have shut the window.

There was another flash of lightning outside and I jumped back from the window in order to avoid becoming a victim of Bertie's skills as a marksman. At that moment Bertie apparently began to take tentative steps down the main staircase with a loaded gun in his hand, his finger on the trigger. I could hear what I took to be his footsteps in the darkness. It took a fraction of a second to realise that, to give Bertie his due, he undeniably had an ounce or two of daring. It struck me that he wanted to distinguish himself in front of Miss Barbara. Judging from what later transpired, it would appear that Bertie was scared out of his wits, but that only makes it all the more admirable that he went down to the hall in total darkness, fully supposing that some robber or murderer was lurking there.

A split second later the silence was banished by an explosion of sound. The tremor that came so quickly afterwards can barely be said to have followed the sound. First there was a terrible flash. Then came a thunderclap right next to the house. A cold draught of air blew through the hall and slammed the window shut with such force that all the panes fell out with a hollow shattering sound. Aunt Catherine let out a shriek and a dull thud could be heard on the stairs. Flames flared up in the darkness and inside the house the report when Bertie's gun went off was so loud that for a moment I too was deafened.

"What the Devil's going on?" Grandpa's roar came from the staircase and before anyone could reply another shot rang out in the darkness. It felt as if someone had blown into my face, while a shower of lead shot embedded itself in the plaster above my head with a sound like a sweeping broom. I couldn't understand what Bertie was shooting at, because it was pitch black and he couldn't have seen a thing. I felt that things had gone too far and decided that come what may I was going to restore the power supply. Bertie must have already emptied both barrels, but I couldn't be sure whether he had further cartridges to hand in the pockets of his pyjamas. I had taken perhaps two steps in the direction of the control panel when I was pounced on by some kind of monster in the darkness and a moment later we were rolling around together on the floor of the hall. I say that it was a 'monster' because of the ferocious nature of its onslaught and because at first I didn't have the least idea that I was dealing with Saturnin. Not until it began to work me over according to the rules of classical ju-jitsu could I just about manage to get a few words out in a rasping voice:

"Is this you, Saturnin?"

"Yes sir," came the bewildered reply while he relaxed his grip.

I stood up with difficulty and took a few steps towards the control panel in the dark. It was only when I stumbled over a wicker chair that I became aware that I was on the wrong side of the hall.

In the meantime Saturnin, drawn by his infallible instinct, found what I was looking for and grasped hold of the main switch. The hall was flooded in light and the chorus gathered on the staircase began their descent to the accompaniment of a madly shrieking bell. It looked like a parody of the Grand Entry of Courtiers in some frightful opera. A look of bewilderment was highlighted on every one of their faces, with only Miss Barbara looking as if she could hardly suppress a laugh. Bertie had an awful bump on his forehead and seemed to be limping a little. Meanwhile the shrieking bell had clearly taken leave of its senses, although I'm not clear whether a bell that is silent makes any sense to begin with.

Grandpa asked who the Devil was ringing and now the eyes of all were riveted on the front door, as if Houdini was about to appear there. Saturnin approached the door, opened it, glanced outside in all directions and shook his head in confusion. Then it was Miss Barbara's turn to surprise us all.

"If you will permit me," she said to Saturnin. Then she went to the front door and in no time the bell had been silenced. She came back and explained:

"I think that I am the one responsible for the alarm going off, but never in my wildest dreams did I imagine that Master Bertie would fire a broadside at the bell."

Bertie mumbled something to the effect that he hadn't been shooting at the bell, and Grandpa said that this was true because Bertie had manifestly been shooting at the wall. The floor was covered with plaster that had been trampled underfoot and the air was thick with the smell of gunpowder. Then Grandpa asked Miss Barbara what she'd meant by saying that she was the one responsible for the bell going off. She showed him a broken match which had been pared down at one end and explained that she'd intended that the bell would disclose to us when the power supply had been restored. She had pressed the bell in and had then used the wedge made from her match to keep it in that position. She had done this because having tried so many times to see whether the power was back on, we had lost track of whether the electrical devices in the house were currently switched on or off. When the power was restored it would be desirable to check the electric stove, the radiators and other equipment at once as a precaution against the outbreak of fire.

Grandpa said that this had been a prudent move, but he was still not clear as to who had deactivated the system in the first place, who had smashed the window, and why I had been grappling with Saturnin. Before I could reply Saturnin's voice could be heard as he threw himself into the firing line. The window had not been properly closed and was rattling in the wind. He had got out of bed in order to close it and just as he was doing so the lights came on and at the same time he heard the bell ringing. Because there was no one at the front door, Saturnin explained, he had come to the conclusion that there was a short circuit somewhere, which was why he had closed the whole system down, concluding that a proper investigation could be put off till morning. He then returned to the open window and failed to hear the sound of voices and doors opening coming from the first floor because of the wind and the noise of thunder. He shut the window and just as he was preparing to go back to bed there was an explosion of sound from Master Bertie's gun. Then he heard the director's voice and immediately afterwards a second explosion from Master Bertie.

He was somewhat taken aback, and before he could recover his composure he was assailed by his master, who had apparently come running down the back staircase in order to tackle the presumed burglar with his bare hands.

It was not in my interest to contradict Saturnin's account, because I would then become even more caught up in the whole affair. I only want to say that never before in my life had I encountered such a bravura performance in the art of lying.

Miss Barbara looked at me with fascination and then pointed out that my hair was full of plaster. This shifted the focus of attention towards the dogged marksman and in the end we discovered that Bertie had never intended to shoot, least of all at the wall as Grandpa had suggested. The first shot happened when he lost his footing and fell down the stairs. At that moment the gun got caught up in the banisters of the staircase and when he tried to pull it free it went off for a second time, even though he apparently had his finger nowhere near the trigger.

Although everything had now been cleared up, Aunt Catherine continued to sit on the stairs casting her frightened eyes round the hall and saying: "Don't try to tell me that. I don't believe a word of it." We shrugged our shoulders and felt that there was nothing left for us to say.

There was a bout of silence and then we looked at each other in alarm. Unknown voices were coming from the living-room. Aunt Catherine groaned and said she'd known as much. Dr. Witherspoon asked her to be quiet.

The muffled voices of two men engaged in a ferocious argument could be heard in the living-room. I couldn't understand a word they were saying, but the presence of strangers in Grandpa's house was enough in itself to unnerve me. Miss Barbara listened attentively and then said in a whisper: "They're talking in Spanish."

"Perhaps we ought to turn off the wireless," said Dr. Witherspoon.

We all looked at him in astonishment and then Saturnin went into the living-room in order to switch off the radio broadcast. We felt a little ashamed at taking fright so unnecessarily and Grandpa brought the night's events to a conclusion with the words:

"Back to bed! The lot of you!"

XIV.

After the chaotic events of the night before I was woken in the morning by a shower of pebbles landing on the floor of my room. I leaned out of the window and caught sight of Miss Barbara below searching for another pebble. With a cloudless sky and blazing sun outside, it would be a crying shame to spend another minute in the room.

Miss Barbara asked me whether I was intending to spend all morning in bed. All the others had already breakfasted and Grandpa would be back from his morning walk at any moment. I dressed quickly and met up with Miss Barbara in the living-room where I drank down some coffee which was already going cold.

I learned from Saturnin that Grandpa had left for the forest probably in order to avoid setting eyes upon Aunt Catherine, with whom he was clearly still in a bad mood.

Miss Barbara informed me that our supply of provisions had gone down appreciably and that she had no idea what we'd do when the last potato had been eaten. She explained that Aunt Catherine had carried out a remarkable raid on the pantry the previous day and that Master Bertie had apparently wolfed down so many of its contents that he might just as well have been locked in his room without food for a week rather than for twenty-four hours. She asked me what I thought the chances were of someone swimming across the river and trying to bring back some provisions from town.

Crossing the river would not be difficult in itself. The problem lay in having to transfer to the other bank the clothing necessary for ensuring that whoever undertook this risky venture could actually put in an appearance anywhere in town. Transporting the purchased food back across the river would also be difficult.

We were surprised in the middle of our discussion by Grandpa returning from his walk. He told us that he doubted whether such measures would be necessary. When the bridge had been destroyed by flooding four years earlier, he had made an agreement with a builder in the town. The agreement stipulated that should the misfortune repeat itself the builder would start constructing a new bridge without requiring Grandpa to swim across and visit him in his office in order first to agree an estimate of the price. Because the water level in the river was now much lower, Grandpa expected to see Mr. O'Reilly's workforce appearing on the opposite bank and getting down to work at any moment. Grandpa even pointed out that the previous summer he'd spotted some wood specifically designated for this work in the builder's storehouse. On that occasion he'd offered Mr. O'Reilly a light-hearted wager on whether it would ever be used or would rot in store before the occasion arose.

Then Grandpa asked Miss Barbara how many days' supply we had left. She replied that we could probably hold out for four days if we didn't eat too much. After a while Aunt Catherine appeared and Grandpa didn't so much as glance at her. She, on the other hand, remained undaunted and the whole day was marked by her efforts to get back on good terms with the old boy.

I have never had much understanding of Aunt Catherine. If I hadn't been personally acquainted with her I would never have thought it possible for one and the same individual to have so many different characters. She could be sweet and sycophantic and then in the twinkling of an eye become unbelievably cruel, arrogant and rebellious. A moment later she would become obsequious and over-considerate all over again before reverting to downright rudeness. She hankered after money with a feverish longing, and then when she had it she threw it away in a manner that I'd consider plain bloody daft, if my own upbringing did not prevent me from using such expressions. The manner in which she tried to ingratiate her-self with Grandpa again was a distinct embarrassment and among other things spoiled his evening story.

After dinner we took our seats in the living room, where Grandpa was preparing to share the memories of his youth. Aunt Catherine sat down directly opposite him and throughout his story spoke when he did. She interrupted him with shouts of admira-tion, making noisy displays of fear when he spoke of danger and of delight when he recorded his triumphs. We were all left wonder-ing why Grandpa didn't banish her from the room. There was only one possible explanation. I have already pointed out that Grandpa took pleasure in observing the intense and desperate competition between his relatives as they strove to win his favour. It is conceiv-able that the frantic efforts of Aunt Catherine amused him. What cannot be denied is that he endured them and continued his tale to the very end.

He knew how to tell a story and the room was soon filled with an atmosphere of wistful recollection characteristic of those with most of their lives already behind them. Ah yes, those were the good old days, weren't they! I used to suppose that this golden age was sometime around the end of the nineteenth century, and that during this particular period all was unusually right with the world. Then I discovered that Grandpa's good old days were quite different from the good old days enjoyed by my father. I also ran across some relatively young people who told me that this golden era dated from a time which I must already be able to remember myself. It seemed confusing and contradictory. I later understood that these golden times stand for the youth of whoever is speaking about them. Which means that our generation must be living through golden times right now. How extraordinary.

So Grandpa told his story and we hung on his every word. We listened while he mentioned the dates of events that took place before we were born. We imagined what an imperial greatcoat might have looked like and guessed how much a golden ducat would be worth in our present currency. My aunt let out a low whistle, inclined her head and voiced the opinion that it must have been a lot of money in those days.

Grandpa spoke of how he joined up and accompanied the armed forces to a marvellous country full of lemon blossom. The world was big and beautiful, the sky was blue, the women had smouldering eyes and Grandpa was at the centre of this world. Everything seemed to be working out for him.

Aunt Catherine commented that everything always turned out well for Grandpa and that fortune inevitably favoured him – as well it should. Then Grandpa told us about the generals and we received the impression that there were two kinds of general at that time: there were the ones on the other side who dashed around the globe simply to enable Grandpa to capture them together with their chiefs of staff, and then there were those on his own side, who were there so that Grandpa would have someone to laud him for his acts of bravery in the presence of the entire army. In white castles surrounded by pine trees countesses lay in wait, hoping to seize the opportunity of falling in love with Grandpa for the rest of their lives. Fate seemed to have been extremely busy just contriving incredible events and unbelievable incidents in which Grandpa could enjoy a starring role. He was only a sergeant, but everyone knew what sort of a man he really was. There was the power of his military moustache and sparkling eyes – and as for women, well, the less said about that the better.

My aunt tried to affect a roguish expression and demanded to know whether Grandma knew about all this. And the wine! Grandpa went on, my God, all that wine they had. Wine also played a major part in the story of how Grandpa saved the life of a general and how a countess fell in love with him. Fell in love with Grandpa, naturally, not with the general.

It was a lovely May night with a gentle breeze and Grandpa, although almost on his own, heroically conquered a deserted village. An abandoned castle stood on a gentle rise above the village, its cellars full of wine. The quartermaster galloped up followed soon afterwards by the commanding general with his entourage. "Ah! It's you, old chap!" he said to Grandpa, with whom he was on first name terms. Then he went into the castle. Despite a whole day in the saddle Grandpa reconnoitred the grove of cypresses and listened for sounds in the Southern night. There was too much silence all around and Grandpa didn't like it. You should never underestimate your foes.

Now Grandpa digressed and moved on to the intrigues and ingenious traps, the chance events and moments of inspiration that had saved so many lives. He recalled lots of secret doors, floors which gave way under your feet and cellars packed with barrels of gunpowder. Death was lurking behind every corner (at this point Aunt Catherine shook with fear for Grandpa's life and Dr. Witherspoon offered her a blanket).

It was dangerous to look into the smouldering eyes of the women because they lured you onto rocks as surely as the Sirens. Grandpa preferred the noise of battle to a conspicuous silence which he judged would be suddenly and inevitably broken by shots fired from an ambush.

Grandpa's tale was gripping and we all started in fear when the reference to gunfire provoked a scream from Aunt Catherine. I wouldn't like to exaggerate, but I think that even Grandpa started. He frowned slightly but went on with his tale.

There was something touching about those memories of an old soldier. His eyes blazed as he recalled the names of the encampments and towns, gave the names and dates of battles and unwittingly made use of military terms which were more than half a century old. I had the impression that the room quietly reverberated to the sound of the Radetzky march.

Now let's return to that beautiful and quiet night. All too quiet. The soldiers were relaxing around dying fires, the fragrance of the cypress groves was in the air and from time to time the horses whinnied. In the hall of the castle some mediaeval nobleman in period costume looked dejectedly down from a black frame upon the officers who were dining at a long oak table. Candles were burning, their flames dancing like fiery red sparks in their goblets of wine. The officers were not drinking, because it was for the general to raise his glass first. But in those days it was not a good thing for the person whose life was most valuable to drink first. That would be dangerous, and because of this Grandpa had come back from walking through the cypress and pine groves in the gathering darkness in order to stay the general's hand as it was lifting the glass to his mouth. There had already been too many cases of wine being doctored, and so it was Grandpa who took the first glass and drank to the health of the general. God alone knew who drank the last glass, for there were too many to be counted.

The candles flickered and burned low, while the nobleman maintained his melancholy vigil from the picture. Wine subdued the longing for home in the soldiers' hearts and brightened the eyes of the officers, summoning songs to their lips and tales of victories to come. Even the eyes of the general lit up under his grey eyebrows and some colour appeared in his ancient face. The blood started to flow in limbs made numb by riding all day. The old gentleman looked at his soldiers with pleasure. He loved them all, loved his men with a passion such as the old harbour for young men full of life, men he expected to raise the banner that would eventually fall from his hand when God ordained it.

The soldiers brought wine, replaced the candles and the nobleman in the picture kept watch and brooded. The wine flowed and the night wore on. Speech became slurred while ideas grew confused and conversation went round in circles. A pleasant tiredness spread through their veins and their limbs grew heavy from wine and the hard day which they all had behind them. The journey had seemed endless and the road had been covered in a white dust that rose under their horses, settled in their eyes and choked

the breath from burning throats. It was an endless road lined with dusty trees and solitary wells, the sort that women went to for water in the Bible. They'd had to keep going until darkness fell, until they were where they were now.

The wine rinsed away the dust lodged in their throats and summoned sleep to close their reddened eyelids. Sunburnt heads fell onto the cold surface of the oak table, leaving the wine undrunk in the glasses. The candles were about to go out. The old general was sitting upright at the head of the table, his eyes still blazing under his grey eyebrows. He gave an approving look to all those who had succumbed neither to wine nor to fatigue.

The pale nobleman in his mediaeval apparel looked quietly down from the portrait. He was watching them all, but no one was watching him. No one except Grandpa. Grandpa had taken a dislike to his mediaeval countenance with those melancholy eyes, and he did not take to the heaviness around his mouth. This aristocrat had definitely not been a good man and the fact that he was sleeping in some church crypt beneath a heavy marble slab was to be welcomed. Without doubt he would have already disintegrated and become dust, while his soul had been carried off to hell by the Devil. No doubt about it, my dear chap, the Devil had every right to you, even if you were a member of the Holy Inquisition during your lifetime. That institution holds no sway on the other side. You look as if having someone burned was right up your street.

Grandpa straightened the wick of the candle and went to top up the general's glass. He returned to his place by the door muttering: "Damn! I spilt it. Because of that fellow in the portrait I spilt it. I'm not plastered but I can't stand the way he keeps looking at me. I'm sick of his repulsive eyes. He keeps on staring and I shall just have to kill him." Rage mixed with foreboding at evil things to come rose in Grandpa's breast and an icy hand gripped his throat. The candles were blazing, the wine sparkling and death was walking in their midst. That was the moment when Grandpa drew his pistol and shot. He really wasn't drunk and kept his hand steady. The bullet made a hole in the nobleman's overbearing forehead. A moment later the portrait fell from the wall and a man came crashing down after it. Yes indeed. There was a niche behind the picture and the enemy was waiting until the wine had managed to achieve what his weapons could not. The officers roused by gunfire, the calm and resolute general, the summoning of the guard, the castle surrounded by their foes and wild skirmishes with sabres under the olive tree, the comrades-in-arms who lost their lives when they fell from their horses into laurel with all its symbolic meaning – the whole story was served up in Grandpa's narrative at an ever-quickening pace. The old gentleman was out of breath and a little confused. He told us, for example, that the bugler sounded for them to mount their horses. Then the bugler reportedly made everyone dismount again because he had forgotten to tell them to saddle the horses to begin with. Then they mounted once more. They rode at a great pace for a long time and found the parched highway with its white dust and the biblical wells along its route. And on that very day the grey general went up to Grandpa in front of the whole army and . . .

Grandpa had quite forgotten that he was also meant to tell us about the countess and how she fell in love with him.

iss Barbara transferred her culinary headquarters to the kitchen. She even said that she didn't want to make the move, it being quite interesting working outdoors. This didn't surprise me. For all the persistent rain that had gone before, the weather had now changed and was staying fine.

Pleasant days went by. You might say that nothing special or important happened, but I could not agree with you. For me these were wonder days filled with extraordinary and miraculous things.

I realise that other people cannot share my feelings, because what I am speaking about concerned only myself and Miss Barbara. Each day the bonds of friendship between us became stronger. Foolish trifles made us happy by providing us with the opportunity to show that we belonged to one another – of course only when nobody was looking. We shared cigarettes, we took bites out of the same apple and we swapped possessions. I wore a red scarf belonging to Miss Barbara round my neck and she carried my cigarette case, lighter and pocket knife in the pockets of her elegant leisurewear. I went around with her metal pocket mirror and we had cogent reasons for seeking each other out, because I frequently wanted to light a cigarette and Miss Barbara urgently needed her mirror.

We rummaged around together in Grandpa's library and always felt a craving to read the same book. Surprisingly enough, this worked out quite well. Our customary silent encounters after dark on the terrace had been interrupted by the rest of our group, who were enticed there by the balmy evenings. It became the location of our soirées, with the telling of a story a compulsory requirement from all those present. Each of us had a designated deckchair and each evening Saturnin arranged them so as to save Miss Barbara and myself worrying about the crucial matter of whether we'd be sitting next to one another.

Saturnin is a most ingenious fellow. I have never discovered to this day how he arranged in such a miraculous manner for Bertie's deckchair to collapse, more often than not in the middle of a story, leaving the arrogant fop buried in the ruins. The first time it happened everyone had the fright of their lives, and Saturnin obligingly brought Bertie another deckchair. After about ten minutes this one disintegrated too and Bertie ended up on the ground once again. It was all too much for Grandpa. "What are you doing now, you stupid boy? Don't you know how to sit properly?" he yelled. Bertie went off feeling insulted.

Saturnin lived up to his promise in another way too. I think Bertie will remember his stay in Grandpa's house for a long time to come. Like a character a slapstick comedy he suffered extraordinary accidents and misfortunes at Saturnin's hand. It was interesting that he stayed silent and did not point any finger of blame at Saturnin. There must have been some reason for this. Saturnin spared no effort and it would be beyond my powers to give an account of everything which he thought up for Bertie. I recall my dear cousin's rage when he sprayed his hair with paraffin from a bottle of birch water. I remember how he went storming round the whole house, his mouth full of curses, during the time when we didn't have any light. He'd gone to bed after dark and had discovered that someone had changed round the furniture in his room in a completely ludicrous manner. He began to doubt his own sanity when he found even the twopenny thriller which he was reading totally incomprehensible. Saturnin had altered the text by inserting pages from other thrillers, making sure that – unlike the content – the page numbers would remain consistent. Interestingly, the first time he read through the doctored volume Bertie didn't notice anything wrong. I even think that he intended to tell that story when his turn came round during our readings after dark. In the evening Grandpa insisted that we should keep them going on a rota basis, even though the electricity was back on. Aunt Catherine readily agreed to this and began her own contribution.

She pointed out that Grandpa and I had taken stories from our own lives, recounting things that actually happened to us. That was not something she could do. Her life had been a hard one, full of daily toil and privation. After Uncle Francis died she devoted herself to her child Bertie. She had never had a bad word to say about her late husband and wanted to remember him only for his goodness. After all, he was Grandpa's son and she respected Grandpa more than anybody else. Even so, she might permit herself to say that where material things were concerned he did not provide for the family in a fit and proper manner.

Grandpa gestured impatiently and my aunt quickly explained that she knew there was the factory and a tidy sum in cash, but it had been necessary to provide Bertie with an education. Grandpa looked at Bertie as if he was trying to cope with an entirely novel idea. He shook his head in disbelief, but Aunt Catherine was not allowing any interruptions.

She told us that even if the family thought otherwise, she had nothing to reproach herself for. The factory had been a small one and didn't produce enough. It had been absolutely essential to buy the building next to it. This had landed my aunt in debt and had forced her to sell both buildings. Any unbiased observer would agree that it was a miracle that she'd managed to keep her head above water for as long as she had, without being crushed by the burden of her worries. Naturally she couldn't have behaved as a man might have done. She was merely a member of the weaker sex and wherever she went she had no support. Bertie was too small for her to depend on him as her protector. Besides, she wasn't made for coping with the crude demands of practical life.

She had never mentioned this to us before, but it was becoming more and more clear to her that she'd missed her vocation and that her true place was in the world of the arts. It was a shame that such a wealth of talent had remained unexploited. Even at school the teachers were astonished at her writing assignments and spoke of her extraordinary creative writing skill. But it was not to be. She had sacrificed her whole life to someone else and nobody had guessed that she saw into the human heart more deeply than other people. Nor had they realised that there was a beautiful song in her soul which she longed to capture for posterity so that it could live on in the memory of future generations. She wanted to write mainly for women, for a woman is best understood by other women. Perhaps her readers would have a better understanding of her than those among whom she'd lived her life. In fact no one understood her. Love had come her way on only one occasion, pure and marvellous as a mountain stream, but she was a married woman at the time and told him that they were unable to travel arm in arm together on life's journey.

Later she often wondered what right she had to wrench the love from her heart and separate two people joined together by the sacred bond of emotion. However, there was the child to consider and that perhaps excused her. Her lover disappeared from her life taking his grief with him and she never set eyes on the man again. She dreaded to think of whether her rejection might have driven him away into the cold arms of death. He loved her too much.

Then she tried to forget. She bowed her head, accepted her fate and patiently bore her cross. She even remained silent in the face of the insults with which she was bombarded by her relatives. She was too proud to respond to their smears, at least insofar as they concerned herself. Naturally when he also became the target of their slanders – and these were people who were not good enough to clean his sandals – then she could no longer keep silent, especially when they pointed out that a broken heart hadn't prevented him from going off with her gold watch and several silver spoons. Such a calumny. You can't begin to understand how awful it all was. Such is the malice of mankind. But a dog howling at the moon carries no weight. His reputation remained unsullied by anything they could dredge up from the past. Perhaps he held on to the watch as a keepsake or sold it for – here my aunt paused for effect – a revolver. There was clearly no point in looking back. Both loves had been lain to rest, the love for him and the love of literature. My aunt told us that she would tell us the theme of the book she'd meant to write. Her account went roughly as follows:

People called her Martha the delicate flower. She used to stand behind the counter among bunches of roses, carnations and lilacs. She used to wrap the flowers in tissue and paper. With a diffident smile she handed them to all the smart men who carried them off for other women. She had eyes the colour of violets, lily-white skin, a bright red mouth like a poppy and little snowdrop teeth. Her soul was deep and her boyfriend steady. The boyfriend was Paul, who was not as smart as the men who used to buy baskets of flowers for the heroines of light opera. He worked in the mines. By day he laboured down the pit and in the evening he waited on the corner of Wenceslas Square for his delicate flower Martha.

Their love for each other was ardent and pure as a mountain stream. Martha didn't care that he was dressed shabbily, if tidily. She honestly loved this big lad with his grey eyes. He lived only for her and no sacrifice demanded of him in order to make her happy was considered to be too great. However, as they say, fate has a fickle finger and it doesn't stay still. Martha's dream of love came to nothing, destroyed by the malice and duplicity of the world, by obstacles placed in the path of their happiness of which that delicate flower Martha, poor trusting soul, had no conception.

As luck would have it, she met up with an attachment from her school days in one of the city's schools – Oscar the demon cynic. He overcame her defences with words of passion, pretending in a devilish way that he had carried her image in his heart since childhood. He promised her undying love and faithfulness unto the grave. Human frailty being what it is, Martha resisted his false promises for a long time but in the end she succumbed. She was so young and inexperienced that it is impossible to condemn her. For is it not written: let the one who is without sin cast the first stone?

After this youthful infatuation was over she would certainly have returned to Paul, seeing that he alone was the sunshine of her life, but fate decreed otherwise. She was spotted by Paul leaving Oscar's flat with the young man in tow. Martha went white and her knees buckled beneath her. She wanted to shout after Paul as he went away, but her throat tightened in anguish and everything collapsed around her. Her dream of happiness lay in ruins and she felt as if there was nothing left to live for. She would have fainted if Oscar had not caught her in his arms. Martha the delicate flower girl shook with disgust, struck her seducer in the face with her fist and ran off.

She wandered the empty streets for a long time, her heart breaking as she came across those places where she used to meet Paul and which were reminders of their happiness together. She avoided only the embankment, because she was uncertain whether she could withstand a summons from the river, luring her into another embrace.

In the meantime Paul was sitting in his room with his head buried in his hands. It seemed to him that all this just couldn't be true. He would wake up and leave the nightmare behind him. His Martha, his delicate flower Martha had forgotten their love for one another and there was nothing left for him to do but accept this blow of fate. Then he stood up and with stony-faced resolve burnt all the letters, photographs and other tokens of their past life together, things that until then had been so very precious to him. One thing alone he didn't manage to burn – the image of Martha which

139

he carried in his heart. Months went by, a year went by and then another year, but the wound in Paul's soul failed to heal. He walked the streets of the city alone and despondent. His friends didn't recognise him. He whiled away his evenings chatting to his landlady, a wise woman of many years and deep roots in her people. She loved him as if he were her own son. She cheered him up as best she could, telling him about the novels she'd read, novels in which a loving heart finally attained peace and joy. But Paul merely smiled wistfully and pointed out that life is not like a novel. It took a long time before he understood from what the wise woman was saying to him that he was not behaving decently and that his duty was to forgive. Only by so doing could he prove from the bottom of his heart that his love was true. His passion for playing chess was the guilty party in all of this. Why hadn't he shown more devotion to his delicate flower? Why had he left her alone every Thursday and hurried off to the cafe in order to play several games? His heart was filled with shame as he recalled the way he used to sink deeper and deeper into total self-indulgence as soon as he sat down at a chessboard, and at the fact that at these times – may God stay His hand from striking him down for it! – creating an opening for a pawn meant more to him than his Martha. Had she not been left alone once a week? This was what drove her directly into Oscar's arms. Yes, that was the reason for it and nothing else. Paul decided with scarcely a moment's hesitation to forgive Martha. His landlady had been in the right every time she'd said to him "My God, 'once' doesn't have to mean 'always'."

But in the meantime life had been moving on. It was late, Paul, it was too late when you understood where your duty lay. And so it turned out that Paul went in vain to look for his delicate flower in the shop where she'd been working two years beforehand and failed to discover her in the flat where she'd been living at that time. He was in a state of total despair, but fate did not even spare him the hardest lesson of all. It led him in front of the Old Town Hall at the very moment when, looking pale and despondent, Martha emerged from the ceremonial hall as the wife of a man whom Paul had never seen before. Paul fainted on the spot, smearing his light overcoat with mud from the street.

Marriage did not make Martha happy. She was not in love with her husband and only the thought that fortune might favour her with a child, whose pure eyes would soothe the anguish in her soul, provided her with the strength to accept her toilsome lot. But her longing was in vain. Months went by and motherhood remained elusive. Music was now her one source of happiness. She composed dirges and wrote long letters to some famous composer Johannes Christophori.

Her husband loved her but was rather too simple-minded. He was unable to fathom the depths and complexity of her sensitive soul. It seemed that Martha's happiness was already lost forever. But then Providence itself delivered her from the bonds of matrimony. Her husband passed away after a short illness. So far as his wife Martha was concerned, although she genuinely regretted his death it also brightened her life with a ray of hope that perhaps all was not lost.

She guessed that Paul still loved her and hoped that the money that her husband had left her would enable her to make Paul's difficult life working in the pits somewhat easier. She read her laborious way through the letters which he used to write to her at one time. She gave herself searching looks in the mirror, wondering whether Paul would still think her pretty. What plans and minor stratagems she cooked up in order to meet him, never guessing that she was about to endure the unkindest cut of all!

It was fate which directed her steps to the Kinsky Gardens, where the two of them had once taken walks together, and there she caught sight of Paul. He was standing right opposite her on the narrow path, silently looking in her direction. Their unexpected encounter had drained the colour from his cheeks. Martha began to tell him about herself, her marriage, how she had never forgotten him and how she was now unattached. Paul listened to her gloomily and then delivered the sentence which put the final nail in the coffin of all her hopes. His voice quivering, he told her in despair: "I'm a married man."

Martha found herself looking at the low-level building in which a department of the Museum of Agriculture was located. Tears were streaming down her face. Then she asked in a whisper: "Are you happy?" He took his time replying and then told her that without love a marriage could never be happy and that only once in his life had he been in love. Nevertheless he could just about describe himself as content. He had a good wife and a sweet little daughter. The old wounds had almost ceased to hurt. It was pointless to remember what had been and was now gone, never to return. Such a step would seriously upset the peace of mind which he had managed to acquire.

Martha made her way home with only a vague idea of where she was going, because her eyes were full of tears. Which explains how a state-of-the-art twelve-cylinder limo was able to slam into her, drag her along for several yards and then dump the delicate flower on the edge of the pavement. A casually but smartly dressed man who was getting on in years leaped out of the car and bent down over the body, but Martha's eyes saw nothing of this. When she came round she was in an expensively equipped ward in a private sanatorium and was very slowly beginning to register what had happened to her. She could dimly recall a big blue limousine, which she'd only spotted at the last moment through a veil of tears, after which everything in her memory went blank.

She was just looking inquisitively around the white room in which she found herself when she heard a polite tap and the same man of advancing years, stately bearing and greying hair came into the room. He introduced himself as 'Mr. Stone, a factory owner' and expressed deep regret at the misfortune she had suffered under the wheels of his car. Luckily her injuries were not serious and the judgement of the consultant was that there would be no after-effects. He asked Martha not to hold back if there was anything at all worrying her. She remained silent. He went on to say that he was sending her books, wine and fruit. If she fancied the idea of a friendly chat he would visit on a daily basis. Naturally he considered it a matter of honour to meet the bill for all expenses connected with her treatment and he hoped that once her recovery was complete she would not refuse an invitation to convalesce in the countryside.

Under normal circumstances Martha would not have accepted such an invitation, but reeling under the blows meted out to her by fate she longed to be in Nature's temple away from the bustling city. She wanted to rediscover the peace which she had lost. She accepted the invitation and that was how six months later the wedding came to be announced between Martha and Mr. Stone, the factory owner, in the society columns of the daily papers. By a twist of fate the death of Paul's wife was announced in the papers on the very same day. Before the wedding Mr. Stone explained to Martha that he was well aware of the fact that he could be her father. However, he added that he had not asked for her hand in marriage without very sound reasons for doing so.

He told her that he was suffering from a serious liver complaint which he supposed would sooner or later be the death of him. He would be content if fate were to grant him a beloved wife at his side for the rest of his life and if it delivered him from his concern that, burdened as he was with considerable property assets, he might have no heirs. He looked so robust for his age that Martha could hardly believe that he was ill. She tried to soothe his anxieties and it can even be said that she succeeded in this, not least when after a year she bore him a son. The factory owner was happy and seemed to be enjoying a second youth. He appeared to have forgotten entirely about his illness.

He had forgotten the illness, but the illness had not forgotten him. Mr. Stone passed away as predicted. After his death it became clear that he had been far more wealthy than Martha supposed. She was almost alarmed at the sums mentioned by the public notary and it took a long time for her to come to terms with the fact that such a fortune really belonged to her. She and little Martin could live without any worries for the future and could even make an occasional donation to worthy causes.

Martha thought about Paul often and it goes without saying that she asked herself whether he was living in poverty. Being in the lap of luxury herself, she was constantly troubled by the unbearable thought that the one man she'd loved in the past and loved still was forced to earn his living as a mineworker. Perhaps his child suffered hardship too. From the moment when she'd read the announcement of his wife's death in the papers she'd had no news of how he was doing. She was determined to meet the manager of the mine where he was employed and try to secure a better position for Paul without his being able to guess that she'd intervened on his behalf. It was not a difficult task to carry out because the manager, Mr. Hill, had been a frequent guest of the late Mr. Stone. Consequently she could approach him as an old acquaintance. Having resolved upon action, she carried it through. Her blue limousine was summoned, little Martin was entrusted to the care of a diligent nurse and Martha set out for Prague.

It was the first time in her life that she'd stepped into a factory office. Martha allowed her arrival to be announced to the manager. She was invited in at once and without any dithering explained the reason for being there. The manager was perfectly obliging, at least initially. He then looked surprised until finally a smile crept over his features. He repeated Paul's name and asked whether Madam meant her request seriously. He went on to say that no one of that name was on the register for his pit but that Mr. Paul Cross, of whom the

144

dear lady was speaking, was the owner of this mine and consequently his employer. For that reason it was absolutely out of the question for him, as an employee of Mr. Cross, to raise his salary. In a flash Martha understood that Paul's lowly occupation had been a pretence in order to put her to the test and she was overcome with emotion. Before she had time to collect herself, in walked Paul himself. Mr. Hill greeted him respectfully and withdrew discreetly from the room. Let us also show discretion and draw a curtain over the encounter between lovers whose hearts found each other through all the vicissitudes of fate and changing fortunes of life, so that they could enjoy quiet happiness in the harmonious union of man and wife. When, a short time later, the delicate flower arrived at the altar beside her beloved Paul, their delightful children walked behind them, their little hands locked together in mutual affection.

When Aunt Catherine's tale was over she fell silent, lost in contemplation of the pattern of the carpet. Then she recalled that a well-known writer, whom she would refrain from naming, had shown great interest in her work and had earnestly advised her not to offend God by failing to make use of the talents with which He had endowed her. My aunt said that perhaps even she could see that it was not yet too late to set out as a writer. The editor of a women's magazine had also given her great encouragement. Of course such a thing could only be possible (here she threw a glance full of meaning at Grandpa) in circumstances where she was financially secure and concerns about Bertie's future didn't apply the brakes to her creative endeavours. "Ah yes!" she said, "you'd see some writing then." She even thought that Bertie could make his presence felt in the literary world. He'd written several very pretty poems and there was a prospect of publication in an edition of authors at the early budding stage. So, then. There's no doubt about the talent round here. It's just a question of having the financial means to let the delicate flowers bloom.

XVI.

My aunt went silent. Grandpa appeared to be mulling over her words until it turned out that he was dozing. Dr. Witherspoon asked my aunt what the delicate flower Martha would have done if Paul had remarried in the meantime. My aunt retorted that any work of literature could be ridiculed in such a manner, and threw a tongue-in-cheek question back at Dr. Witherspoon. She asked him what he would have done if he had died before completing his doctorate. Dr. Witherspoon told her that he would be lying peacefully in the cemetery, leaving others to reflect on what might have become of him. My aunt got up and left the room with her bored crown prince in attendance. Grandpa immediately emerged from his slumber and was quite breezy for the rest of the evening. The doctor then held forth on the fact that a great deal of ink had been spilt concerning the pernicious influence of bad adventure stories on immature youth. He explained that by way of contrast he had read very few articles directed against so-called women's novels, the disastrous consequences of which for the public at large

147

could hardly be matched, in his most humble opinion, by the admittedly pernicious impact of twopenny thrillers on their young readers.

He pointed out that even the most dim-witted youth must understand that he cannot lasso the police in Wenceslas Square and that the golden age when the gunslinger plied his trade is now long gone. It was far more dangerous to put into the heads of many of our young female readers the idea that there was nothing final about marriage and that it was one of the very few ways for a woman to make her fortune, not to mention the pernicious notion that it was never too late to see one's marital mistake, shed any matrimonial ties and follow the summons of the heart to eternal bliss. It is much easier to demonstrate to an immature boy that he is not a bloodthirsty pirate than to prevent a not-so-intelligent young lady from finding some parallel between her own destiny and that of a romantic heroine in a novel when such a comparison will only lead her into a lot of trouble.

Young girls' heads are filled with preconceptions about manufacturers, landowners, bankers and millionaires who only offer their hand to poor dressmakers, telephonists and salesgirls. Judging from the novels, on the rare occasion when a millionaire does not marry a seamstress he is doomed to marital unhappiness and soon repents, getting a divorce only to seek out the loving embrace of a poor girl. Of course it sometimes happens that the heroine of a romantic novel falls in love with a poor but decent lad, let us say a conductor on the railways, but in the end this awkward situation is resolved when it turns out that being a conductor is merely the young man's hobby and in fact he's the owner of the whole railway network. "So that's the explanation!" exclaims the female readership and lapses into contentment. Otherwise those readers would not be able to sign up to the idea of perfect bliss which washes through the final pages of the novel. After all, their husbands may be railway workers too and they know that living with them is far from perfect.

The form of influence wielded by these publications over many women is certainly quite scandalous. Dr. Witherspoon explained that about five years back he'd been treating a young man who'd tried to kill himself. The reason for his attempt was a girl he'd been engaged to for several years and who had now started a relationship with someone else. This was hardly anything special. Such things happened all the time. However, there was something peculiar about the behaviour of this girl. She continued to be friends with her former fiancé and to meet him. She informed him that her heart was torn between love for Fiancé Number One and love for Fiancé Number Two. She told him all about her encounters with number two and appealed to him not to give up hope and to fight for her affection.

The young man was totally disconcerted by all this. He was in distress, unable to sleep and finally shot himself. The girl went to visit him, shed some tears and it seemed as though, in her own words, he had won her heart by puncturing his lung with a bullet. Yet no sooner had he recovered than she somehow relapsed into her old ways and the game began all over again. With a trust that I found touching the chap came to me asking what he should do. While he was ill I had become something of a father confessor to him and now I had to give him advice.

I suggested that he find another girl, but you know how youth in its folly responds to advice like that. It had to be her! There could never be another! He left me with a heavy heart and I fully expected to be summoned to inspect his corpse. Instead of which he turned up again about a week later. He brought me some kind of magazine for women, opened it near the middle and asked me to read it. I would rather have thrown it away, but in the end I complied with his wishes.

It was an extract from some novel being serialised and was entitled 'Caught Between Two Men' or something like that. The episode which I read concerned some girl called Angela who proposed to a certain Peter that they split up because she was in love with a Luke. This suggestion apparently drained the colour out of Peter's face and he replied: 'To be continued next week.'

I folded up the magazine and asked why I was supposed to read it. My patient rose to his feet and shouted: "She is playing at being Angela!" Then he resumed his seat and told me that this meant the end of everything. He explained that he had suspected for some time that some outside influence was at work affecting his fiancée's behaviour. Her manner of speaking had undergone a transformation. She indulged in phrases full of highfalutin words. Following the dictates of my heart. The universal writ of emotion. The deepest reaches of the soul. You and I are on different wavelengths. The pinnacles of passion. And so on. He'd thought she'd got all this from Suitor Number Two, but then he'd come across this wretched magazine in a cafe. He was astounded to read in it the very same sentence which she had used with him a few hours beforehand. It was absolutely identical, word for word.

His first thought was that perhaps his fiancée was the author of this novel and found inspiration for it in her own vacillation between suitors. But then he rejected this idea. Apparently what had happened was this. His fiancée had simply transposed the realm of fiction into that of reality. He was Peter and Luke was Suitor Number Two. He got hold of all the back issues of this magazine and carefully read through every instalment of Caught Between Two Men. Everything tallied. There was no room for any doubt. He tried to guess the ending of the story in order to assess his chances of defeating his rival. Unfortunately it wasn't clear where foolish Angela's final choice would lie.

He tried to find the answer out from the editors of the magazine, but was told that the author delivered the novel instalment by instalment. Perhaps even she had no idea of how it was going to turn out. The next issue was still hot from the press and his fiancée had not yet read it, but it was clear that the moment she did she would insist on a separation.

Dr. Witherspoon said that to him it had all seemed like a bad dream. He attempted to talk his patient out of his ridiculous conjecture, but in vain. In the end they parted with an agreement to see how the girl would act after reading the latest sequel.

The very next day the wretched young man burst into the surgery like an express train flying through a station, hurled himself into an armchair and shouted out: "It's exactly as I said! Word for word. She even got mixed up and called Suitor Number Two Luke, even though his real name's Francis. That's everything finished now."

It upset me that he was so clearly distraught. I explained the basics of eugenics to him, which rules out marriage to a lunatic, and once again advised him not to compete with his rival for the dubious honour of setting up a sanatorium for the mentally ill at home.

He went off and I heard nothing from him for a long time. When I met up with him again he was married and just about to go abroad with his wife. I didn't want to ask whether he'd married the same scatterbrained girl but he confirmed it to me himself. Yes, it was she and everything was fine. The situation had simply required some clever thinking. He had found out the address of the perpetrator of Caught Between Two Men, had written her a letter and had described to her his unfortunate situation. He had assured her that everything hung on the outcome of her novel and implored her to hitch Angela up with Peter. The authoress was moved by his tale and willingly complied with his wishes. She told him that it was hardly a difficult task, since Angela had to marry someone in the end and there was no reason why it shouldn't be Peter. In the very next issue the scales fell from Angela's eyes, she saw through the dishonest character of Luke and recognised that there was a place in her heart only for Peter.

That, of course, was a different story. The fiancée did a volteface and they got married after all. The happiness of the young newly-wed was marred only by one thing. He was tormented by the thought of what would happen if some novel was serialised in the magazine describing how a married woman discovers that she made a mistake in tying the knot – and so on. The editor refused any guarantee that no such novel would crop up in his pages, but on this occasion the young man knew how to be resourceful. He found out which European countries received the magazine and went off with his wife to live in one that wasn't on the list.

When Dr. Witherspoon had finished, we failed to conceal our suspicion that he'd invented this story. However he clambered onto an armchair, held up three fingers and shouted that he would take an oath that it was so. It all made him look like some ancient seer and Miss Barbara started to laugh. The enthusiasm of the doctor drained away. He climbed slowly down from the armchair and moodily informed us that he was hungry. No wonder! Miss Barbara had apportioned the food in such a way that we could hold out for another three days, and the amounts were really very small. We discussed what would happen if on the following day – or at the very latest the day after that – Mr. O'Reilly's workmen were nowhere to be seen building a new bridge.

Doctor Witherspoon told us that he had a few supplies in his log cabin, and that it would perhaps be a good idea if he despatched someone to fetch them. In his opinion they amounted to at least a day's rations for everyone. Miss Barbara commented that this was no solution, since we would simply consume the provisions and be in the same boat all over again. It was possible that Mr. O'Reilly wasn't even aware that the bridge had been destroyed. In any case it was necessary to think of something that would get us out of this difficult situation. Grandpa agreed with Miss Barbara.

We could have been lighthouse keepers waiting in vain for supplies from a ship, members of a polar expedition coming to the end of their rations, a besieged garrison in a town facing starvation or I don't know what, but in any case our plight was tinged with a sense of adventure. We came up with a host of madcap schemes aimed at getting us into town in order to buy fresh provisions.

Finally Dr. Witherspoon thought of a fairly sensible plan. He proposed that we wait two more days to see whether they started to rebuild the bridge. Then we should take the last day's provisions with us and make for his log cabin. It was an easy hike with beautiful views, and if we set off at around eight in the morning we would be there early in the afternoon. There was room enough for us all to spend the night. Naturally it wasn't as comfortable as the place we were currently staying in, but we didn't have any alternative. The following day we would leave early in the morning for White Saddle Ridge, skirt around the source of the river, and descend via Heather Springs into the valley, after which we would attempt to make it as far as the town on the same day. It was a fairly challenging enterprise, but one well within the bounds of possibility. In the town we would bear down upon some hotel, have a proper meal and then while it was still night drag Mr. O'Reilly out of bed so that he could get working on the bridge.

Grandpa declared that he looked forward above all to the final item on Dr. Witherspoon's itinerary and commented that it was quite a sensible plan. A vote was taken and everyone was in favour. Dr. Witherspoon pointed out that it was doubtful whether Aunt Catherine would agree with the scheme. Grandpa said that it didn't make any difference if someone didn't like the plan. Let all those against stay where they were without food and we'd bury them when we got back.

Then he took out a map on which he and Dr. Witherspoon plotted out our proposed route. In the end we decided what it was necessary to take with us. Dr. Witherspoon said that we should take blankets in case fatigue prevented some member of the group from being able to complete the journey within a single day. Two or three would suffice, since we could get hold of the rest in his log cabin.

But Grandpa declared that dragging blankets along with us was out of the question. It would simply weigh us down on our march. Whatever the cost we must make it to the town. We were in a situation where any kind of sentimentality was damaging. Anyone who couldn't go on would be left to their own devices. Grandpa was full of the Spartan spirit that evening. I was waiting for him to suggest that we disposed of the weaker members of our party before setting off. I made some comment along those lines myself and Grandpa appeared to give it serious consideration before turning the proposal down. Perhaps he was afraid that he'd find himself among those categorised as disposable.

We discussed our escapade long into the night. We were possessed by a strange feeling of excitement for which there wasn't the slightest justification. Under normal conditions such a trek would have been no more than a popular tourist outing which we would have enjoyed without there seeming to be anything specially exciting about it. The mere fact that we had been compelled to make this journey because of a dangerously low level of provisions was enough to alter our whole understanding of the trip and turn it into a great expedition born of despair. A matter of life and death! The weak will be left to the wolves. Forward march, onwards and upwards and it's every man for himself. I think that we all went to bed that night hoping that Mr. O'Reilly was not going to spoil our adventure. Now that the bridge had stayed down for so long, let it stay that way. We're just not interested in that bridge of his any more! It came home to me, just before dropping off to sleep that night, just how much our plight must appeal to Saturnin.

XVII.

he next day passed without any noteworthy developments. Mr. O'Reilly's workers were nowhere to be seen. As I had anticipated, Saturnin was enthusiastic in his assessment of our enterprise and coined the phrase 'hunger march'. He claimed that such things took place in China, although on a larger scale. Over there such a march would probably involve a million people. Grandpa claimed that this was nonsense, because if one million people were to stand in a row they could simply pass the provisions along the line from the town to where we were. Saturnin objected that each one of them had to eat. If everyone in the row took a single bite as the supplies were moved along we'd end up dying of hunger at our end all the same.

It goes without saying that Dr. Witherspoon entered the fray at this point and wanted to calculate what would happen if each person in the line wanted to eat and only passed the provisions on when they couldn't consume any more. I don't like this sort of banter. They always begin by talking about something in what initially seems to be a sensible manner and then they take it to insane lengths. It would at least be tolerable if you knew that they were making light of the topic. Instead they wear serious expressions throughout and sometimes end up in a quarrel. I am referring here to Grandpa and Dr. Witherspoon. Naturally Saturnin never becomes involved in argument, though he usually manages to fan the flames all the same.

In the afternoon I set off with Miss Barbara looking for blackberries, but failed to find any. We came across some brambles, but couldn't be sure whether it was the sort that meant blackberries were growing there. Otherwise we drew a complete blank.

When we returned with empty jugs Grandpa told us that he'd guessed as much, because when certain people go looking for something together it's out of the question that they'll find anything. Miss Barbara blushed and Grandpa smirked at her.

While we were sitting on the terrace in the evening Aunt Catherine urged Bertie to offer us a story, it being his turn. Bertie said that he wasn't interested. Let someone else do it. "You see how it is," said Aunt Catherine, "what a timid young man! He's always shy like this, mainly because he's embarrassed in front of Miss Barbara. I've begun to wonder whether she's turned his head. It's now clear to me that she has."

Miss Barbara denied responsibility for turning any head at all, but then she looked taken aback and my belief is that she was thinking at that moment of me. My aunt raised her voice to say that she'd only meant her comments as a joke. But I wasn't listening to her. I was looking at Miss Barbara and waiting to see whether she looked at me. Look she did. She recognised why I was smiling. It was because I knew from my own experience that it was untrue to say she couldn't turn a head. The realisation made her blush to the roots of her hair. Even so she did not lower her eyes which sparkled from the joyful fires within.

Grandpa proceeded to challenge Saturnin to tell a story. He said that from what he'd heard Saturnin had lived through many an adventure. So let him recount something interesting.

Saturnin responded that he would be very happy to comply with the director's wishes, but he would like to point out that his life had not been adventurous in any way. This was a cause of genuine sorrow on his part, because he always longed to be wherever anything out of the ordinary, unusual or dangerous was happening. However, in this domain he was unable to have what he wanted. He often found himself envying those of his colleagues who had the chance to join their employers in living through unforgettable experiences. Those colleagues usually failed to appreciate their good fortune and longed for the sort of employment where nothing happens. He could never understand this attitude of theirs.

He told us that some years before he had been in the service of a very staid and sober gentleman. One day this gentleman showed him a letter he had received from a former manservant which was overwhelming proof of the fact that some people cannot stand the slightest hint of excitement. The contents of the letter were roughly as follows:

Dear Sir,

When I left your service some years ago, I never guessed what dastardly deeds and predicaments I was about to run into. It is true that Mr. Gustin offered me a better-paid position than the one I enjoyed in your service, but what I had to go through in his employment was something for which no amount of money can provide adequate recompense.

Perhaps it might all have turned out differently if Mr. Gustin had remained in Prague and had held on to his position for longer, or if he had not inherited enough money from his uncle to be completely independent where material circumstances were concerned. In any case let me come to the point: my first disappointment came when I learned that Mr. Gustin's Christian name was Augustine. Augustine Gustin! Perhaps you consider this a trivial matter, but I do not feel that it is suitable for a man of his social standing to be given a name which mimics an echo.

I was yet more taken aback when the first thing Mr. Gustin did after taking up his inheritance was to buy a castle. It is a matter of the greatest regret to me, sir, that I must refer to certain events transpiring which you will perhaps find it hard to believe took place, but I can assure you that what I am about to say is the truth. I have never been able to understand how a private businessman and an employer who benefited from such a good upbringing could see his way to buying a castle. I have always considered castles to be merely municipal property. Perhaps the only suitable owner of such a building would be the Czech Tourist Association, but never a private individual and certainly not one of Mr. Gustin's standing.

I have to say that my employer is of a very sensitive disposition. Ensconced in the grand halls of a castle he was and is affected in a special – I would say in a suggestive – manner. There is no other way in which I can account for those most unusual ideas of his which caused me so much embarrassment. I realise that it is among the duties of a gentleman's gentleman to carry out all the commands of his employer with meticulous care, naturally so long as they do not exceed the limits of his physical strength. Please forgive me if I sound somewhat distraught, but judge for yourself: how could I procure for him such a ridiculous thing as a ghost? He got it into his head that once autumn mists were drifting through the region, logs were crackling in the hearths of vaulted chambers and the soft music of a creeping draught was sounding through the silent corridors, the ambience was conducive to a supply of strong alcohol and a spectre. He asked me to fetch him a cognac and a ghost at once. He told me that I could bring them in reverse order if I so desired, the apparition first and then the cognac to dull the fear. He would leave the order of appearance to me.

From then on the household was so full of gossip about ghosts that the other servants managed to convince themselves that there really was one haunting the main tower. A host of sightings were reported in which the phantom assumed an ever more concrete form. In the servants' quarters they knew exactly what the ghost looked like.

They also knew why it was haunting the tower, the hour at which it chose to disclose itself and the time when it vanished into thin air.

Then a strange thing happened. Some furniture was damaged in the corner of a room on the first floor. By and large I can say that I've no idea what happened or where the rest of the servants got their information from. Unfortunately I cannot rid my mind of the suspicion that it was the work of Mr. Gustin himself. In any case the view from the servants' quarters concerning what took place was as follows:

Mr. Gustin was sitting at his fireside late at night and drinking what he presumed was cognac. On the stroke of midnight a ghost appeared in the hall. It was dressed in some kind of period costume and sported a severed head which it carried under its arm. It took a seat in an armchair opposite Mr. Gustin and arranged the head in its lap.

My employer retained his sangfroid and offered the spectre a drink before starting to tell him some hunting yarn. He paused frequently, partly because words began to fail him under the influence of drink and partly because the apparition was pouring the cognac into the mouth of this head on his lap, an event which proved somewhat challenging to Mr. Gustin's tranquil state of mind. Understandably so. Nonetheless he returned to his tale for another full hour, ignoring the fact that the ghost, intoxicated by cognac, put such unprecedented effort into frightening him, trying to scare him with bloodcurdling special effects, that an old oak wardrobe began to shriek in terror and proceeded to escape from its normal position and shut itself inside the cellar.

Allow me to make it clear once again that I am merely reporting what I heard and cannot guarantee that everything happened exactly as I describe. Nor can I associate myself with the crude terms apparently used by the exasperated spectre in order to describe my employer and I present them only for reasons of completeness. The apparition had exhausted every weapon a headless aristocrat can have in his armoury in order to scare Mr. Gustin. Yet still my employer's bored voice as he rambled on, and then his beginning to hum to himself, made it clear that every effort had been in vain. The desperate ghost apparently made a comment to the effect that frightening the wits out of a blockhead like this was a job for a real assassin rather than a decent, self-respecting spectre. Then he set off a terrifying explosion.

Perhaps you may recall, sir, that a sceptical frame of mind is my preferred philosophical disposition. I cannot allow myself to accept the existence of the supernatural, including such phenomena as ghosts, loose heads in laps and runaway wardrobes. Nevertheless, you may perhaps permit me to point out to you that the following day I was compelled to acknowledge certain facts which forced me to reflect further. In the first place the room in which the event transpired was literally demolished and I couldn't even begin to ascertain the cause. An old oak wardrobe, chock-full of heavy books, was missing and I located it later in the wine cellar. I had to make my way into the cellar by means of a window, since the door was locked from the inside. Mr. Gustin had disappeared and they found him in a hunting lodge in the middle of a forest. Permit me to observe that the journey to that forest takes several hours by bicycle and as to how Mr. Gustin came to be there I haven't the slightest idea. He was in nothing but a dressing-gown and bedroom slippers, had not yet fully recovered his sobriety and was holding forth in a confusing manner about his failure to understand how a ghost could be so horribly frightened of itself.

Repairing the wrecked room cost a lot of money and my employer, put out by the unnecessary expense involved, imposed a ban on any further talk about a ghost. I welcomed this as a sign of more peaceful times to come, but I was to be disappointed. The thing was that Mr. Gustin's younger brother had died not long before, leaving behind him an eight-year-old boy. My master took charge of this child and we received him into the household. This boy possessed such a pronounced fondness for dramatic incidents that we all, the master not excepted, think back upon the period when we were governed by a ghost as an era of idyllic peace. Mr. Gustin says that he has not had a good night's sleep since he resigned from the civil service.

Master Xavier – the young gentleman in question – claims that this is an exaggeration because, for example, on the occasion when he locked the governess away in the dungeon his uncle slept so soundly that he didn't even hear the roar of the Chief Fire Officer when he

broke his leg on the staircase because he was being pursued by a four-teenth century suit of armour. I can well remember how confusion reigned on that particular occasion. None of us knew what was actually going on. Then Master Xavier explained that there had been a case of spontaneous combustion in the library in the tower. He had wanted to assist the firemen and had gone there in a suit of armour in order to avoid being burnt. He had no idea why the Chief Fire Officer ran away from him.

Then Mr. Gustin, in order to calm himself down, spent such a long time walking around the battlements of the tower that he began to go out of his mind and started yelling that he'd rather be saddled with a dozen phantoms than such a little monster, by which he meant Master Xavier.

I dare say that it will seem to you, sir, that I am overstating the case, but I can assure you that I could relate to you many other events of a similar nature and that the one which I have chosen quite at random to acquaint you with is by no means the worst. We all, with the exception of the Chief Fire Officer and Mademoiselle Poisson, recovered from this particular incident relatively quickly. The lady in question was the governess whom the young man had shut away in the dungeon. Into her prison cell came some very disconcerting sounds – screaming, the arrival of the fire brigade and similar noises – and she later had to undergo treatment for her nerves at Mr. Gustin's expense.

Perhaps you wonder why I am telling you all this. Sir, I would simply like you to have some idea of my present conditions of employment and to be assured that I would greatly value the more peaceful surroundings which would return to me should you be able to accommodate my humble request to be taken back into your service.

I remain your faithful servant,
Balthasar Crisp

Saturnin pointed out that he had never enjoyed such a stroke of good fortune himself, though he was once employed by a private detective. He'd relished the thought of life in the fast lane confronting danger at his master's side and devoting his talents to solving cases.

Unfortunately he'd discovered that a bailiff or a conductor on the trams would have lived a far less prosaic life than that of his new master. The only riddle for him to solve was the mysterious case of why his employer had engaged his services in the first place. The man lived in a hotel, whiled away his time in a pub and was disastrously under-employed, which was just as well. The results of his investigations brought him nothing but trouble and they usually ended with the presumed offenders taking him to court. Saturnin's work consisted in visiting the courts in order to announce that his employer was unable to attend the hearing owing to sudden indisposition. Otherwise he had the whole day to himself with the exception of Friday afternoon, when he was obliged to bring his master further supplies of detective stories from the public library.

Never mind, said Dr. Witherspoon. At last you've now managed to enter the service of a real adventurer, a man who lives on a boat, hunts lions in Prague's zoo district by night, and makes insanely daring journeys in cars driven by impulsive and irresponsible young women. To cap it all you'll now be able to starve to death with them on this inhospitable island.

Saturnin commented that over the course of time the word 'adventurer' had acquired certain pejorative overtones. For that reason he supposed that it could not be used as a description of his master, that is to say myself. He suggested that a much better expression would fit the bill, that of 'Gentleman with a Relish for the Stirring and the Sporting'. He was fully aware of the fact that his present position was the best of all those which had come his way, and he hoped that his employer would confirm the fact that he showed due appreciation for the circumstances he found himself in. He supposed that Dr. Witherspoon somewhat exaggerated the danger of starvation, but if that was what it came to he believed that he would find enough moral courage to make a peaceful and dignified exit.

Aunt Catherine went pale and asked whether things were really that desperate. Dr. Witherspoon calmed her down and explained that at least some of us would be saved, of that he was certain. Unfortunately our bodily resistance had been somewhat weakened by the low rations of recent days, and this could have fatal consequences. Nevertheless, we must not allow ourselves to despair. The firm belief that we would successfully make it to town before it was too late was the first prerequisite of survival. On the other hand it made no sense to conceal the seriousness of our situation. Starvation did not represent an easy exit from this world and he had decided that were there no other way out he would use his revolver in order to end the agony.

It is possible that Dr. Witherspoon did not manage to deliver this last sentence with sufficient gravitas or even over-egged the pudding with it. My aunt gave him a searching look and then announced that she was going to lie down. She bade us goodnight and went out. We stayed sitting a while longer and then we too dispersed to our various rooms. A sudden storm sprang up during the night, but morning brought a cloudless sky. Bathed in sunlight the mountains rose huge and glorious in the fresh, ozone-rich atmosphere.

XVIII.

We devoted the last day spent in Grandpa's house to preparations for our emergency expedition. Many things were stuffed into haversacks and then pulled out again on the grounds that we couldn't even sustain their weight for an hour. Grandpa assumed command and took on the mantle of a general on the eve of battle. He demanded that all the remaining rations be fetched. At that point Miss Barbara discovered that some of our supplies had gone missing. They had been in the larder the previous evening. Grandpa asked whether she was quite sure about this. She answered in the affirmative and explained that from the moment when we had been forced to start rationing food in exact quantities she had kept a written record of the remaining supplies. Grandpa responded that this was a very serious matter and that he would never have expected to find any of us so devastatingly lacking in communal spirit.

Then he asked us one by one whether we had raided the larder. He began with Aunt Catherine, who took offence. She said that it was typical of the way she was treated in the place that she was the first to be asked this question. Grandpa pointed out that he had to begin with someone and there was no need for her to feel insulted. He asked the question once more and she replied theatrically: "No!" Then he asked Dr. Witherspoon, myself, Bertie and Miss Barbara, in each case eliciting the same negative response.

The one person who wasn't present was Saturnin. A while before he had asked Grandpa for permission to check whether Mr. O'Reilly's workers hadn't made a last-minute appearance on the opposite bank. I now found myself in a most unpleasant situation. For my own part I was convinced that Saturnin would not have done something like this, but I felt that it would be inconsiderate towards the others if I were to say so, since someone must have taken those provisions and I would be indirectly accusing one of those present of being a liar.

Grandpa told us that he would ask Mr. Saturnin as soon as he got back. Aunt Catherine suggested that it would be better if we didn't involve the servants in such unsavoury matters. It would be highly embarrassing and perhaps it would be preferable to say nothing about the affair in front of Saturnin.

I protested against this. I objected that after the denials of all those present suspicion had fallen upon Saturnin and it would be most unjust if we said nothing about the matter to him and failed to provide him with an opportunity to defend himself.

My aunt said that no one suspected Saturnin and the whole affair was a storm in a teacup. With all that we had to climb, why make another mountain out of a molehill. If someone raided the larder if was because they were driven to do so by hunger. It was in bad taste to say anything more about it. For her own part she had no objection to everyone receiving reduced rations, and proposed that we have done with this ridiculous parody of a courtroom drama.

Grandpa objected to this, saying that he fully agreed with my view that it would be unfair to Saturnin, and made his mind up to ask him the same question that he had asked the rest of us. My aunt said that she was used to having her wishes ignored and would therefore defer to his.

Then we all fell silent. My aunt alone paced round the room pulling scornful faces. From time to time she shook her head and added a few comments of her own in an undertone such as: "The tastelessness of it all", "I don't want to have anything to do with it", "Phooey!", "They're quite shameless", "Who would ever have believed such a thing", "They must have rhinoceros hides" and so on. At one point Grandpa asked her to get off the stage but his request simply met with some desperate arm-waving gesture.

When Saturnin came into the room he felt the eyes of us all upon him, but assumed that the explanation of our interest lay in what he'd discovered at the river. At that very moment it flashed through my mind that Saturnin might have taken the provisions for myself and Miss Barbara. I often had the feeling that he would be capable of acting in a somewhat unscrupulous manner on my behalf, and this new thought banished the peace of mind I had felt up to this point. I wanted to leave the room.

Saturnin stood to attention before Grandpa, an expression of complete calm on his suntanned face. He informed him that there was no sign of Mr. O'Reilly's men or for that matter anyone else on the opposite bank. A preoccupied look on his face, Grandpa replied that he'd thought as much. He then explained to Saturnin in a few words what had happened. He went on to ask him whether he'd taken the provisions. Instead of a firm denial from Saturnin an embarrassing silence filled the room. Saturnin looked at Grandpa, made no reply and appeared to be reflecting on the matter. This went on for quite a time and the longer Saturnin maintained his silence, the stronger became the unpleasant suspicion which I'd entertained earlier. Then my aunt went up to him and told him in a curt tone of voice: "You can go!"

Grandpa told her to stay out of this. Then he asked Saturnin whether he understood the question. Saturnin answered that he did. Then he apologised to Grandpa for having to leave, but he believed that Madam would wish to impart some information of her own to the director. If necessary, the director could put the question to him once again. Saturnin bowed and left the room, which was filled once more with an embarrassing silence.

Then Aunt Catherine told Grandpa that she wanted a word just between the two of them. He vehemently refused any kind of private exchange and told her that the matter concerned all of us. He was not going to take part in any discussion behind closed doors. He asked my aunt what exactly she wished to say. In an offended tone she replied that in that case she had nothing at all to say. Grandpa swore and ordered Bertie to bring Mr. Saturnin to him. At this point my aunt had a change of heart. With a powerful sweep of the hand she held Bertie back and declared that she would tell us what she'd wanted to say. Saturnin had taken the supplies from the larder. He'd taken them to the kitchen on her orders. From there my aunt had taken charge of them herself. Saturnin had supposed they were to be used in order to prepare supper or would be packed into the haversacks as provisions, and there was nothing to reproach him for. She said that she had never imagined that this house would live to see the day when an exact reckoning was made of how much food each guest was eating. She had never been so humiliated in her life. She had taken the provisions for herself and for Bertie. It had been necessary to act in this way because the male members of our company did not act in accordance with their moral obligations. Wherever and whenever civilised people find themselves in danger, an unwritten law comes into play: Women and Children First.

On the other hand, the principles that reigned in this place were of such a primitive nature that those who were incapable of further progress on an exhausting journey were to be left to their fate, without any special regard for women and children. It was clear that since the time of the sinking of the Titanic opinions had changed on this subject. The natural rights of women and children had been ground into the dust. My aunt illustrated the grinding by stamping on the carpet. Then she remarked that if one of the 'gentlemen' present was able to harden his heart enough to ask for the return of these provisions, she would be happy to inform him that they had already been consumed by Bertie and herself. They had both been so famished that there was a serious danger of their not being able to withstand the rigours of the journey, and just let anyone dare to criticise what she'd done. She had been driven to it by the fact that people today have started to neglect the most sacred of their obligations. Then she wished us well in an ironic manner and swept out of the room.

There was another embarrassed silence for a while, punctuated only by the grandfather clock. The first to speak was Bertie, who had a minor surprise in store for us all. He said that he'd had no idea where his mother had got hold of the provisions which she'd brought to his room, and he much regretted the fact that he'd wolfed them down. He did not consider himself to be a child and would refuse to be the beneficiary of any special treatment, even were it to be offered him. He announced that he would give up his rations for the following day and asked us not to speak about what his mother had done.

Although I didn't care for Bertie, I had to admit that his words sounded different from the empty gestures that Aunt Catherine's speeches amounted to, and I felt a smidgen of affection for him. Dr. Witherspoon responded to the effect that there was no need for him to sacrifice his share because the provisions we'd find in his log cabin would be more than enough for two whole days. He pointed out that we'd all been to blame the previous evening for exaggerating the danger we found ourselves in, and my aunt had had no idea that we were speaking tongue in cheek.

Bertie replied that if his mother had really believed things to be that bad then her actions were even less excusable. Dr. Witherspoon said that it was Bertie's own wish we would say nothing further about the matter, and we ourselves longed for nothing more than to change the subject.

Then he asked whether all our boots were in good working order. During our two-day trek we wouldn't exactly be walking on tarmac. Furthermore he advised us that now was the time to have everything ready for the next day, since we were setting off early in the morning in order to get the major part of our climb behind us before the heat became too severe.

So it turned out that by around three in the afternoon our state of preparation could have suited a departure time not the following morning but half an hour hence. Having nothing to do any longer, we sat on the terrace and chatted. Bertie and Aunt Catherine had gone to their rooms and so our conversation turned in part to them. We agreed that Bertie's expression of sincere regret at Aunt Catherine's selfishness had taken us all by surprise and that we would not have expected it of him.

Dr. Witherspoon argued that our opinions of others should never be offered as final judgments and that a person was too complicated a being to be classified and confined by a formula. He told us that it was not out of the question that in other circumstances Aunt Catherine, for example, might be willing to lay down her life for someone else, while on the other hand one of us might be capable of some bad deed which would surprise us all. How can others be expected to know what is in us, when we ourselves often fail to do so!

He then related to us some interesting experiences on the part of those of his colleagues who were psychiatrists, and claimed that usually much less attention was paid to mental than to physical health. If some normal person had been affected by nausea and possibly dizziness, he would not be satisfied with the assurance that it had already passed but would seek out a doctor and submit to a thorough check-up. At the same time there were people among us who were mentally ill and yet would be insulted if someone told them that they required treatment. No one would be offended if they were told, for example, that they were suffering from poor blood circulation and that they must regulate their behaviour by doing this and not doing that. The problem lay in the fact that anyone suffering from some mental illness was hardly seen as distinguishable from a raving lunatic. This was a gross error, because insanity amounted to being mentally dead and it made no sense for this to be the only circumstance in which it was recognised that something was actually wrong with a person.

The other great mistake came from supposing that it was some kind of disgrace when mental or nervous illnesses manifested themselves in relatively young people and that they should be ashamed of their disability. Dr. Witherspoon told us that he knew of a case where the manager of some office refused to allow one of the clerks any leave for convalescence. Instead he told him: "Neurasthenia at your age! Shame on you!" It would certainly never have occurred to this gentleman to say to someone: "Appendicitis at your age! Shame on you!" Nevertheless both remarks should be regarded as equally foolish.

Having completed his discourse, Dr. Witherspoon asked what we we were getting for dinner. That day we went to bed at an unusually early hour.

XIX.

hursday, 26th August was a day like any other and nothing seemed to suggest that this could be a significant milestone in our lives, that the die was cast, the Rubicon crossed and it was Anchors Away! Nothing like that.

The sun rose as normal and the mountains seemed impervious to our resolve to climb them. It was an unusually hot August. Grandpa turned up in some travelling outfit which he probably used to sport in the times when the Czech Tourist Association had around 110 members, and Aunt Catherine was spotted early in the morning by the river, dowsing her calves in cold water and from time to time attempting a few tentative knees bends with her arms outstretched. She carried out the performance to a tune, giving Saturnin and Dr. Witherspoon the chance to argue over what she was singing. Dr. Witherspoon was of the opinion that she was offering *Baa Baa Black Sheep had a Little Lamb*, whereas Saturnin was sure that he could recognise the words of some 13th century canticle in which John the Baptist splashes about in cold river water.

Speaking for myself I consider Saturnin's explanation the more probable one, because it was more in tune with the rhythm of my aunt's ritual ablutions than a sheep in labour. My aunt had a very high opinion of her own figure and would certainly not make such a comparison in this context.

Miss Barbara appeared in her sportswear, competing in appearance with the freshness of the morning. Bareheaded and with her hands in her pockets, she looked as if she was looking forward to a half-hour foray in the forest rather than a two-day trek. She asked me whether I had a cigarette and whether I wanted to bring along the guitar from the living-room. We all found her sparkling mood infectious.

By this time Bertie had returned from the river, having been sent there by Grandpa who was once again trying to find out whether Mr. O'Reilly's workers had put in an appearance. At this point the decision was made that in twenty minutes' time we would take our leave of Grandpa's hospitable home. We then helped Grandpa to lock all the windows, doors and other entrances. Miss Barbara's white car was squeezed into the garage, taking up space which had been freed up owing to the sad fate of Grandpa's Ford. We set off at twelve and a half minutes past the hour of six o'clock, heading for Castle Hill. That's the time noted in a thick exercise book which Saturnin had come across, goodness knows where, and in which he carefully wrote down each and every piece of idiocy that took place during the course of our journey. He called it 'the logbook'. On the first pages he wrote down the names of those making the journey, drew caricatures of us all and asked us whether we would sign our names beneath the rather unfamiliar figures. He described our venture as an expedition, naming Grandpa's house the base camp, the doctor's log cabin the initial destination and the weather atmospheric conditions and so on. Naturally Dr. Witherspoon gave him every encouragement and helped him to think up more nonsense.

Slowly we made our way up the stony mountain path bordered by grassy slopes. Slender fir trees stood like ramparts on either side of us and it was still pleasantly cool. There wasn't a cloud in the sky, the dew glistened in the sunlight and there was a fresh and cheerful aspect to everything around us.

We found it easy going. Our knapsacks were nowhere near full and became even emptier as our journey progressed. At first we were all bunched together, but later on the caravan started to spread out. At its head went Grandpa and Aunt Catherine, moving at such a pace that the others couldn't keep up. My aunt's characteristic prancing gait took her uphill while she talked incessantly. She expressed admiration for Grandpa's vigour, saying that she was amazed by the way he tackled mountains like a young buck. Grandpa kept silent and increased the pace. Perhaps he wanted to amaze her even more or just get rid of her.

A second group was made up of Dr. Witherspoon, Bertie and Saturnin, who were arguing about something. I think the issue related to the upper reaches of the Amazon, but I'm not completely sure. Miss Barbara and myself brought up the rear of the procession. The scent of pine resin and mushrooms filled the forest, while the moss-covered tree trunks looked like the numberless columns of a cathedral. Barbara chatted happily and every so often played football with the pine cones.

From your own experience you will doubtless be aware of the fact that time drags at some moments and at others flies like the wind. When I am in the company of Miss Barbara the hours are unbelievably short and the day hurries through its course as if I'm in a dream. We had hardly managed to have a proper chat before the stony path changed direction, the bronze trunks of the pine trees drew aside and Dr. Witherspoon's log cabin was revealed ahead of us. It lay beneath several tall pines and was a far more splendid affair than I had imagined it to be. From the small clearing in front of it there was a marvellous vista of tree-covered hillsides leading to the valley below in which the river sparkled soundlessly beneath the noonday sun. Just below the clearing a babbling brook accentuated in its mild way the ravishing silence of the mountains beyond. The chalet had already filled up with the other members of our party. They had opened the windows and shutters, and proceeded to welcome the two of us by asking us where we'd got to, even though they could plainly see us standing right in front of them. It was pleasantly cool inside. Dr. Witherspoon played the part of host and with the help of Saturnin and Miss Barbara he served up a lunch which surpassed all our expectations. While we enjoyed a postprandial siesta our whole expedition began to take on the appearance of a pleasant country ramble. Our good mood was fortified by the reading of an unusual letter which Dr. Witherspoon dug out from some archive he kept in the log cabin. We seated ourselves in very comfortable if rudimentary armchairs and our surroundings were filled with the dulcet tones of Miss Barbara's alto, for Dr. Witherspoon had requested that she read the letter out loud. Shut your eyes and listen:

Dear Doctor,

While I am still fragrant with the scent of pine-needles, the thorny signature of the raspberry bushes is still on my hands and the varnish of the hill grasses still marks the soles of the feet that walked on them, I am sitting down to write in order to thank you and at the same time to scold you. My thanks are for the most wonderful holiday that I have ever had, and the scolding is for the malice hidden inside your every act, even the most warm-hearted.

A month ago, when you responded to the concerns I had about my state of health with a lecture on returning to nature and the life of prehistoric man, I objected that you might as well be advising me to climb trees. It was a perfectly reasonable observation and I did not like the way you reacted to it. I recall the malicious glare in your eyes as you examined my figure and told me that such an activity couldn't do me any harm. I had a crushing retort on the tip of my tongue, but held it back in the face of your surprising and generous offer to let me spend my holiday in your mountain retreat. What a strange mixture you are, half Spanish Grandee and half mischievous sprite! I had to reflect on whether I owed this offer to a friendship which goes back such a long way or to that spirit of mischief which, when it couldn't make me stoop to the demeaning task of climbing trees, rejoiced in forcing me instead to make my way 700 metres above my starting-point with a haversack on my back.

As you can see, I underestimated both these factors – I mean your friendship and your malevolence. But what wouldn't a person do in order to improve his state of health. I followed your advice to the letter in everything I did. I even purchased all those books which you recommended me to buy, although the names of the authors and the titles meant nothing to me and they didn't hold out any great promise for me. I know now that I did rightly, but there's one thing that I'd still like to ask you: books are wonderful things, doctor, but are you aware how much they weigh? Do you realise that I lugged my load up these mountains like a pack animal? When I had trailed about halfway up your hill from hell, the terrible thought occurred to me that you were less concerned about whether I had sufficient mental stimulus for my holiday (a consideration that is hardly consistent with extolling the virtues of prehistoric men) than with making me drag fifty kilos to the summit. It is infuriating that one never knows where one is with a person like you. I gritted my teeth and knuckled down to the challenge of ascending step by step. Only the thought that I'd soon be at the top and that you'd be there to offer me a decent drink enabled me to perform like a competent Sherpa serving his Sahib.

I'd presumed that you'd be staying in the log cabin until the Monday morning, and so it came as something of a surprise when the welcome awaiting me consisted of a note pinned to the door with a brief message informing me you'd had to return to Prague and that the key was hanging on the first pine tree on the right. How thoughtless, I said to myself, to leave a key in such an easily accessible place. I was soon to stop saying it.

When I discovered that you'd hung it about seven metres above ground level I was extremely surprised. I was engaged in a fruitless search for a ladder when all of a sudden I remembered the malicious glint in your eyes when we talked about climbing trees and at this point I swore like a trooper. It was just the sort of thing I could and should have expected from you. When I look back on it now, I am tempted to acknowledge that the situation had its funny side, but

I certainly didn't see it at the time. The only sensation that shook my body was rage. My first idea was to about turn, return to the station and go home. Then I would have sent you a pointed letter of thanks for your hospitality. Perhaps I would have done just that, had not the first signs of twilight in the valley reminded me that it would soon be night. Then it occurred to me that I could hunt around for an axe in the outhouse of the cottage and try to cut the pine tree down.

I can vividly imagine you flying off the handle at this last sentence of my letter. Pray go ahead and start to sermonise on how this is the clearest evidence that I have allowed my vital forces to degenerate. What else can it be when a person is willing to submit to several hours' work with some instrument that he has perhaps never in his life laid hands on before, rather than carry out a straightforward and insignificant task such as climbing five metres of tree. To which I will respond: Seven metres, doctor, seven and possibly even higher. Permit me this interruption and allow me to deny you the chance to continue with your lecture about the mad bull which, in your opinion, would possibly be the only means of awakening in me the capacity, inherited from my distant forebears, for shinning up trees.

The fact that I decided to consider climbing as the very last resort is understandable. It was an act of defiance designed to prevent you having things your way. Lest your perverse sense of humour feels short-changed by events, let me confess that I finally did indeed climb that tree. Amuse yourself even more by knowing that the first ferocious attack aimed at laying my hands on that key was launched in hobnailed boots and with that absurdly heavy haversack still on my back. You are welcome to snigger or even chuckle at the thought of me, coatless and barefoot, eventually conquering those seven metres and wresting hold of the key. I have never worked so hard in my entire life and it was the first and last unpleasant experience during my whole vacation.

Everything else was marvellous. I slept very well from the very first night and woke up to a magical morning in the mountains, to be followed by twenty others, each more exhilarating than the one before. The days passed in a spirit of blissful contentment. I tried to decide what I admired most. Was it the way your little chalet was fur-

nished in such an original and comfortable style? Was it the grace-ful fir trees and romantic wilderness providing a forest enclosure for the tarn? Or was it the authors of the reading matter which I had supplied myself with on your advice? I went raspberry picking and mushrooming, and often lay sprawling in mountain meadows. My eyes were drawn for hours on end to the valley below while my mind reflected on what I'd been reading. The cool evenings spent in shades of violet, the dewy mornings and noondays filled with the fragrance of pine resin, the sunsets and indeed all the charms of my holiday harmonised in some strange manner with the pages of the books I was reading. I am convinced that in years to come I will still be able to recall which chapter I read in your log cabin and which right next to the tarn. Certain chapters will still exhale the aroma of wood in your chalet or will resonate with the pitter patter of raindrops on the roof. I do not know whether I lived like a prehistoric man, but I surely had a wonderful time.

About halfway through the holiday I came to the conclusion that your disquisition on the charms of catching trout with imita-tion flies can be reckoned among those sweetly scatterbrained notions with which you like to entertain your fellow man. The only common characteristic of these bizarre opinions is their improbability. To cut a long story short, I couldn't manage to catch a single fish and firmly reject the idea that the world contains a single person who could man-age it. I put the fishing tackle back where I found it and the most I got out of that tarn was a swim. I really did swim! Every single day! I can see you shaking your head in disbelief, but this is the truth and you'll never guess the favourable effect it had on my state of health. My con-dition improved day by day. And don't think that I did no more than dip a toe, as they say, into that cold water, or that I splashed a little water on my back a few times and called it bathing. I dived right in, doctor. Do you understand what I'm saying? Even the head went un-der. Right to the bottom of that tarn!

As a gesture of goodwill I shall forget the fact that telling me to climb trees was not the advice of a friend or even of a doctor but of a jesting knave, and I will reciprocate according to that proverb which says that if someone gives you a stone, repay him with bread: Doctor, *follow my example and your tarn will make an Olympic athlete of you. Once again I thank you for your hospitality and wish you all the best as you dive.*

> *The key to your log cabin is in the tarn.*
> *Yours truly,*
> *Archibald Gibbon*

XX.

AN EVENING IN THE MOUNTAINS
COOL AIR AND COLD WATER
WHAT WOULD HAPPEN IF I LOOKED
INTO A WELL THROUGH BINOCULARS
CAESAR DIDN'T WEAR A FLANNEL SHIRT
GRANDPA MAKES A SPEECH WITH DISASTROUS
CONSEQUENCES

he sky over the Western horizon was a riot of colour. Small clouds edged with burnished gold drifted into the bright beyond. The scene in all its splendour put me in mind of an explosive display of coloured fountains or the outpouring of some demented painter who had flooded the canvas with golden oranges swimming in their own blood-red juice. It was as if a rainbow was glowing inside an open furnace. But most of all it was like the sun setting in the mountains and beautiful to behold. On the other hand, Miss Barbara was also beautiful to behold. She was sitting next to me on a low wall which supported the doctor's log cabin and looked into the heavens with sparkling eyes.

From the open window above us we could hear the sound of cards being slapped down on a table top as Grandpa, Dr. Witherspoon and Saturnin played whist. From time to time we could hear the patois of the gambling den inspired by their high spirits. The brook babbled away and muffled snippets of a row between my aunt and Bertie made their way over to us from the direction of the tarn. My aunt was washing her calves in the cold water and trying to induce Bertie to do likewise. Although it was so lovely there and Miss Barbara was at my side, my spirits were a mite low. I was

180

thinking of the fact that my holiday would soon be over and with it days like this one which, once gone, would never return, days when I had the opportunity of savouring Miss Barbara's company from dawn to dusk. I thought of all those dazzling young men in every corner of Prague, dashing fellows with talents that I could never discover in myself. Apart from anything else they could fire bullets with their tennis serves and their forehand smashes would be unreturnable. All those minuscule and delightful triumphs through which I had won the friendship and affection of Miss Barbara could be of merely passing significance. I was cast down by the idea that nothing more would remain of all our wonderful days together than a few memories and a couple of decapitated matches.

"The flaming seven!" yelled Grandpa from within the log cabin. Miss Barbara smiled roguishly, put her clenched fist to her mouth and imitated the siren of a fire engine come to douse the flames. She stretched out her legs to reveal her sensible walking shoes, thrust her hands into the pockets of her skirt and leaned back against the wall of the log cabin. She occasionally arranged herself in awkward and somewhat ungainly positions of this kind, and at such moments the lithe elegance of her usual poise would give way to the appearance of a little teddy bear. Her eyes sparkled and I felt myself driven to distraction by my feelings for her. Aunt Catherine rose out of the brook and started marching towards us, the vexed expression on her face contrasting in a peculiar manner with her bouncy gait. She pranced by without noticing us before disappearing inside the chalet. The voice of Dr. Witherspoon came through the open window: "Queen of Hearts! Hide the tarts!"

The disc of the sun had already disappeared below the horizon and all at once the clouds in the heavens were almost black. The colour of the sky was changing all the time and at the moment when Grandpa reacted to a ten with the cry of "My bonnie lies over the ocean!" it was turning light green. A thin mist rose from the tree-covered slopes of the mountains. The air in the valleys was still crystal-clear but in colour it was starting to resemble the dewy skin of ripe plums, and soon afterwards the hills below began to

181

sink away into the twilight. Heralded by the sound of displaced scree, Bertie made his way from the brook. The first stars were coming out in the sky.

It was still virtually dark when we got up in the morning. We were still groggy and everything around us felt unpleasantly chilly. I folded the blankets I'd slept under while my teeth chattered from the cold. Dr. Witherspoon lit the samovar and placed a large pot on it so full of water that I thought it would never begin to boil. Grandpa was putting on his boots, whistling while he worked up to the point where he broke a lace. Then he gave himself over to swearing in an undertone. The women could be heard rousing themselves from sleep in the attic room above. My aunt was determined to sing, perhaps supposing that this would warm her up. Saturnin came in from outside with a towel around his neck. He wished us good morning with a cheery smile and told us there was fine weather ahead. How he knew this to be the case I have no idea. Judging from the view through the window it looked like one of those November days when it leaves off raining only in order to let the snow come down.

The idea of going to wash in that stream appealed to me very little, but there are certain principles that a well brought up gentleman never departs from. In any case Saturnin was already handing me my toothbrush, toothpaste and a clean towel.

I sallied forth into the great outdoors intending to get the necessary ablutions over and done with as soon as possible. Silently and with bated breath, Nature was lying in wait, anticipating sunrise. As I ran down the stony slope making for the tarn, I struck blow after blow against Nature's soundless splendour with my hobnailed boots and the noise of scree slipping down in my wake.

If you will allow me to offer you a piece of advice, never do what I did. Don't even try to run down a steep, scree-ridden slope in hobnailed boots, at least not if it's a damp morning. Make no mistake, the fact that I didn't kill myself was just one of those unbelievable strokes of fortune that sometimes happen. I flew down the slope in a manner that strongly suggested a natural disaster. As I slid, the stones I trod on reacted angrily and took evasive ac-

tion from under my feet. Curiously enough, my desperate efforts to come to a stop had precisely the opposite effect. I tumbled down among the trees bordering the brook, gathering speed at a lunatic pace as I went.

I have no idea how I avoided knocking Miss Barbara into the tarn, but it was decidedly not through any merit of my own. I spotted her at the last moment. Her mouth was full of toothpaste, her eyes were wide open and she was obviously wondering what was going on. I passed her in a flash, accompanied by a terrible din and an avalanche of stones. I flew straight into the middle of the tarn and the surface of the water closed over my head. Miss Barbara said later that she'd never heard anyone make such a splash.

When I rose to the surface, spitting water in all directions, the sweet girl asked me in a calm voice: "Did they send you for the key, or is that the way you freshen up every morning?" I clambered onto the bank and explained to her that there were people who no sooner saw water than they threw themselves into it. Nothing could stop them. Under certain circumstances they might happen to be sitting in their cars, in which case they'd take the car with them into any lake or river at hand. I hardly need to tell you what a sight I was. Of course I was not in the water long and didn't stay a moment more than I had to, but even so it was long enough. To my amazement Miss Barbara didn't look much better than I did. She was drenched from head to foot. She explained that my diving technique was absurd. She was surprised that there was any water left in the tarn, but without a doubt most of it had escaped and had hosed down any object within a fifty-metre radius. She couldn't understand why she should be dry when even the trees in the vicinity looked as if there had been a rainstorm. She proposed that we move away before the water that had risen vertically upwards came crashing down again and left us saturated. I was also of the opinion that we shouldn't remain there a moment longer than was necessary. I was shivering from cold and I don't think that Miss Barbara felt very warm either. We climbed up to the log cabin, Miss Barbara scurried to the attic and I went into the living room. Everyone there fell silent and looked at me in surprise tinged with confusion. Dr. Witherspoon said: "Well done!" To tell you the truth I was distinctly pleased that no one plied me with questions. I do not find it easy to put up with people who consider it necessary to inflict the question "What are you doing?" on a man who has fallen face first onto slippery ice with a splat.

Saturnin might have had certain peculiarities as a gentleman's gentleman, but one thing couldn't be denied him. By means of some inscrutable thought process he anticipated most of the mishaps which his master might encounter, and was prepared to face them. Let's suppose I was looking into a well through binoculars. I know that this is a ridiculous thing to do, but let's allow it for the sake of the argument. And let's suppose that I would let the binoculars fall into the well. Saturnin would hand them back to me. With an elegant flourish he would pull them out of his pocket like a performing magician. Naturally I would be very surprised and even a little shocked.

I would receive the thing into my hands with the feeling that this pair of binoculars needn't have an absolutely definitive shape. On the contrary, it might suddenly turn into a rabbit or a flower, and perhaps I would get ready to fling the magic binoculars back into the well while mumbling some incantation to ward off evil spirits. At this point Saturnin would quietly observe that it was naturally not the same pair as the binoculars which I'd allowed to fall into the well. From the ensuing remarks it would then become clear that dropping binoculars into wells was such a natural and frequent mishap that it was his duty to anticipate its occurrence. His assertion would be backed up by a brief statistical presentation of the relevant data, focusing on the number of binoculars lost in wells since the time of the Crusades and the odds of such a thing happening to me.

I think that I only have Saturnin's peculiar talent to thank for the fact that I didn't contract pneumonia. Of course I'm not referring at this point to binoculars but to my drenched clothes. He invited me to make an immediate change of outfit and then took my breath away by extracting from his haversack a huge selection of dry clothes and underwear belonging to me. I am convinced

185

that the previous day he already knew without a doubt that I would find an opportunity to fall into water somewhere. The one thing which he did not have in the haversack was a spare pair of shoes, and this gave him an opportunity to perform another of his parlour tricks on my behalf. There is no other way of describing what he did with my shoes. With the aid of several flannel rags and a brush he dried them out so effectively that no one could believe I'd landed in a tarn only a few minutes beforehand.

What a useful chap he is. He also had space in his haversack for a bottle of cognac and forced me to drink a substantial part of the contents. I must say that this did me a lot of good. My spirits were raised appreciably by something so exquisite and yet so full of strength. I am referring to the cognac, of course, although I dare say the same could be said of Saturnin.

At the very moment Dr. Witherspoon finished preparing the tea the sun came out and Miss Barbara came in. When I saw that the downpour I'd arranged by the tarn had been no more than a harmless passing shower, I breathed a sigh of relief, because this was the one thing that still prevented me from seeing the funny side of the whole episode. I gave myself over to a bout of laughter, something I should not have done. Grandpa and Dr. Witherspoon had behaved with great tact up until this point and I cannot say that they intended to exploit my situation in order to make fun of me. However, the moment my sullen face brightened up they went onto the offensive and the whole of our breakfast together was given over to their comments and ironic questions. I think that I defended myself quite well, but when they were joined by Miss Barbara I understood why Caesar hid his face behind his toga and departed this life. This was not something I could do, because our clothes are not suitable for the task. Any impartial observer will admit that it's not possible to hide your face in a flannel shirt, certainly not when there are ladies present. Saturnin naturally refrained from making remarks of any kind, but on the other hand he was writing assiduously and drawing some pictures in his wretched logbook. Then he started talking in an undertone to Dr. Witherspoon. He collected all the blankets in the log cabin, folded them carefully and crammed them into his haversack. I was convinced from this point onwards that we were going to find ourselves in a situation where the use of blankets would be vital. Bertie gave his moustache a nervous tweak. Aunt Catherine showed her impatience and declared that she was going to take a breath of fresh air. Grandpa growled that she'd have quite enough breaths of it to take later. With a toss of the head my aunt went out to take her first gulps.

Dr. Witherspoon divided the provisions between us and then we set out on our memorable journey. We locked the doors and padlocked the shutters of the log cabin and the doctor tucked the key into his pocket. It was clear from the fact that he didn't suspend it from a pine-tree or throw it into the tarn that there were limits to folly. We set off for White Saddle Ridge.

I do not know whether Saturnin recorded our progress in his thick exercise book, but should he have done so then the events of that morning could have been encapsulated in a single short sentence: "Everything shipshape." We felt fresh and full of high spirits.

Our first goal had been to reach white sandstone rocks above the source of the river and we could see that we were getting closer and closer to them. From clearings and intersections fresh vistas opened up, the horizon expanded and the landscape behind us fell away into the depths below with nothing blurred to sight. The sun was blazing and our faces began to darken with suntan. Miss Barbara had put on a pair of very dark glasses which made her look like a cute little beetle. At about one o'clock we'd reached the source of the river and ten minutes later Saturnin could have summed our position up in his logbook with the sentence: "Everything shipshape excepting Grandpa." He could have said that everything was fine including Grandpa, but only if the old gentleman hadn't made up his mind to deliver an address. I have never been enamoured of speech-making, and have often wished that the perpetrators of oratory might meet the same fate as Grandpa did on White Saddle Ridge. I long for their speaker's platform to collapse beneath them, a gale to blow them away or for the ground to swallow them up.

I do not mean to say that all this happened to Grandpa. I merely want to express my distaste for people who, faced with the fiftieth anniversary or centenary of something, consider it an appropriate gesture to launch into a speech, explaining that the bridge was built to be walked on, or that the trees were planted in order to grow and provide shade, or that they would contribute to the autumn harvest, always assuming they had not been struck by some catastrophic drought.

Once we'd made our way round the source of the river and had reached the spot from which we should begin our descent, Grandpa took it upon himself to clamber onto a large pile of boulders and treat us to a whimsical speech. Among his surprising disclosures was the fact that there were seven of us, that we had been compelled by circumstances beyond our control to act as we were doing, that we were high up and now heading downhill, and that a substantial dinner was waiting for us in town. At this point Saturnin yelled out as if he'd taken leave of his senses. Everyone started and Grandpa began to stammer. Saturnin later claimed that he'd shouted "Hurrah!", but none of us believed him. So far as I know the sound he made was nothing like an expression of joyful appreciation. This was not a thought that detained us at the time, however, because Grandpa didn't allow us any opportunity for reflection. He was executing a few desperate movements on a round boulder, waving his hands about as if he wanted to fly away into the valley, and then with a hollow thud disappeared behind the boulder. For a moment we stood frozen with horror and it was only the sound of Grandpa swearing that galvanised us into movement. We ran round the entire pile of stones and discovered Grandpa wedged between two boulders, curses spluttering forth in an impressive range of languages.

The next few minutes were taken up by the rescue operation. We struggled to extricate Grandpa from his precarious position, each of us adopting a different method. We pulled him by the arms and legs, thrown into a panic by the constant stream of curses. Saturnin shouted at Bertie "Pull him upwards!", Dr. Witherspoon shouted at the lad "Pull him to the right!" and Grandpa shouted: "Damn your pulling, you'll break me in half!"

When Grandpa had at last been extracted, he sat down on the grass, snapped at our questions asking where he was hurt and in general gave us to understand that everything would have been all right had we not interfered and instead had left him to disentangle himself of his own accord. He told us that he absolutely refused to be rescued by anyone in the future. Then Aunt Catherine inadvisedly asked him why in God's name he'd leapt off the rock, whereupon he let out an angry snarl that had us all instinctively withdrawing from his vicinity. Although the bright sky above was an untarnished blue, we felt the clouds already gathering over our expedition.

XXI.

A NIGHT IN THE FOREST
I AM ON SENTRY DUTY TILL ELEVEN O'CLOCK
WHAT HAPPENED NEXT THAT NIGHT
BERTIE SURPRISES ME
I OUGHT TO HAVE A SHAVE
IT RAINS
WE LOOK LIKE VAGABONDS
A BRIEF REFLECTION ON OUR ADVENTURES
JOURNEY'S END

So it transpired that till our dying day we wouldn't forget the descent from White Saddle Ridge. Grandpa, supported by Saturnin and myself, gritted his teeth in pain at every step he took, and a sombre mood overtook the whole party. The way down was steep and even for someone in good health strenuous. In half an hour it was already clear to us that if anyone was going to spend the coming night in the *Blue Globe Hotel*, it definitely wouldn't be us. We stumbled over tree roots and stones in the dazzling sunlight and I recalled Grandpa's harsh words to the effect that those who couldn't carry on should be abandoned to their fate. I was aware of the fact that they were spoken in jest, and I would never even have dreamed of reminding him of them. Nevertheless I thought of how easy it was to proclaim one's principles from the deckchair of a terrace after a good dinner. Step by step we made our descent, while now and then Grandpa needed to have a rest.

I wondered whether it would be better for Saturnin and myself to remain with Grandpa, while the other members of our party went ahead to the town. Alternatively, Dr. Wither-spoon, Aunt Catherine and Bertie could go on while Miss Barbara stayed with us. I thought that this would be the best solution, but didn't dare to propose it.

We were perhaps one quarter of the way down when at around six o'clock we reached a small mountain lea and Grandpa timidly remarked that we could perhaps spend the night there. He pointed out that it would be rather romantic to spend a night in the bosom of nature and that we could make a fire to keep out the cold. He was worn out and glanced in embarrassment from one member of our group to another. I was sincerely sorry for him and I think that the others shared my feelings. Dr. Witherspoon remarked that it was the most sensible thing we could do in the circumstances. It was perfectly clear that we wouldn't reach town that day, and if we were going to be forced to spend the night under an open sky we had to be prepared for it. It would be necessary to accumulate adequate supplies of wood and we should turn in as soon as we had the chance, in order to get as much sleep as possible before we started feeling the cold of the small hours. Besides he doubted whether we would find any place on the stony slopes ahead of us as suitable as this meadow for an overnight stay.

We all agreed to the proposal. I was pleased with it, both for Grandpa's sake and because I was exhausted myself. Grandpa is a gentleman who carries some weight and it is no mean thing to have to support him down a steep mountain slope. My whole body ached and I felt as if I would never again straighten up. In an hour we had prepared a heap of brushwood and had created a fireplace where we sculpted a shapely woodpile which was quietly awaiting the ceremonial lighting of the camp fire. Provisions were distributed and Saturnin divided the blankets between us.

Despite what lay ahead of us, I must say that it was a pleasant evening. Grandpa calmed down and only occasionally complained of a pain in the small of his back. Miss Barbara brought him a handful of blackberries and then we lit cigarettes. When the sun had set majestically and Saturnin was ready to light the fire, Dr. Witherspoon asked Grandpa whether this mightn't be the moment for him to deliver his speech. Grandpa growled something in a sour voice, wrapped himself up in a blanket and was soon asleep.

It was a peaceful evening. The smoke from our fire rose vertically and was high above us when it turned and drifted slowly towards Castle Hill before slowly dispersing. From somewhere in the valley came the bleating of a roebuck, after which it was peaceful once more save for a muffled snoring, testimony to the fact that Aunt Catherine also was in the land of nod. Dr. Witherspoon quietly fed the fire, lost in thought as he watched the flames. Miss Barbara explained to me that there were sleeping bags which you could apparently even use in snow. Speaking for myself I have to say that I would never try such a thing. This August night under White Saddle Ridge was quite enough for me. Dr. Witherspoon walked round the fire, sat down next to us and and in a low voice explained to me that he'd been speaking with Saturnin and Bertie. We would have to take turns at keeping the fire going. It would be a pain in the neck for the one who minded the fire during the evening watch. This person would enjoy very little rest, because as the night wore on it would probably become too cold for any of us to sleep. It should be pointed out that Saturnin had offered to stay awake all night, but we couldn't accept an offer like that. A duty rota had been determined by lots. I would be watching the fire until eleven at night. If I preferred to have my turn after midnight, Saturnin was willing to swap with me. He was on duty from one till three in the morning. From eleven until one Bertie would be stoking the fire, and from three till five it would be Dr. Witherspoon.

I told him that I wouldn't be able to sleep before eleven in any case, and I would prefer to opt for what had been chosen for me by the drawing of lots. Dr. Witherspoon told me that at eleven o'clock I should wake up Bertie. He bade us goodnight and returned to his place. There was a quiet crackle to the fire. The darkly looming presence of the mountains, silhouetted against the night sky, hadn't changed in thousands of years. This land of ours was asleep. I was tired, but the stirring presence of a young girl for whom I had such strong feelings excited me and banished slumber. Miss Barbara and I continued to talk in muffled voices for a long time, while the stars slowly shifted position in the dark skies above. Everything around us lay dormant. Only the two of us stayed up, feeding a fire and watching the shadows of night from our high mountain lair. Although I would have loved to spend the whole night like this, I said to Miss Barbara that it would perhaps be a good idea if she tried to get some sleep. She replied with a docile "If you say so" and then said "Good night" before offering me her lips in a movement of charming naturalness.

It was a more wonderful moment than anything I could have imagined. I rearranged her blanket, stroked her hair and then kept watch alone. I added a little firewood to the red-hot ashes and savoured one of those rare moments in a person's life when one is completely content. At that instant everything in the world seemed to have been arranged in the best possible way and life was undoubtedly sweet. I have no idea how long I sat staring at the glowing embers, but long enough for the fire almost to go out. I got up in order to replenish it, and as I looked at all the others tucked up in their blankets asleep, I noticed that Bertie was shaking. At first I assumed that he was cold, but then I realised that he was crying. I didn't have the foggiest idea why he was in such a state. I put a hand on his shoulder and he looked up with a tear-stained face. I didn't ask him anything, but he broke the silence himself. "I saw what happened," he said, before burying his face in the grass. The penny dropped that he was speaking about the goodnight kiss which I gave Miss Barbara. I realised that the image of Bertie which I had formed for myself bore little relation to reality. This man lying here was the cynical seducer of women, the young puppy who incited me with indecent wagers, the man of the world who ruffled feathers with his coarsely knowing turns of phrase – here he was in tears because he saw that I had kissed a woman, one about whom he liked to express himself with the casual indifference of a white slave trader.

I did not know what to say to him. I stoked the fire and returned to my place. Memories of Miss Barbara's kiss mingled with thoughts of Bertie's tears to put me out of sorts. Although what had happened was rather embarrassing, I felt all the same that New Bertie was more likeable, and I wondered whether his crying had washed away his pompous affectation. Sometimes tears are the best teachers. By eleven o'clock Bertie was sleeping like a log, tired out from travelling and tears. I couldn't quite find it in myself to wake him. I sat on the grass beside Miss Barbara and watched her sleeping. Light from the fire roamed across her temples and entangled itself in her hair. I put my blanket on top of hers and gave her a light kiss on the cheek. Her eyes opened very slightly. She smiled and whispered: "You ought to have a shave." Then I sat by the fire in order to take over Bertie's watch.

It began to drizzle just before dawn. One after another we woke up, tired, stiff and tetchy. The blanket which Saturnin presented me with at the changing of the guard was small, and during these cold, small hours I understood that it needn't have been humility that inspired one of our poets to write of his longing to become smaller and smaller until he'd shrunk into the smallest thing of all. Chilly weather and short blankets have an astonishing capacity to influence human yearnings. The rain soon stopped but we had already suffered enough of it. The fire hissed and the pungent smoke brought tears to our eyes. Our clothes were creased and the faces of the men were coming out in stubble. Between our teeth we ground biscuits which Dr. Witherspoon had handed out to us the previous day and cast depressed glances at the forest which was cloaked in a light mist. Miss Barbara sat down next to me and asked in a low voice whether I was planning to go for another bathe today. I told her that I would be neither bathing nor shaving that day. She blushed a little, but with a good-humoured sparkle in her eyes. I wondered what would have to happen for this young woman to be put out of her good mood.

Grandpa was sitting wrapped in a blanket, looking straight ahead with a gloomy expression on his face. When Dr. Witherspoon asked him whether he had at least managed to sleep a little, he brushed the question aside with his hand. He seemed to have shrunken somehow and looked as if he had aged twenty years overnight. Saturnin produced a bottle of cognac from somewhere and handed it to Grandpa. Tapping his forehead in exasperation, Dr. Witherspoon confessed that he could have made the same offer, since he had a bottle of the very same kind in his log cabin. Saturnin drily observed that it was in fact the very same bottle, and began to fold up the blankets. Dr. Witherspoon said that in that case everything was all right. I assumed that it was not all right for Saturnin to take something without the knowledge of its owner, and I meant to say so. I did not get as far as doing so, however, because the bottle had been handed round in the meantime and I was waiting in line for a tipple. I decided to remain silent, because I am as keen on cognac as I am disinclined to argue, especially in circumstances when a person needs something to get the blood flowing through tired and stiff limbs. The bottle made its way back to Grandpa and we all felt that the weather had noticeably improved. Grandpa took another melancholy swig and sent the cognac on another circular tour. In the meantime the fire blazed up again pleasantly and the smoke didn't disturb us so much. Dr. Witherspoon's biscuits were not so entirely tasteless as they had initially seemed, and the mist hovering over the woods seemed strangely picturesque. Everything was fresh and a spot of early rain had certainly perked up the forest. The Eastern sky was brightening by the minute and we felt that the sun was waiting in the wings behind the mountains, ready to go on stage in all its dazzling glory at a signal from the Director in the skies.

The half-empty bottle of cognac was removed from circulation and Miss Barbara skilfully and shrewdly put out the fire. Grandpa struggled to his feet and threw an embarrassed glance in the direction of Saturnin and myself. We went over in order to support him on his journey, and the whole caravan got under way. Grandpa seemed to be a little better than the previous day, but that was only at the start. As the day wore on he started to tire, and from then on our progress seemed even slower than the day before. This time we were not disconcerted by it, because the whole day lay before us and it was likely that so long as Grandpa was capable of any movement at all we would reach the town even at our present slow pace. At around nine o'clock Grandpa demanded a rest. We sat beneath a copse of pine trees and watched the river in the valley below. The morning mist had vanished without trace and the sky was entirely cloudless. Once again the sun was blazing hot.

A sleepless night, the silence of the mountains, the warmth, our fatigue and the morning dose of cognac had combined to make us desperately sleepy.

When we later looked back on this journey, it seemed to have been full of adventures, but to be honest it wasn't a lark in any way. It would be much more appropriate to say that it was full of minor discomforts. Naturally I don't want to press my opinion too far, because the concept of 'adventure' is very vague. You and I and many other people beside us might consider a voyage at sea an 'adventure', but to the captain of a transatlantic liner such an activity would probably seem completely different. It is quite possible that he would find it no more diverting than the train journey from Prague to Brno is to the ticket inspector. Both of them are likely to have the same sense of satisfaction, when the journey is over and their duty with it. If a sixteen-year-old boy dreams of adventures, then his fantasies are full of palm trees, rain forests and sandy deserts. To me there's nothing more exciting about a palm tree than, shall we say, a pine tree and if a person is looking for adventure then the suburbs of Prague may provide a much better place to find it than the rubber plantations of the island of Sumatra. To the best of my knowledge the level of excitement to be encountered in the tropics is such that the white civil servants over there usually go mad with boredom. I refuse to honour accidents, hardships and discomforts with the title 'adventure'. If your sleep is disturbed by mewing cats roaming across the rooves of Prague's Lesser Quarter, you will not enjoy the experience as an escapade, and I fail to understand why it should be any more thrilling to be woken up by the roar of a lion. It could be explained by the fact that lions are less common than ordinary cats, but if that were the case then it would lead to the most ridiculous conclusions. It would mean, for example, that nothing could be so exciting as being woken up by the Archbishop of Torquay and Paignton, because as a matter of fact no such creature exists. It is clearly the case that we would get nowhere with such an argument, so perhaps we should go back to describing our journey.

When we had been resting for about ten minutes, Bertie came up to me and asked me sulkily why I hadn't woken him during the night when it was his turn to keep watch. I explained that I hadn't wanted to sleep. He told me that he didn't need to be treated like a little boy and no special allowances had to be made for him. I replied that I would be guided by his advice in future and that it was unnecessary to mention the matter, because no one else was aware of it anyway. He gave me a distrustful look and went off without saying another word. Aunt Catherine was affecting breathing exercises, intervening every minute a dozen times over with the words "Fresh air! Fresh air!" and then as a variation on this routine "Fresh air – the Spirit of God". Grandpa started to talk a little, indicated to us the place in the valley below where the river looped round and proceeded to tell us some story about it. I was in desperate need of sleep, and so all I can recall of this yarn is that it concerned Grandpa, a fishing rod and an absurdly high catch of trout. It was a story that appealed to Dr. Witherspoon, who began to go on about his tarn, claiming that there were masses of trout there as well. Miss Barbara expressed her doubts about this, on the grounds that the previous morning I had thoroughly examined the tarn in person and had made no mention of any trout, even though I would have been bound to spot any that were there. I heard Dr. Witherspoon making some other remark but it seemed to be coming from very far away – and then I nodded off. I have no idea how long I slept, but I think it was only for a few minutes. I dreamt that I was supporting Grandpa while Saturnin and I carefully ushered him one step at a time in the direction of the tarn. Grandpa had a horrific beard which tickled my face as we went. Then I woke up and discovered Miss Barbara leaning over me, tickling me with a grass stalk and smiling. Once again we stumbled along the stony path which had been worn away by rainwater, Grandpa's condition going from bad to worse. He was breathing heavily, moaning and shaking from fatigue. We weren't surprised, since we'd all had enough of the trip. Even my recently repaired ankle began to make itself felt. It was late afternoon when we caught sight of the church tower, but it seemed to be too far away to give us hope of ever reaching the town. At that moment Grandpa announced that he could go no further. Dr. Witherspoon took out a map and we

199

deliberated on what to do. We found out that we had further to go than we'd thought in order to reach the town, because the route across fields which we had to take in order to get there meandered along in a ridiculous way, full of twists and turns. In the end we decided that we would go along the riverbank as far as the highway which led to Grandpa's destroyed bridge. Then the group would split up. Those who were able to would carry on into town and hire a cab, sending it to fetch Grandpa and the rest of our party. Grandpa agreed to this plan. With effort we struggled to our feet again and continued our trek on sore legs. At around six o'clock we spotted Grandpa's abandoned house on the far bank of the river. Shortly afterwards a terrible oath issued forth from Dr. Witherspoon. We followed the direction of his staring eyes. At that moment our wretched three-day expedition seemed to have been the most foolish enterprise ever undertaken. Both banks of the river were joined by a new bridge, its fresh wood gleaming in the glow of the evening sun.

XXII.

When I woke up the next morning in a proper bed I stretched my legs in utter contentment and remembered Dr. Witherspoon's saying: "Too long a period of bliss blinds us to our good fortune. Fate would then do us an inestimable service if it took us by the scruff of the neck and chucked us out into the cold for a while." I think that something similar happened to us, and if it hadn't been for Grandpa's injury I would have agreed with Aunt Catherine's shrewd pronouncement that every cloud has a silver lining. I remembered how our three-day journey had concluded and that day it seemed ridiculous. When we crossed the bridge and arrived at Grandpa's house we found the cook and Maria the maid sitting on the steps in front of the entrance. Their bicycles were leaning against the wall, weighed down by their hand luggage which was bulging with a range of provisions. These women hadn't the least idea of where we'd been or were coming from. Concern and surprise were all over their faces as they took in our dissolute appearance. Then the instinct of the common people came into play and recognised what was most important: Quickly they set to and prepared us a hearty dinner.

Grandpa was put to bed and Aunt Catherine took on the job of looking after him. I think that he didn't exactly enjoy this arrangement, but he was too downcast to put up any resistance.

I was just thinking that I would take a look at him and ask him how he was, when there was a knock at the door and in came Saturnin. He wished me Good Morning, laid out one of my grey lounge suits and explained that Miss Barbara had been inquiring whether I'd go shopping in town with her after breakfast.

Then Saturnin asked whether I would be taking a bath. I wasn't sure how to take this question, but the expression on his face suggested that it was in no way intended as an allusion to my dive into the tarn, so I replied in the affirmative. I asked him how Grandpa was, and he told me that according to Madame Catherine he was seriously ill. The dear lady had insisted that he must not be disturbed and had even refused to admit Dr. Witherspoon to his presence. Dr. Witherspoon had taken offence and had asked Aunt Catherine whether he was the doctor or she was. Ignoring her protests, he had gone in to see Grandpa. The old gentleman was apparently in pain and grumpy. He'd entreated Dr. Witherspoon not to let Aunt Catherine go anywhere near him. Saturnin said that a sharp exchange of words between Dr. Witherspoon and the dear lady could be expected in the foreseeable future.

If someone had asked me what I would judge to have been the result of this encounter, then my bet would have been on Dr. Witherspoon as the winner. I can say that it was a great surprise to me to discover later on that my favourite in the contest had been completely trounced. In the days that followed Aunt Catherine ruled the roost and Dr. Wither-spoon sat on the terrace, smoking his cheroots and lost in thought. I do not understand why he capitulated. Perhaps the cause lay with a man's natural distaste for embarrassing scenes, or perhaps he expected Grandpa to rise up in rebellion of his own accord and show Aunt Catherine the door. Whatever the explanation, I took away from the affair the recognition that in a contest with a hysterical woman a man, even a forceful one, doesn't stand much of a chance. Although I was disappointed in him, I couldn't hold it against Dr. Witherspoon. I am certain that had he been able to anticipate the effect on Grandpa of my aunt's nursing regime he would have fought more tenaciously.

Bathed, shaved and dressed in my grey lounge suit I went down to breakfast. About an hour later I was sitting beside Miss Barbara in her white *Rapide*, reading through a long list of the things we had to buy in town. In the stores they addressed Miss Barbara as 'Madam' and evidently assumed that we were husband and wife. If I may offer my own opinion, it was a rather charming error, and even Miss Barbara didn't seem to be put out by it. We returned in time for lunch and went bathing in the afternoon.

For the following few days later it was strangely quiet in Grandpa's house. Our group had somehow fallen apart and each of us was doing something different. Grandpa was confined to his bed and my aunt hardly ever emerged from his room. Bertie had sunk into a melancholy torpor from which he only emerged when he began to show an interest in Maria the maid. Dr. Witherspoon went fishing and I went for swims with Miss Barbara or accompanied her on rambles through the woods. Saturnin spent all his free time in Grandpa's library. A soporific air of calm penetrated the whole house, but in spite of that we could sense that something was in the offing. However, none of us even began to anticipate what was actually about to take place.

It began one morning, when Aunt Catherine discovered a sign on the door of Grandpa's room which read like an absurd parody of a sentence you used to find on metal doorplates attached to a special make of door which could close automatically behind you. I quite understand that my aunt looked at the notice and didn't know what to make of it. She pointed out herself that on catching sight of it she thought she was seeing things. The sign read:

Do not enter, this door is self-entering

I will never forget Aunt Catherine's startled face when she came running into the living-room asking for one of us to go in to Grandpa. The request surprised us, because until that moment my aunt hadn't wanted anyone to see him. We were afraid that Grandpa's condition had perhaps deteriorated and Dr. Witherspoon asked my aunt what was going on. At the same time he relieved her of the sign which she had found hanging on the door handle outside Grandpa's bedroom, read it and went in to see the man himself. My aunt later informed us that she naturally hadn't paid any attention to the notice and had gone straight into Grandpa's room. The old gentleman had sat up in bed in a fury and had shouted at my aunt to let him know how Great Dunsinane to high Birnam hill shall come against him. He ended his peroration from the Scottish Play by throwing a pillow at her. She could still hear his yelling as she fled downstairs. I do not understand why Grandpa chose that moment to speak about Dunsinane, and to be honest I wasn't certain who went where along this famous route. Saturnin said that it was all the stuff of theatre. It could not be verified by historical research and indeed his guess was that it was the other way round. It was Great Birnam Hill that to high Dunsinane shall come against him. He even suggested something along the lines that armed soldiers rushed off there to deal with some overbearing minor ruler. His explanation of moving woods was highly confusing. Apparently the one place with no room for more woods was Bohemia, though Saturnin assured me that in Shakespearean theatre it was possible to sail there.

Dr. Witherspoon came back looking glum and said that Grandpa had addressed him as 'Holy Father'. I asked whether the old boy had a temperature, but Dr. Witherspoon shook his head. From the start I'd had my suspicions that Grandpa was using unorthodox methods in order to liberate himself from the company of Aunt Catherine, but over the next few days I couldn't fail to notice that the old chap was losing his marbles. He came out with a host of nonsensical remarks and asked us questions that made us feel he was going out of his mind. We became a band of people in downcast mood. It was a strange, unexpected and sad conclusion to our holiday. Saturnin had to replace Aunt Catherine at Grandpa's bedside, because the moment he saw her he gave way to fits of rage. The most interesting thing about all this was the fact that it was Aunt Catherine, of all people, who disputed the notion that

204

Grandpa had taken temporary leave of his senses. She told us that he made more sense than the rest of us put together, that we were distorting his remarks on purpose and that it was understandable if he was irritated, seeing that he was after all an elderly gentleman who wasn't well.

It was pointless arguing with Aunt Catherine, but I believe that to any reasonable person the situation was clear. For example, Grandpa happened to ask the time and when he was told it said that we would soon arrive in the city of Pardubice. That sort of thing cannot be explained in terms of 'irritation'. The old boy evidently thought he was on the train heading somewhere.

My own view was that he should have had treatment straight away. It annoyed me that Dr. Witherspoon did not take the necessary steps to this end. I advised him to do so, but he still maintained that some rest would serve as the best therapy. Grandpa's mental equilibrium had been damaged, on the one hand by the hardships of our three-day ordeal and on the other by the ministrations of Aunt Catherine.

The descent from White Saddle Ridge had weakened the old boy's bodily defences and the rest had been achieved by Aunt Catherine herself in record time. Dr. Witherspoon explained that he wasn't himself a member of the family. He felt very uncomfortable laying himself open to the venomous attacks of Aunt Catherine. For that reason he had not tried to stand up to her and attempt to bar her from seeing the patient. Her therapeutic regime was the strangest form of nursing care he had ever encountered. He did not know whether Aunt Catherine was acting from motives of religious piety or for some other reason, but what he did know was that she reminded her patient several times a day that the Grim Reaper was drawing near. Once he caught her crawling on her knees towards the patient's bed, arms waving and voice wailing. Dr. Witherspoon had no explanation to offer for this performance. He simply mentioned it so that we could understand why things could not have turned out any differently. Such scenes could drive a healthy person out of his mind, let alone an elderly gentleman who was not well. Given that Grandpa now enjoyed peace and quiet in the care of Mr. Saturnin, Dr. Witherspoon was hopeful that we would see a substantial improvement in the patient's condition.

Dr. Witherspoon finished by saying that he had an idea of his own as to why Aunt Catherine claimed that Grandpa was a gentleman with all his wits about him. He did not want his view to be spread around, but if his suspicions were confirmed he would put his foot down where Aunt Catherine was concerned and show her no mercy.

I didn't know what Dr. Witherspoon had in mind and couldn't press him for more details because our conversation was unexpectedly interrupted by the arrival of Grandpa. We were surprised to see him out of bed. It appeared that walking no longer gave him pain and for a moment I was cheered by the thought that he might come out with some of his favourite jokes, showing no trace of the befuddled brain that had affected his thinking for so long. He was wearing a camelhair dressing gown and sported several days' stubble on his face. He seemed to be in low spirits and his first sentence banished all our hopes when he came out with:

"I am very sorry to have to inform you, gentlemen, that all the single rooms are taken."

His eyes had a look of fixed concentration as he stared at a point somewhere between us. We followed the line of his gaze and noticed the arrival of Aunt Catherine. I have already mentioned the fact that my aunt had an unusual gait made up of prancing movements. Perhaps this is what Grandpa was referring to when he lifted his forefinger and jabbed it in the direction of my aunt, exclaiming:

"If the frog still hops we'll call the cops!"

My aunt was taken aback. Then she asked him:

"Is there anything you'd like?"

Grandpa clenched his fist, drew it over his chest and asked her:

"Are you ready?"

A look of incomprehension appeared on my aunt's face.

"Why?"

"Look out!" shouted Grandpa.

My aunt started and looked around her.

"Ready, Steady, Go!" yelled the old boy, and with his hands flexed in front of his chest he scurried off at the double to his room.

When I mentioned these events to Miss Barbara later, she blinked her eyes and said:

"When was the last time Grandpa was in Prague?"

I told her that it was two years back and asked why she needed to know.

"I thought he only travels by car," she remarked and said no more on the subject.

For a moment I wondered whether Grandpa's nonsensical statements and strange questions had become infectious. At that point I remembered that Dr. Witherspoon had said to Aunt Catherine after Grandpa's departure:

"Quo usque tandem, Catilina?"

I believe that this is an example of the Latin language, but I haven't the slightest idea what it's supposed to mean. Aunt Catherine turned purple with rage but controlled herself and commented in a sweet voice that she could not recall when Dr. Witherspoon had sought permission to call her by her Christian name. Dr. Witherspoon chuckled and left the room.

Grandpa spent the next day back in bed. As the rest of us sat down to lunch, Dr. Witherspoon had news to impart. Grandpa, he informed us, had announced that he intended to write his will. Aunt Catherine's eyes lit up and she responded that this was quite right. Someone old and sick should arrange his affairs in time. She did not want to suggest that Grandpa would soon be dead, and naturally so far as she was concerned she wished that the old chap might remain with us in good health for many years to come. On the other hand we all know that what the young may do, the old must do. Besides, you should not put off till tomorrow what you can perfectly well do today. Grandpa always had the right ideas, and it was for this very reason that she valued him so much.

The doctor went silent for a while and then declared that in his opinion she was talking baloney. After what we had all observed in recent days, it was regrettably necessary to state that Grandpa's mental condition was not such as to allow us to presume that he could sensibly deal with his affairs. We had to face facts, painful though it was to do so. For that matter Grandpa's previous last will, written three years ago, was still in the keeping of the notary called Gribble in a nearby town. However the old gentleman had decided to dispose of his property at that time, it was clear that he had done so then in full possession of his faculties.

"Well then . . . isn't this a funny turn of events!" My aunt was looking venomous.

Then she said that it was now clear to her why everyone had recently been pretending that Grandpa had taken leave of his senses. She had been wondering all the time what we were up to, and now it was all clear to her. She declared that so far as she was concerned the elderly gentleman was behaving perfectly normally, and she would see to it that no one prevented him from exercising freedom of choice in deciding who would benefit from his will. She threatened to contact a lawyer and Dr. Witherspoon gave in. He said that he had merely been expressing his personal opinion. His testimony concerning Grandpa's unusual recent mental condition was available at any time for the use of members of the family who might have some kind of objection against the will being drawn up that very day. My aunt looked as if she was repressing a smile. She told us that she would like to see a man so audacious as to dare to challenge the respect due to the senior member of the family by offering objections based on conjectures about mental illness. At that point Dr. Witherspoon asked Miss Barbara and myself whether we would be present as witnesses at the drawing up of the will, and all three of us repaired to Grandpa's room.

The old chap was sitting in bed propped up by pillows. In physical terms he seemed to be in fairly good health. Sa-turnin had just cleared away the tray on which the patient had taken lunch. When we entered the room, he asked us what day it was. "The twelfth," Dr. Witherspoon told him. Grandpa lifted a forefinger and declared: "The glorious twelfth! Get shooting! The bird has not yet flown."

I threw an awkward glance at Dr. Witherspoon. I could not understand how in such circumstances it was possible to set in motion something so serious as the writing of a will. The doctor avoided my glance. When I looked at Miss Barbara I discovered that she was looking Grandpa straight in the eye and smiling. Grandpa was rubbing his unshaven chin with his hand and smiling back at her. Then he took a gold cigarette case from his bedside table and offered Miss Barbara a smoke. The sudden gleam of an act of gallantry on the part of a person whose mental horizons were clouding over so moved me that I could scarcely hold back the tears. Dr. Witherspoon was saying something to me at that moment and it took me some time to realise the meaning of his words. I became aware of what he was saying for the first time when he explained that we were not going to write any will and that he would explain everything to us later. To compound my confusion Miss Barbara declared that she thought so too. I had no idea what was going on, but when everyone started talking in hints and allusions like suburban sibylline oracles and then someone added that of course she thought so too, it really made my day! I have to say that so far as I was concerned I didn't think so too and hadn't the slightest inkling of what Dr. Witherspoon was up to. Assuming that the information which I received later concerning further developments was correct, the following things happened:

About an hour later Dr. Witherspoon left for the living room, where Aunt Catherine was lying in wait. He threw himself into an armchair and announced that it was all done and dusted. Everything had passed off smoothly and Grandpa's decision, though a little surprising, was certainly evidence of his wisdom. He supposed that there would be no objections on the part of his relatives, since all of them were already well off in material terms. Aunt Catherine was taken aback. She said that they were not all well off and hoped that Grandpa was aware of that fact. He was always a generous man and would certainly not fail to show this trait in his will. After all, it shouldn't be necessary to call upon his generosity because there were certain moral obligations that a person of Grandpa's stature would never shirk. If it was not Grandpa's duty to see that Bertie and herself were provided for, then she really didn't see what doing one's duty meant.

Dr. Witherspoon told her that the elderly gentleman was obviously of a different opinion. Of course there was nothing strange about this. It was in the nature of opinions to differ from one another. So far as generosity was concerned, the old fellow had shown by his latest will that he possessed this quality to a surprising degree. Then he added that Grandpa had bequeathed his fortune to charitable organisations. Dr. Witherspoon later explained that he had never in the course of his medical career seen anyone go quite so pale as Aunt Catherine did when he uttered this last sentence. The whole of her face went rigid as her lips tightened and her eyes somehow narrowed. When she began to speak, her voice shook with resentment. In that case, she said, she had made a mistake when she claimed that Grandpa was of sound mind. Only a person who'd gone soft in the head could behave in such a cruel manner.

Dr. Witherspoon said that in his opinion there was no reason to consider it cruel for someone to leave his fortune to good causes.

In icy tones my aunt declared that she had no intention of discussing the matter any further with him. She was leaving at once in order to seek the advice of her lawyer. She was determined to summon a psychiatrist to take a look at Grandpa, and she would show no mercy in moving heaven and earth in order to have this latest weak-minded will declared invalid. Dr. Witherspoon rose to his feet and with unconcealed sarcasm repeated the statement that my aunt had come out with not an hour before, to wit that that he would like to see a man so audacious as to dare to challenge the respect due to the senior member of the family by offering objections based on conjectures about mental illness. He added that he had never seen anyone who lacked integrity to the extent the dear lady did and left the room.

In the corridor he ran across Maria the maid and remarked to her whimsically:

"Oh Hebe, Eris is not well. Give her two spoonfuls of brandy in a minute's time and take care that you prepare the others. She'll be drunk within the hour."

"What? How . . .?" began the astonished girl.

"Terribly drunk," said Dr. Witherspoon, a look of mocking contentment on his face as he lit his cheroot.

XXIII.

Our holiday comes to an end
Miss Barbara thinks for herself
Recalling a man who didn't know
how to tell a story
Tomorrow at the National Theatre

Small villages with red-tiled rooves looked like beads on the white-grey string of the highway, along which Miss Barbara drove her *Rapide* with the control and assurance of a professional chauffeur. A large billboard promoting some make of tyres struck us in the eye with its slogan and then disappeared behind us. Magnificent lime trees aside the highway whooshed past at regular intervals. Reflections of clouds and trees flew into the distorting mirror constituted by the chrome-plated eyelids above the car's headlights. The passing sound of barking dogs attacked our ears and then vanished along with several deserted houses.

Our holiday was almost over. There are always wistful feelings on an occasion like this, but I have to confess that just then the end of the holiday was the best part of it. After the hurried departure of Aunt Catherine a sigh of relief went through the mountains. Miss Barbara was so nice to me that the posers of the tennis court with their cannonball services made ever more infrequent guest appearances in my dreams. I gradually became aware of the fact that I had qualities of my own which could perfectly counterbalance my insufficiencies and I told myself that there was no reason why I shouldn't meet Miss Barbara from time to time in Prague. Indeed our encounters needn't always be on court. She told me that she liked the theatre and I hoped that she would not refuse a polite invitation to go there in my company.

I leaned back comfortably in the seat and gave myself over to memories as the flat landscape came and went in its predictable way. I felt that I would remember the last three weeks for a long time. Lunches prepared on an open fire, two headless matches, a morning dip in the tarn, a night spent on the slopes of a mountain under White Saddle Ridge and – this memory came with a little malevolence attached – Aunt Catherine receiving her come-uppance. The one thing that disturbed my peace of mind was thinking about what had happened to Grandpa.

"Poor Grandpa!" I said out loud.

"Why?" asked Miss Barbara. "He could have done far worse than you so far as grandsons are concerned."

"I didn't mean to comment on his grandsons. I'm thinking of the mental breakdown which Grandpa suffered."

"Don't tell me you take that seriously!" Miss Barbara responded. "I don't share the views of your esteemed aunt in other ways, but she struck a chord when she declared that your Grandpa had more sense in him than the rest of us put together. I admit that he's been making fun of us in a somewhat unusual manner lately. But that's all there is to it. Anyway, he might have had a reason for acting as he did."

"You mean to say that Grandpa's derangement was feigned?" I asked in astonishment.

"Just so," replied Miss Barbara. "If you were to think about it for a moment you'd come to the same conclusion. Do you remember my asking you when Grandpa was last in Prague? You told me that it was two years ago. How do you explain the fact that this dear elderly gentleman has been bowling us over for several days with rhetorical flourishes in verse form that first appeared in the windows of the city's trams just a few weeks back? Who taught them to him? If I remember rightly, you examined that notice on the door at the same time as I did. The one that read: *Do not enter, this door is self-entering*. I'm sure it crossed your mind at once that your grandfather couldn't have written that. A person with a shaking hand can't show such precision with a drawing pen. When we were packing this morning, you found that the cover of your shoe-box was missing. I told you that I knew where it was and you thought I was joking. But I wasn't. Your Saturnin used the cover to make that notice and wrote the inscription with a pen used for technical drawing – one with a nib one-and-a-half millimetres thick – the very pen with which he wrote the title-page of his logbook about our journey to White Saddle Ridge. Your man's sense of humour has its own unique character, and if the old chap dubbed that aunt of yours awash with sayings a 'Prancing Dictionary of Slavic Proverbs' then with all due respect to your grandfather I submit that the idea was Saturnin's. Besides, the elderly gentleman knows that I don't believe he's mentally unbalanced. I saw it in his eyes when he said that the twelfth was the time to start shooting and I couldn't suppress a smile. That cigarette which he offered me was a bribe so that I didn't spoil his fun."

"Good Lord," I said, "It never occurred to me and yet it's all so simple. It's so obvious when you point it out and that's the greatest compliment to your own ingenuity. You should become a detective. And drive more slowly, please. A cyclist going uphill often swerves unexpectedly and ends up under the bonnet. You can't imagine how much you've cheered me up. If Grandpa's still of sound mind then everything's for the best and that's wonderful."

"He is," said Miss Barbara. "Your grandfather's splendid. I really like him."

I went quiet for a moment and then rejoindered: "But he's no good at tennis."

Miss Barbara smiled and replied softly: "I love him all the same."

Poplars replaced lime trees beside the highway and a series of lakes appeared on our left, shining like giant mirrors. Our ears buzzed as we shot through a short underpass below a railway embankment. It released us onto a long straight road that was as flat as a table top. A woman working in the fields waved a sunburnt hand at us and the small child next to her followed her example a moment later. A large furniture van chugged past panting with effort. We passed a gleaming petrol station set amidst green meadows and an employee lifted a hand to his peaked cap. Prague fifty miles away. Another sign warning of a dangerous bend in the road. The tyres squealed and the road ahead was straight once again.

It occurred to me that even a man who wasn't in love with Miss Barbara must acknowledge that the girl had a sense of humour. I regretted the fact that we hadn't dragooned her into giving us a story on one of those evenings when we were sitting around after dark. She'd excused herself on the grounds that she didn't have any tale to tell, but that had certainly not been the case. There are very few people who really cannot manage to spin a yarn.

I myself have met such a person only once. It was wintertime and I was sharing a ski chalet overnight with several other people. A man with a weather-beaten face was sitting on a bunk in the corner smoking a pipe. I had no idea who he was, but he looked like the star of some film about skiing. His windswept appearance had such a magnetic effect that one of us asked him to tell us a story. We were expecting something about avalanches and alpine rescues, but what was in store for us was quite different. He said that he would be only too happy to oblige us, but couldn't tolerate any interruptions. If we promised him that we wouldn't butt in, he would tell us a tale of misunderstanding between a friend of his and a certain Miss Vera. The misunderstanding was full of interest and led to Miss Vera's marriage to some commissioner rather than to his friend, who had loved her since he was a child, but about whom she thought he loved her younger sister instead. At least that's what she later said it had looked like. She said that the whole thing made her cry a lot and that she'd only married this commissioner in order to step aside on behalf of the more fortunate sister when she'd realised there was no point in competing against her sister's youth. Her sister was sweet seventeen and as for her, she'd already seen eighteen years of her life go away. And anyway marrying a commissioner, she supposed, was something rather romantic like taking the veil. She was convinced that commissioners spent their time preaching religion to cannibals before suffering a martyr's death. The bronzed man with the pipe explained that he'd never come across anything so hopelessly complicated – not he, that is to say, but his friend. It was worse than the riddle of the

215

red and black hats in a darkened room, you see. Vera had always been a scatterbrain for as long as anyone could remember and considering he was her brother he'd be the one to know.

We were taken aback by this and asked the tanned narrator whether he meant to say that he himself was Miss Vera's brother. He was surprised that such a thing could occur to us and explained that his friend was Miss Vera's brother. We pressed him to tell us whether he had two friends. He replied that he had three and wondered why we were asking. We told him that everything was fine and that we had actually known all along that he must be referring to two different friends in his story. He came back at us saying that he couldn't understand why he should mention the third friend, because that one lived in Pilsen and had no connection with his story whatsoever. Of course we hadn't insisted on a mention of the third, but it was evident to us that the friend who was brother to Miss Vera couldn't be the friend who had made amorous advances towards her. We simply wanted him to clarify this. We hankered after some clear distinction between one friend and another. Let's put it this way, we said to him. Let's call one of the friends Friend X. The man asked us whether we were talking about Charles. Yes, we said, that's the one. Then we asked whether Charles was in love with Miss Vera. He said he didn't know the answer to that, but thought probably not because the two weren't even acquainted. In order to make sure that we understood, we asked whether Miss Vera was acquainted with her brother, and this made him annoyed. We swore that we hadn't meant to provoke him and explained that we understood this Charles to be neither Vera's brother nor the unfortunate suitor, so he was probably the one who lived in Pilsen. The man replied that Charles did not live in Pilsen but in a suburb of Prague known as Vysočany. He then refused to tell us any more.

I merely wanted to say that I have a certain mental picture of people who lack the skills of a raconteur and that try as I might I couldn't make Miss Barbara fit it. I looked at the way she drove the vehicle without the least sign of tiredness and thought over what she'd said to me about Grandpa and Saturnin. I was aware of the fact that very little had happened recently without the guid-

ing hand of my employee somewhere behind it, and I was almost relieved at the fact that I was returning to Prague without him. I should explain that Dr. Witherspoon had told me of how Grandpa had become very partial to Saturnin's services. He'd therefore asked me to leave Saturnin with Grandpa for at least as long as it took to see a real improvement in the patient's health.

A faint smile had appeared on Miss Barbara's lips and I asked her what was amusing her. She told me that she was trying to envisage how I'd manage on my schooner alone, and that I could perhaps invite Aunt Catherine to help me. I must admit that this thought had also occurred to me. Not the idea of inviting Aunt Catherine, of course, which would be an act of madness, but the reflection that it would not be pleasant to live alone on a boat like a castaway. It occurred to me that I could inquire about whether my former flat under the auspices of Mrs. Sweeting was still vacant.

The spires of Prague appeared on the horizon. Our journey was slowly coming to an end. I was touched by a feeling of unease. Just an hour before everything had been so clear. I had told myself: this is what I will do – I will thank Miss Barbara for the lift and then I will ask her for a date. I will do it calmly and casually. After all, I'm not a little boy. There are many things that look easier than they really are. You get much the same feeling when you watch the effortless performance of a champion athlete on the bars. My God, you say, there's really nothing difficult about that. Just you try to do it yourself. I had already gone over the moment of parting from Miss Barbara in my mind. I could see myself becoming flustered and tangled up in all the carefully chosen words I'd prepared in advance. I'd end up making an embarrassing spectacle of myself. I would get out of the car, thank her for a pleasant ride, and then out would come some inappropriate phrase. Miss Barbara would brush it aside with a wave of the hand, saying that a lift was the least she could offer to a friend. She would offer me her hand, say goodbye, step on the accelerator and overhear my stumbling effort at arranging a rendezvous as she drove off in her *Rapide*.

I could see it all so vividly in my mind's eye that I was already imagining what I'd do when I failed to summon up enough courage at our parting to arrange a meeting between us. I told myself that I could arrange to come across her at the tennis club as if by chance encounter, or I could leave a letter with the ball-boy Joe. That should provide every member of the club with a week's amusement.

Red light! Stop! Miss Barbara slammed on the brakes and I realised that we were within the city limits. The engine of the *Rapide* turned over quietly. A stream of traffic, trams and pedestrians crossed our path. Orange, green and we were off again. Miss Barbara stopped on the embankment and inspected the houseboat with a smile. I got out and at just that moment realised that the girl couldn't drive off prematurely because there were several of my cases in her vehicle. As I was straining to pull out the first, some young fellow appeared at my side saying: "Need a hand, guv?"

While this helpful chap was extracting my cases, I nervously lit a cigarette while Miss Barbara watched me with a probing smile. I think I blushed a little and hastened to offer her a cigarette. She lit one but it did nothing to alter the expression on her face. I do not know how many means of asking a girl out have been stored in the annals of sophistication, but I doubt whether mine is among them.

"You wouldn't like to meet up, would you?" The voice that asked could hardly be described as being firm and controlled.

"I would," said Miss Barbara, that smile forever upon her lips.

"When?" I asked, exhausting all the breath left in my body in getting the word out.

"When you like," replied Miss Barbara, without even making an effort to ease my plight.

I looked at my watch and said: "This time tomorrow I'll be at the National Theatre."

Her eyebrows went up as she inquired: "On stage?"

"Off stage," I explained. "I'll be there waiting for you."

"Done," said Miss Barbara cheerfully, "and I think we might be on first name terms from now on, don't you?"

And so it came to pass that a while later the porter doubted my sanity. I'd rewarded his efforts on my behalf as if I'd just become a millionaire.

XXIV.

A buzz of muffled conversation filled the cafe while the rain kept falling outside. A stream of hurrying umbrellas was reflected in the wet asphalt. The tyres of passing cars sent volleys of fan-shaped rainwater into the air and a policeman's black oil-skins gleamed as if they'd been freshly varnished. Anxious about their tights, girls skipped round puddles and dived into passage-ways at the approach of cars.

Inside the cafe the aroma of coffee and cigarette smoke filled every nook and cranny. The two letters I'd received were lying in front of me on the marble table while I put off opening them. It wasn't the prospect of bad news that concerned me. I simply enjoy that pensive pause over an unopened missive. Both envelopes were the same size and bore the same postmark. On one the address had been penned by Grandpa. It remained as neat as ever despite an unsteady hand. The second was the work of Saturnin.

I tried to think of what they'd written to me. I decided that Grandpa was evidently no longer in need of Saturnin's services, which meant that Saturnin would be announcing his return.

I ordered a coffee and proceeded to open the letters. Grandpa's began with a form of address that I do not intend to divulge. I don't mean that there would be anything wrong in doing so, but it is a nickname from early childhood and I don't suppose that it's suitable for communicating with the mature and grown-up man I consider myself to be. Whenever Grandpa used it my reaction was like that of an attractive eighteen- year-old girl when, during the visit of some man, the family photograph album is raided for snaps taken when she was too young to protest against being captured lolling around in her birthday suit on some fur.

We will therefore suppose that this letter kicked off with the words 'Dear Grandson'. The rest of it I will leave unaltered.

Dear Grandson,

One day, when you're as old as I am, you'll realise that you care very little what people think of you, even your own flesh and blood. Nevertheless I find it hard to bear the thought that you seem to believe I am really away with the fairies. I feel that I owe you an explanation as to why, during those last few days we spent here together, I behaved in a way that could make you think such a thing. I will reveal all. Try to listen carefully just like you did as a boy when I was telling you a fairy story. By the way, I used to tell them so badly that you ended up believing that Little Red Riding Hood was a princess turned into a wolf who lived in a gingerbread house. But you probably don't re-member that any more, so let's get back to the subject.

I apologise for the fact that I have to begin by discussing your aunt and my daughter-in-law Catherine. I do not know whether you have ever realised what money means to this relative of ours, and if it wasn't such a harsh thing to say I would surmise that she'd do any-thing in order to get her hands on some. Even so I'm definitely near the mark in pointing out that in pursuit of money she's capable of most things which a decent person would refuse to countenance.

Those days during which she was looking after me following our return from White Saddle Ridge are among the worst I have ever known. I really had severe pains in my bruised back and dear Cath-erine judged that my days were numbered. By the way she expected me to put my affairs in order she made it obvious, in what I dare say she deemed a gentle way of getting her message across, that the Grim Reaper was knocking at my door. That alone would not have greatly disturbed me. I'm getting on in years and I realise that I shan't grace this planet with my presence forever. Although I quite enjoy this world and think that I still have some time left here, nonetheless the thought of death does not fill me with terror. I am prepared quietly and with a suitable degree of dignity to pass behind the veil of shadows into that supposedly better world, after I am summoned by the dear voices of those who have gone on ahead of me.

Unfortunately, on this occasion I was being sent on my way by the rather disagreeable voice of your dear Aunt Catherine. As I've already pointed out, it would not be too much of a torment for me to accept that she considered herself obliged to remind me that I should dispose of my property in good time. What was much worse was the fact that she also told me how I should dispose of it and tried to influence me in a way that I don't wish to talk about. In all my life I have never known such embarrassing scenes, hysterical outbursts, disagreeable panderings and fits of false pique, not to mention the dramatic performances similar to some kind of dismal hypnotic rite, all of which filled the days when I was under her care. Time and time again she stood over me like some tragic fury from Greek drama, alternately weeping floods of tears and delivering rousing speeches. Then there were the countless performances on her knees in front of me, arms imploringly outstretched.

Once she even compelled Bertie to take part. Seeing the evident unwillingness with which the lad knelt down on the floor, with Catherine urging him on from the rear, was the one breath of fresh air where all else was unsavoury. I was completely defenceless at this time. Catherine had cut me off from all of you and not even Dr. Witherspoon managed to live up to the expectations I'd had of him. On one occasion, when things had gone beyond the limits of my endurance, I told Catherine that I would bequeath her everything I had, provided, for God's sake, she gave me some peace and quiet. She reminded me that fine words butter no parsnips and asked me to summon the notary without delay.

It goes without saying that I didn't do so, but when desperate for some respite, I cried out that I was willing to do anything she wanted, something happened which we will call a defining psychological moment. *From that point on I didn't believe that I had strength enough to withstand the relentless pressure of her iron will, and I wasn't even certain, by the way, that I wouldn't soon be pushing up the daisies. Perhaps you find it hard to understand my state of mind at that time. It now, thank God, seems almost incomprehensible even to me, but I can assure you that I was in the depths of despair. I thought that I'd have to kill Catherine or else be driven out of my mind by her, killing her later in some mad frenzy.*

In the end I found a way out through taking leave of my senses. I don't want to claim that this was my own idea. I am grateful from the bottom of my heart for the fact that your Saturnin spent his free time in the library where he overheard so many of those activities, which to Catherine went by the name of nursing care, that he resolved to act. I think that he was the one who later suggested to Dr. Witherspoon the idea of pretending that I'd written a new will and so liberated me from Catherine once and for all.

At that moment I could have stopped playing games and this letter would have become unnecessary (you know that I don't like writing). But I continued pretending because it amused me, although you were the one person I could still deceive. Both Dr. Witherspoon and Miss Barbara saw through me right from the start, but you were kept out of the real world by the fact that you had eyes only for the lovely Barbara. I am not surprised at you and it gives me great satisfaction to recall that even years ago I knew and said that you had perfect taste.

By way of finishing, I have a request to make of you. I would like you to let me have your employee Saturnin.

I dare say you imagine that with the cook and my housemaid Maria, not to mention the fact that I have managed so long without him, I don't have any need for Saturnin. The fact is that I do need him. My soul yearns for him, as does a brain that has been worn out by a long professional career. It needs his support. The fellow's flights of fancy show that he has been touched by some Muse and his sense of humour is close to my heart. His power of imagination and his remarkable mental dexterity could turn a timetable into a crime thriller. He makes a person realise that he needn't have grown old so quickly if he hadn't forgotten to play games. I am having fun as never before in my life. A few days ago we launched a jihad against writers. We raided the library and now we are rendering novels into the language of sober reality.

When that is over and done with we are going to write a book about how reality is in fact romantic. Come to that, you can read all about it in Saturnin's own letter.

Your extraordinary aide-de-camp is willing to stay in my house if you have no objections, and I hope that you don't have any.

This is the first favour that I have asked of you in the thirty years of your life. I am not counting that time twenty-eight years ago when I asked you not to batter your wooden horse on the hat box because I wanted some shut-eye after lunch.

Your old Grandpa

I put down Grandpa's letter and finished the coffee which had grown cold in the meantime. The buzz of conversation filled the cafe while the rain outside was relentless. You can read the beginning of this chapter to see how the scene was painted.

Rainwater flowed down the spacious cafe windows as I reached for the letter from Saturnin.

XXV.

SATURNIN'S LETTER
"WITH GOD AT OUR SIDE, WE SHALL
NOT DIE OF THIRST"
A PASSAGE FROM A POPULAR ROMANCE
WHAT REALLY HAPPENED
MR. DALE, A GAME OF POKER AND WHAT
IT LED TO
HEAVEN HELP WRITERS

ear Sir,

Your esteemed grandfather asked me to supply you with more details concerning the work which we are now embarked upon together. Permit me therefore to say a few words by way of introduction.

Perhaps our project seems foolish to you and leads you to ask why we are actually pursuing it. I could reply that we are acting in the interests of culture and humanity, but that is a grandiose expression in whose name many crimes have been committed. I will explain it to you in another way.

You will certainly be aware of that exasperating feeling which grows inside you when someone tells things not as they actually happened but in a way that suits his own purposes, while he takes it for granted with an offensive self-assurance that you believe his account. It was precisely that feeling which tried the limits of our patience and which compelled us – I am referring to your grandfather and I – to go into battle against writers.

When as a lad I read some adventure story written for young people, the trusting nature of a child who has faith in the veracity of an author's tale was put to the test in a thoroughgoing way. I read about a shipwreck which several people survived by making it onto a tiny island. Among their number was a small child of about six. From the very beginning they suspected that the island did not abound in drinking water. It caused them to lose heart, whereupon the child came out with a sentence that at the time of reading made me feel that it was the most amazing thing in the whole book. Out of the mouths of babes and infants came the remark: "With God at our side, we shall not die of thirst."

There are two possibilities here. Either our author cooked up such a story, which is unbelievable, or some child really came out with these words, which is even more unbelievable.

A six-year-old child who says "With God at our side..." and so on is a creature from the supernatural realm, one that is even more terrible than a headless count, the ghost of a walled-up nun or the hound of the Baskervilles. I am convinced that it was only because all this happened on a very small island that the other castaways didn't flee the child, scattering in all directions and screaming in terror.

This was the first occasion on which I began to lose faith in the veracity of story-tellers and over the next few years I came to the view that it was necessary to take the contents of novels, novellas and short stories with a large pinch of salt, whether in terms of grand overall themes or the most insignificant details.

You will certainly have noticed already how often in novels young men and for that matter even spirited girls are described as thrusting their chins forward in a belligerent manner. I challenge any one of the thousands of readers of these books to stand in front of a mirror and thrust forward a chin. What the reflection will show is not a young man looking belligerent but some kind of retarded ape. This goes to show that aggressive forward thrusts of the chin are downright idiocy, and it's a good thing that in real life no one performs any.

Authors often assert things which a person with common sense can only consider improbable, but which once printed in black and white do not allow for any doubts. Your esteemed grandfather and myself consider this to be an unacceptable state of affairs. In order to prevent that irresponsible tampering with the facts which our worthy writers of fiction have grown accustomed to, we have established *an 'Agency for Introducing a Sense of Proportion into Novel Writing'. Our institute works in the following way: a reader who doesn't believe the claims of some author, usually with justice, will send the relevant text to our agency and will receive absolutely precise and correct information on how the story measures up to reality. Permit us to furnish you with an example. We have subjected an extract from a well-known popular novel to* close examination:

The manufacturer Oakley was sitting in his lavish workroom subjecting his bookkeeper Straw to a cool reception. His round eyes watched the accountant without a spark of excitement and from time to time transferred their attention to the face of an onyx clock on the desk.

A burning cigar lay on the ashtray, sending plumes of bluish smoke upwards in the hot, stuffy air of the office. Oakley the Manufacturer's personality was calmness itself at that moment.

The bookkeeper Straw, on the other hand, was choking with rage. His temples were throbbing and his whole body was shaking. He had just learned that the manufacturer wanted to give his daughter away in marriage to a banker called Wilde, something that caused him so much agitation that he couldn't bring himself to speak. He felt that he couldn't manage a coherent sentence. He longed to strike the smug face behind the plume of cigar smoke. He yearned to cry out and at last give vent to everything he thought about this.

Oakley was sitting and looking as if he couldn't begin to imagine the tempest convulsing Ernest Straw. There was an oppressive moment of silence and then the bookkeeper shouted out:

"Scoundrel!"

The manufacturer rose slowly to his feet and asked in an icy tone of voice: "What was that you said?"

"Scoundrel!" Ernest shouted once more, and it was as if the cry had opened the floodgates to everything that had been building up in his soul. He unleashed a torrent of sentences in Oakley's direction with passion and speed, as if afraid that he would be silenced before everything he wanted to say had found expression.

The flood of words struck the plume of cigar smoke in such a way that it went into a flutter of panic, lost its cohesion and dispersed into tiny greyish cloudlets.

"You're an unspeakably selfish oaf! Your daughter loves me and you're only dragooning her into an unhappy marriage in order to save your firm with the money of that banker Wilde, a firm that you have brought to the brink of disaster through your dissolute way of life. You want to sacrifice your own child, but I will not permit it! Do you hear what I'm saying? I shall not permit it!" As Ernest shouted these words he struck the manufacturer's desk with a blow of his fist, making the onyx clock jump into the air. Oakley went pale. No one had ever spoken to him like this before.

We had our doubts as to whether the scene between the manufacturer Oakley and the bookkeeper Straw could have taken place as written in the novel, and our 'Agency for Introducing a Sense of Proportion into Novel Writing' reached the following determination on the matter:

The manufacturer was not called Oakley but Briggs. God knows why so many authors feel compelled to lace their books with these Oakleys, Ashleys, Pursleys and Chumleys. They would go out of their minds if the hero of their novels had a name like Chick. It is true that the manufacturer received the bookkeeper coldly, and there's nothing surprising about that. It is not customary for an employer who sees his accountant several times a day to launch himself into a tirade of welcome along lines like "Goodness gracious me, who's popped in to see us? Who do we have here? My friend, I am delighted to see you! To what do I owe the pleasure of this visit?" and so on.

It is also true that Straw the bookkeeper was very hot under the collar, but this is as far as the reliability of the account goes. Everything else happened in a quite different manner to that portrayed.

Ernest Straw's concerns about being able to come out with a coherent sentence were well founded. From childhood he'd suffered from the fact that when he was upset his words and sentences became garbled. He had very unpleasant memories of his schooldays as a time when any distress caused him to confuse the names of rulers, get his dates the wrong way round and give phantasmagorical names to chemical compounds which would have the whole class, including the teacher, in stitches of laughter.

This was another of those occasions when distress paralysed his powers of expression and he caused genuine panic in the manufacturer Briggs by yelling at him: "Groundrail!"

This was the word that made the perplexed boss get out of his armchair and ask: "What was that you said?"

The bookkeeper, scarlet with rage and a piteous fury at his own wooden speech, cried out: "Groundrail! You're an untreatably elfish loaf!"

It is true that the manufacturer went pale. No one had ever spoken to him like this before. Admittedly he was aware of the fact that the bookkeeper was a scatterbrained fellow, but he'd never expected his outbursts of lunacy to take this form. He turned over in his mind the possibility of summoning an ambulance. Then he tried to quieten Ernest Straw down himself and succeeded to the extent that the furious accountant stopped raving and advanced to the point where his nerves brought on fits of crying. It ended with a longer speech from Mr. Briggs in which he explained to Ernest that he had two daughters. The elder one, Olga, was soon to be married off to this banker Wilde. In no way had this been done in order to conform to her father's will. It was her own decision, on the whole understandable if we take into consideration the fact that Graham Wilde was a young and handsome man.

The younger daughter, Lydia, had no current marriage plans, and Mr. Briggs didn't even know whether she was interested in having any in the future. The bookkeeper's claim that Lydia was in love with him he considered a trifle presumptuous. He had no desire to interfere with the way his daughters chose to live, but he would certainly entertain doubts about having a son-in-law who was subject to such theatrical displays and as manifestly unable to exercise any self-control as Mr. Straw.

'The Agency for Introducing a Sense of Proportion into Novel Writing' adds that it has not succeeded in determining whether the

torrent of words released during the argument between the two men
really succeeded in striking the plume of smoke from the cigar in such
a way that it went into a flutter of panic, lost its cohesion and dis-
persed into tiny greyish cloudlets. Perhaps it did.

The aforementioned agency furthermore draws attention to
the fact that this is only one of countless cases where an author turns
reality on its head. Kindly note that the scene in the novel between
the manufacturer and the bookkeeper is portrayed in such a way that
from a moral point of view Ernest Shaw overwhelms his employer. Re-
ality, on the other hand, presents the bookkeeper as a doubtful hero,
a fellow who's not all there – one might even say he's slightly round
the bend.

The following passage from a novel set in the Wild West may
well provide an even more striking example of unreliability:

Dale overturned the card table with his foot, told his fellow players to their faces that they were cheats and let them look
into the barrels of his guns. That was when a feeling of cold terror
told him that after the shoot-out in the canyon he'd failed to re-
load.

Now he was holding five dangerous men at gunpoint with
empty pistols, and those five men included the sharpshooter Stone.
He could see his own horse hitched to a post outside the saloon
door. Dale was busy guessing distances. Out of the corner of his
eye he could see that the one person on his side, old Jesse, was
prepared to cover his retreat.

Meanwhile Jim Stone was slowly getting nearer to Dale and
there was murder in his eyes. The powerful fingers on those hairy
paws of his were opening and closing while the narrowed eyes
stayed fixed on Dale's throat.

"Get those hands where I can see them." Dale's voice was
ice cold.

A mocking sneer played around Stone's lips and then Dale
understood. His enemy knew there were no bullets in the guns he
was looking at. At that moment old Jesse leaned back and in a jiffy
had Stone on the floor from a knock-out blow.

"Get out of here!" he shouted at Dale and took a dive of his own through the open window on the other side of the saloon. Dale moved like lightning. He flew through the door with both pistols in his hands, leapt into the saddle of his horse and had disappeared in a cloud of dust before anyone could stop him. Back in the saloon the men yelled out in disappointment.

From the investigation it has conducted into this case, 'The Agency for Introducing a Sense of Proportion into Novel Writing' observes, on the basis of eyewitness reports and other pieces of information, that events took a rather different turn to the one described.

Mr. Dale lost a considerable amount of money, not because his fellow gamblers were swindlers but because he was very bad at poker. He knew perfectly well that he was lying when he accused the other players of cheating, and that he would not be able to escape certain painful sanctions against misconduct which would have been imposed if things hadn't gone on to happen in the way they did.

Mr. Jim Stone was indeed aware of the fact that Mr. Dale's pistols were empty. For that matter everyone there knew it. At that time it was already the case that very few men carried loaded weapons, and to those who did Peer, the saloon keeper, strictly applied a rule admitting of no exceptions: all cylinders must be emptied, and the ammunition handed over to the barman. The empty pistols can then be kept for sundry purposes such as cracking nuts. The owner of the saloon was compelled to introduce this law when they shot dead a bottle of cherry brandy standing on a shelf.

The course of events was determined by two important circumstances: Mr. Dale had offended honourable men and then wanted to hold them at gunpoint with empty pistols. Mr. Jesse, a foreman ripe in years, knew that Mr. Dale didn't have right on his side, but he'd been looking after that fellow since he was a child. His affection for Dale was so strong that he decided to save him from a beating.

What he hadn't counted on was the fact that Jim Stone was a professional hoodlum. When he saw Mr. Jesse discreetly leaning back, he knew that the old man was preparing to strike. So in the split second which Jesse's fist needed to connect with Stone's jawbone he jerked his head backwards and poor old Jesse's clenched fist made contact with the column supporting the roof of the saloon with such force that he blacked out.

At that moment Dale rushed out of the door and if no one prevented him that was simply because all the men in the bar, with the exception of Mr. Jesse, had collapsed into their chairs, were propping each other up or were grasping the edges of the table, roaring with laughter.

So it happened that only two people spotted Mr. Dale's sensational departure: Mr. Jim Stone, who at that precise moment was already standing at the saloon door, and a little boy with freckles who was trying to palm off a vending machine selling chocolate in front of Peer's saloon with a metal button.

Both of them agreed that they had never seen anything like it before. Dale found himself in the saddle, both pistols in his hands, after some kind of wild straddle jump only seen in films, and dug his spurs into the flank of his horse. Both witnesses were somewhat confused about what happened next.

The boy claimed that the horse reacted to the impact of Dale by neighing violently and trying to jump onto the roof of the saloon, He said that this caused Dale to fall out of the saddle, injuring his head on the hitching post and denting a piece of metal advertising Singer sewing machines, before he ended up lying on the ground. It looked like a 'clean kill'.

The boy added that the unruly horse then fled in the direction of the railway station. There was nothing good about that horse, he observed. He would never want a brute like that himself. Cross my heart, he explained, they could have been offering up a critter like that for free and he wouldn't have took one.

Jim Stone took the view that it was a hell of a good horse, a much better one than Dale deserved and that it probably made off in the direction of the station in order to board a train and get as far away from its owner as possible. He added that anybody who jumps into the saddle and digs his spurs in with his hands full of pistols, without first untying the horse, is a moron who deserves to have his goddamned head broken.

'The Agency for Introducing a Sense of Proportion into Novel Writing' is unable to identify itself with the vulgar language of Mr. Jim Stone. Nevertheless it grants that Mr. Dale Dorson behaved in a somewhat unusual manner and in a way that was fundamentally different from that presented in the aforementioned novel.

Sir, your grandfather and I hope that the examples given have managed to convince you it was high time for 'The Agency for Introducing a Sense of Proportion into Novel Writing' to come into being. The task awaiting us is a huge one, but we will approach it with enthusiasm. Nothing will escape our watchful eyes and every transgression will be punished.

We will provide regular bulletins on the results of our work and we can assure you that you'll be surprised. You will learn that the three musketeers were not four but two. We will provide you with precise information concerning what happened when Louis Bromfield described the rainy season (at the moment it seems that the only significant event was that it rained). You will be forced to agree that Jules Verne's mysterious island was not full of mystery, and even if it was the mystery lasted only five weeks, and unlike his Five Weeks in a Balloon never got off the ground. We will expose the truth of why Three Men in a Boat is silent about dogs despite Montmorency, and we will prove that the Czech author who believed on maternal authority that a town could be held in the palm of a hand was as unaware of dimensions as Shakespeare, who believed that a hamlet could be bounded in a nutshell.

Before concluding this letter, sir, there is something else which I should like to say. The one rebuke which I received from you during my time in your employment concerned the fact that I behaved as if the houseboat belonged to us. You expressed concern as to whether the owner had agreed to the alterations which I carried out. I would ask you not to allow yourself any such concerns now and to forgive me for deceiving you in a certain manner. The boat is actually mine.

It would be ungrateful of me, after the pleasant days spent in your service, to say that the boat is a memento of better times, and I would therefore ask you to be content with the assurance that I bought it some six years ago. I would be delighted if you decide that it *will remain your residence. I would like to ask whether I might return to your employ when your esteemed grandfather has no further need of my services.*

With respectful greetings from your faithful bo's'n,
Saturnin

XXVI.

I AM AWARE OF THE FACT THAT
A WEDDING IS THE ONLY APPROPRIATE
ENDING FOR EVERY TALE, AND IT GIVES
ME PLEASURE THAT I NEEDN'T DISAPPOINT
MY READERS IN THIS IMPORTANT REGARD
A LITTLE LATER IN PRAGUE'S GRANDIOSE
CHURCH OF ST. LUDMILA
AUNT CATHERINE REMARRIED
INTO MONEY

AFTERWORD

Saturnin has always been a great favourite of Czechs. It has also proved popular with those who read it in translation (it now exists in at least nine languages). It is not uncommon for visitors to the Czech Republic to ask their hosts for a Czech writer to read on their return home and in many cases Jirotka's *Saturnin* is the book recommended. This is not just because the visitor doesn't look up to the challenge of Hrabal or Kundera. It is because they are asking for something 'typically Czech'.

Given this association, it is understandably irritating to Czechs when they hear *Saturnin* described as 'another Jeeves'. The tendency can even move towards accusations of plagiarism. It is observed that demanding family members (fearsome aunts, in particular), quick-witted servants and somewhat clueless employers in need of a helping hand inhabit Jirotka's world as much as that of Wodehouse – but so what? Plagiarism lies not in the cast of characters itself but in how those characters behave. As the author of a bilingual edition of Wodehouse entitled, in an amusing turning of the tables, *Jeeves aneb anglický Saturnin*, ('Jeeves, or the English Saturnin') remarked in the preface to his work, the cast list in West Side Story is similar to that of Romeo and Juliet, but one doesn't hear too many remarks about the plundering of Shakespeare by Arthur Laurents and Stephen Sondheim, or the Jets and the Sharks as a pale update of the houses of Montague and Capulet.

In fact, there are important differences between Jeeves and Saturnin. The differences are reflected in the fact that although young women play an important role in the affairs of both servants, Jeeves is usually required to get his master out of romantic encounters rather than into them. After all, were Bertie really to fall in love and find his life transformed by one of these young women, the settled world of the master and the gentleman's gentleman, the morning pick-me-up in bed to prepare him for a cracking day at the Drones Club and doubtless a scrape or two requiring deft handling from Jeeves along the way, would be interrupted by something far more destructive than the intrigues of a couple of aunts calling each other up, in Wodehouse's immortal expression, 'like mastodons bellowing across the primeval swamps'. Jeeves is capable of some dodgy manoeuvres, but his mission is to preserve the ordered calm of the Wooster household. His reward is to see a garish waistcoat jettisoned alongside a threatened engagement and the secure world of a proper gentleman restored.

Saturnin is not like this. There is an element of mischief bordering on the dangerous about his strategems. He declares himself one who 'always longed to be wherever anything out of the ordinary, unusual or dangerous was happening' (p. 157). This is hardly Jeeves, who would bristle if Bertie's tie was 'out of the ordinary' and avail himself of the first opportunity to give the offending item to charity. He is a dangerous fellow, this Saturnin. He battles burglars with mediaeval flails, teaches old men Ju-Jitsu (rather than bringing them their slippers), fails to give an aunt the proper greeting and plucks the cigarette from the mouth of her wastrel son before throwing it into the River Vltava.

The most famous passage in *Saturnin* is the doughnut scene. Dr. Vlach (Witherspoon) divides people into three categories based on the way they would react to a plate of doughnuts in a busy café (Prague's *Hotel Imperial*, to be precise). There are those who would never dream of hurling doughnuts around the room, those who would dream of it but never do it, and those who would do it. Saturnin is one of the few (they are apparently 'as rare as white crows') doughnut-throwers.

Saturnin is a doer, and the rules of decorum can be the victim. But he has a mission – to make his master a doer too. His mission, unlike that of Jeeves, is not to rescue his employer from matrimony but to lead him into it. The object of desire is not a gormlessly affectionate pretty young thing like Madeline Bassett, from whom Bertie Wooster frequently has to be extricated. Wodehouse tells us that though physically 'in the pin-up class', with blonde hair, attractive curves, and 'all the fixings', Madeline still believes that every time a fairy sheds a tear a new star appears in the Milky Way and that the stars are God's daisy chain. The young woman in *Saturnin*, Barbara, on the other hand, doesn't just excel in the kitchen but also on the tennis court and unlike the men can recognise when a conversation is in Spanish. She drives a white *Rapide* and offers to power it over a bridge about to be swept away by floods (her offer is accepted, enthusiastically by Saturnin and with some reluctance by her suitor). She has a different view of the stars to that of Madeline Bassett, admiring them with the narrator without any references to fairies or daisy chains – the text tells us that they look for shooting stars without speaking. She is (at least within the context of a book written in 1942) a modern woman and Saturnin has to make his master worthy of her.

This is the setting in which the master is sent to recapture Marcus Aurelius (an escaped lion, of course), finds himself homeless without his houseboat, is taken to hospital, trapped in a secluded country-house when the bridge is indeed swept away in a flood (a couple of hours after Barbara has taken them on their daredevil drive across it), runs out of supplies, treks up and down mountains, bathes in tarns, spends nights in the forest and then returns at last to 'civilisation'. These adventures form the backbone of the story. Through all this he gets to know himself as much as he gets to know Miss Barbara. And though it is true that Saturnin is behind it all, he is behind it less as master strategist than mentor, an example that his master is inspired to follow.

Once the prospects come to fruition, Saturnin can withdraw from the scene, handing over to his employer what turns out to be Saturnin's own houseboat and taking up new employment working for his Ju-Jitsu pupil, Grandpa. It's true that he promises to return when his services are no longer needed by the old gentleman, but the sense is that his work is now done.

Jirotka spent much of his long life in journalism, as a contributor and as an editor, and he also worked in radio and television, writing a number of radio plays. Though he produced other books beside Saturnin, the most well-known being a parody of a detective novel entitled *Muž se psem*, (Man with Dog), published in 1944, Saturnin is by far the most well-known. In 1994 it was made into a mini-series for Czech television and later into a film (*Muž se psem* was also made into a film, but in Polish by a Polish director), and as recently as 2009 it was pronounced an all-time favourite in a Czech television survey. Whatever the psephological reliability of this survey, there is no doubt that *Saturnin* is the work for which Jirotka will always be remembered.

He is sometimes seen as a one-book person in the manner of Joseph Heller. But it needs to be borne in mind that an author may be remembered for one book above all, not because he only wrote one good book, but because one book spoke to a particular time and for that very reason endured even when times changed. Heller's book is famous for the relentless and futile bombing campaign in Vietnam. Hence the well-known Catch-22, that you can escape the bombing run only if you are insane and if you apply to avoid the bombing run, then by definition you must be sane. Jirotka's book, written in 1942, was composed while the Czechs were under German occupation during wartime. Jirotka had served in the army as an infantry officer himself before the occupation, and then from 1940 worked at the Ministry of Public Works.

The political context does inform the text. That is is not to say that *Saturnin* is in any manner of speaking an allegory of wartime resistance. Rather, the wartime resistance lies precisely in the affectionate way in which it gathers around itself traits and mannerisms of indissoluble Czechness. And this brings us back to the plagiarism issue. The point is that despite a range of influences from abroad, the book was intended to encapsulate a national character – which is partly why it is still popular, and why visitors find themselves encouraged to take this particular book back home with them rather than the work of writers that are more well-known outside the Czech Republic. It was not simply a work of escapism, written to make people forget occupation. It was a reminder of what must be preserved, even under an occupying power. It is this that makes the accusation of plagiarism (which admittedly has very few supporters nowadays) rankle. After all, the Czechs were not trying to be like the English. They were trying to maintain themselves as Czechs, initially through German occupation and later under communism (note that the television series appeared shortly after the collapse of communism in 1989). Only by such means could empires sustained by bombs eventually be undermined by doughnuts.

Of course Wodehouse was an influence on Jirotka, but so were other writers like Jerome K. Jerome. Saturnin has passages reminiscent of the reflections on the foibles of modernity and civilisation found in *Three Men in a Boat*, such as the wonderful disquisitions on 'how to conduct oneself at a funeral' (Chapter XII) or the decline of craftsmanship (Chapter III). One can easily imagine (to recall one of the most famous passages from *Three Men in a Boat*) Dr. Vlach making his own way through a medical dictionary and concluding from the symptoms listed that he has every ailment in the book, with the exception of housemaid's knee.

Some of the inspired rants of Dr. Vlach have a contemporary resonance. He describes a lost world in which shoemakers were determined to refer to themselves as 'Shoemakers' on a sign which 'would hang next to a picture of a lady's laced boot'. Now he was forced to live in a world in which shoemakers (without in any way expanding their premises or number of employees) had transformed themselves into 'Manufacturers of Footwear'. But we could equally think of a more recent world in which every public servant has acquired officer status, from the binmen in the street (Refuse Disposal Officers) to the secretaries (Programme and Communication Officers) in the buldings above.

Everyone knows that translation carries with it an element of interpretation. Saturnin is a minefield in this respect, because it contains a wealth of puns, proverbs and metaphors, a number of difficult cultural references and a smattering of dialect and irregular word order. There are also a couple of rhymes. I have tried to do justice to all of these without interrupting the flow of the text. But it can be difficult and it is important not to try to be too clever. The natural rhythm must not be compromised.

For instance, Czech can give emotional colour through the use of diminutives in a way that English on the whole doesn't. Hence, in the sentence '*Sluníčko pálilo a já jsem si všiml, že slečna Barbora má trochu spálený nosík,*' (The sun was scorching and I noticed that Barbara's petite nose was a little sunburnt'), I decided that I could give Barbara a 'petite nose' in order to register the diminutive 'nosík' of 'nos' meaing nose. But what about that diminutive of 'slunce' meaning sun, 'sluníčko'? 'Little sun' doesn't work and something folksy like 'The dear old sun' would be too much like Madeline Bassett's stars appearing to be God's daisy chain, especially if it was going to start shining upon Barbara's 'little nosey'. So I stayed with 'the sun was scorching' and the force of this particular diminutive was lost. Sometimes you have to accept that you cannot carry everything over into another language.

Or at least, not into all of them. It is now a decade since the hardback version of *Saturnin* was published and in that time it has been translated into many languages, not only those like Spanish and French which are spoken around the world but also some that are largely restricted to particular places, like Latvian and Estonian. Interestingly, there have been several academic studies of the translations, including comparisons between renderings of *Saturnin* into different languages. English may struggle with the force of diminutives, because it tends to use them only when lacing a description with a heavy dose of sentiment. Other languages offer much more flexibility. One must not forget that what we often call an 'untranslateable' expression may in fact be translatable into some languages but not others.

Looking at my own translation a decade on, I cannot avoid a feeling that I might do some things differently. Maybe I would now keep the original names (always a difficult decision, especially when they will be changed anyway through the way they are pronounced). My one hope is that any flaws in the translation will at least inspire the reader to learn enough Czech to read the original, while any merits will at least enable the wit and insight of the author to shine through.

Mark Corner
Brussels, 2022

ABOUT THE AUTHOR

Zdeněk Jirotka (1911–2003) was a master of comic prose, the author of radio plays, and the writer of Saturnin, a great favourite among Czech readers, a book translated into over a dozen other languages.

Jirotka joined the army as a young man and during the Nazi occupation worked in the Ministry of Public Works. After 1942, when *Saturnin* was published, he devoted himself exclusively to his writing. He contributed short stories and other pieces to several magazines. In 1940 onwards he began a close collaboration with *Lidové noviny*, and in the 1950s became an editor at Czech radio and edited the satirical weekly *Dikobraz*. He contributed to television and radio programmes and wrote a number of plays for Czech radio and television.

The works which managed to reach a wider reading public are the novels *Saturnin* and *Muž se psem* (Man with Dog), in which he was inspired by the Anglo-Saxon comic prose of writers like Jerome K. Jerome and P. G. Wodehouse. His leaning towards English comic writing represented a form of protest, because both books were written under Nazi occupation. Jirotka can also be linked to a tradition of humour characteristic of the Czech lands and of writers like J. Hašek, K. Čapek, and K. Poláček. Like them he criticises a small-town mentality, snobbish behaviour and pretence. His novels are composed in a characteristic manner, built up around the feuilleton style of writing – marked by extraordinary situations, heightened language and wordplay – representing a parody of various literary forms and genres. Both *Saturnin* and *Muž se psem* have seen successful transitions onto stage and screen.

CONTENTS

MODERN CZECH CLASSICS

The modern history of Central Europe is notable for its political and cultural discontinuities and often violent changes, as well as its attempts to preserve and (re) invent traditional cultural identities. This series cultivates contemporary translations of influential literary works that have been unavailable to a global readership due to censorship, the effects of the Cold War, and the frequent political disruptions in Czech publishing and its international ties. Readers of English, in today's cosmopolitan Prague and anywhere in the physical and electronic world, can now become acquainted with works that capture the Central European historical experience – works that have helped express and form Czech and Central European identity, humour, and imagination. Believing that any literary canon can be defined only in dialogue with other cultures, the series publishes classics, often used in Western university courses, as well as (re)discoveries aiming to provide new perspectives in the study of literature, history, and culture. All titles are accompanied by an afterword. Translations are reviewed and circulated in the global scholarly community before publication – this is reflected by our nominations for literary awards.

PUBLISHED TITLES

Zdeněk Jirotka: *Saturnin* (2003; pb 2016)
Vladislav Vančura: *Summer of Caprice* (2006; pb 2016)
Karel Poláček: *We Were a Handful* (2007; pb 2016)
Bohumil Hrabal: *Pirouettes on a Postage Stamp* (2008)
Karel Michal: *Everyday Spooks* (2008)
Eduard Bass: *The Chattertooth Eleven* (2009)
Jaroslav Hašek: *Behind the Lines: Bugulma and Other Stories* (2012; pb 2016)
Bohumil Hrabal: *Rambling On* (2014; pb 2016)
Ladislav Fuks: *Of Mice and Mooshaber* (2014)
Josef Jedlička: *Midway upon the Journey of Our Life* (2016)
Jaroslav Durych: *God's Rainbow* (2016)
Ladislav Fuks: *The Cremator* (2016)
Bohuslav Reynek: *The Well at Morning* (2017)
Viktor Dyk: *The Pied Piper* (2017)
Jiří R. Pick: *Society for the Prevention of Cruelty to Animals* (2018)
Views from the Inside: Czech Underground Literature and Culture (1948–1989), ed. M. Machovec (2018)
Ladislav Grosman: *The Shop on Main Street* (2019)
Bohumil Hrabal: *Why I Write? The Early Prose from 1945 to 1952* (2019)
Jiří Pelán: *Bohumil Hrabal: A Full-length Portrait* (2019)

Martin Machovec: *Writing Underground* (2019)
Ludvík Vaculík: *A Czech Dreambook* (2019)
Jaroslav Kvapil: *Rusalka* (2020)
Jiří Weil: *Lamentation for 77.297 Victims* (2021)
Vladislav Vančura: *Ploughshares into Swords* (2021)

FORTHCOMING
Jan Procházka: *The Ear*
Ivan M. Jirous: *End of the World. Poetry and Prose*
Jan Čep: *Common Rue*
Jiří Weil: *Moscow – Border*
Jan Zábrana: *Lesser Histories*
Libuše Moníková: *Verklärte Nacht*
Ján Johanides: *The Crime that Punishes* (Modern Slovak Classics)

ZDENĚK JIROTKA

SATURNÍN

Translated and afterword by Mark Corner
Illustrations by Adolf Born
Graphic design by Vladimír Vimr
Published by Charles University, Karolinum Press
Ovocný trh 560/5, Prague 1
Prague 2022
www.karolinum.cz
Set by Karolinum Press
Printed in the Czech Republic by Těšínské papírny, s. r. o.
2nd English edition

ISBN 978-80-246-5074-6

Also available in paperback and ebook edition.